EVEREST TRILOGY

SPECIAL EDITION

EVEREST
TRILOGY

SPECIAL EDITION

GORDON KORMAN

SCHOLASTIC INC.

New York   Toronto   London   Auckland   Sydney
Mexico City   New Delhi   Hong Kong   Buenos Aires

The Contest, ISBN-13: 978-0-439-40139-5, ISBN-10: 0-439-40139-9.
Copyright © 2002 by Gordon Korman.

The Climb, ISBN-13: 978-0-439-40506-5, ISBN-10: 0-439-40506-8.
Copyright © 2002 by Gordon Korman.

The Summit, ISBN-13: 978-0-439-41137-0, ISBN-10: 0-439-41137-8.
Copyright © 2002 by Gordon Korman.

12 11 10 9 8 7 6 5 4 3 2 1   8 9 10 11 12 13/0

Printed in the U.S.A.   23

ISBN-13: 978-0-545-09309-5
ISBN-10: 0-545-09309-0

First compilation printing, June 2008

Contents

THE CONTEST vii

THE CLIMB 139

THE SUMMIT 295

BOOK ONE: THE CONTEST

EVEREST

For Brandon VanOver

PROLOGUE

It was a funeral in every way but one: The body was missing.

Not *missing*, exactly. Its location was common knowledge — that was the most horrifying part of all this. The body was nine thousand miles away in a country called Nepal, twenty-seven thousand feet up Mount Everest, the highest point on planet Earth.

On Everest, everything above twenty-five thousand feet is known as the Death Zone. There, overpowering wind gusts approaching two hundred miles per hour can wrench a strong person clear off the mountain, and bone-chilling nighttime cold of one hundred degrees below zero causes frostbite and hypothermia. Wherever the body was, it was surely frozen solid.

Twenty-seven thousand feet is above the range of any helicopter. At that altitude, the air is simply too thin to provide the rotor blades with any lift. A stranded climber would have a better chance of being picked up off the surface of the moon than in the Death Zone. Atop Everest, you are your only rescue squad — you and the others who take on the mountain with you.

It was easy to spot those teammates among the mourners, and not just because of their young age. Their physical bodies fidgeted in the chapel, constricted by grief and tight collars. But their minds were still on the other side of the globe, five miles straight up, in the Death Zone.

They had that much in common with their unfortunate friend. It was a place they might never truly leave.

CHAPTER ONE

Dominic Alexis arranged the caps and wrappers on his bedroom carpet and examined them for at least the hundredth time:

E E R E S T

He rummaged through the shoebox, searching for the V he knew was not there. R's. T's. Dozens of E's. He had counted once — more than fifty, and that was weeks ago. Even a few extra S's. Not a single V.

That was how these contests worked. Millions of the other letters were stuck under the caps of Summit Athletic Fuel and on the inside wrappers of Summit Energy Bars, distributed to stores all around the country. Then they printed up a grand total of three V's and shipped them to nonexistent addresses in Antarctica, fourth class.

He was exaggerating, of course. There were V's out there, even if just a handful. Over the past weeks, the TV news had shown clips of ecstatic young climbers who had spelled out EVEREST to qualify for the five wild-card spots at boot camp.

THE CONTEST

Four of those places had been filled. Only one chance remained.

At boot camp, the five lucky winners would join the American Junior Alpine Association's fifteen top young mountaineers for four weeks of intensive training and competition. It promised to be a brutal month of six-hour workouts, night climbs, and marathon hikes carrying heavy packs. But the end result was worth it. The top four climbers would earn places on SummitQuest — Summit Athletic's Everest expedition, the youngest team ever to attempt the world's tallest peak.

A shout from downstairs interrupted his reverie. *"Where's my sand?!"*

It was Christian, Dominic's older brother. Chris didn't have to scramble around garbage cans and recycling bins, scrounging for caps and wrappers. His place at boot camp was already secure. He was the number-two-rated under-seventeen climber in the country — second only to the Z-man himself, Ethan Zaph.

Chris was talking about his good-luck piece — a small glass vial of sand from the Dead Sea. It had been a gift from their grandmother, brought back from a trip to Israel when Chris was a baby and Dominic hadn't even been born. Chris loved the idea that the sand was from the lowest point on the globe. When he started climbing, he strung the vial on a leather cord so he could wear it around his neck. "I'm taking this sucker *vertical!*" he would say before an ascent. And at the top of the rock, or cliff, or mountain, he would talk to it: "Far from home, baby! You're far from home!"

It was natural that, as Chris became more accomplished as a climber, it would one day cross his mind to take his good-luck piece from the bottom of the world to the top of the world at the summit of Everest. Now, finally, he was getting his chance.

Pounding on the stairs. "Come on, Dom! I'm packing up my stuff for boot camp!"

There was no question that, right then, Dominic needed luck more than Chris did. The vial of sand clutched in his fist, he opened the sash of the window and expertly eased himself outside.

In many neighborhoods, it would probably raise eyebrows to have a thirteen-year-old climbing out a second-story window, but it was a fairly ordinary occurrence around the Alexis home. Sometimes it was just the easiest way down. Vertical was a forbidden direction for most people; for Chris and Dominic, it was as simple an option as left or right. Years before, as little kids, Chris had become the town hide-and-seek champion by

THE CONTEST

scaling a fifty-foot tree for aerial surveillance every time he was "it." Even Mr. Alexis, when he needed to go up on the roof to check a flapping shingle, never bothered with a ladder. He had grown up in Switzerland, in the shadow of the high Alps, and was responsible for introducing his two sons to "this climbing foolishness." (Their mother's opinion.)

And anyway, a thirty-second climb was better than a face-to-face with Chris over a stolen — ahem — *borrowed* good-luck charm.

As far as degree of difficulty went, the front of the house was pretty pathetic. Dominic started down, jamming the edges of his sneakers into the narrow spaces between the bricks.

As he passed the picture window in the living room, he caught an exasperated look from his mother. He couldn't actually hear her, but instead read her lips as he dropped to the flower bed:

"We have a door . . ."

But Dominic was already sprinting along Mackenzie Avenue. Preparing for an ascent of Everest required workouts in the five- to seven-hour range, and he had been matching Chris step for step, pedal for pedal, and stroke for stroke. Only when climbing did Chris still hold an advantage. He was almost sixteen, bigger, taller, and stronger than Dominic. He could haul himself up a top rope as naturally as a yo-yo returns to the hand playing with it. Dominic was just a month past his thirteenth birthday, and small for his age.

The Mackenzie Avenue 7-Eleven was his home away from home. Dominic estimated he had drunk more than forty gallons of Summit Athletic Fuel in the process of spelling E EREST. He'd tried his share of the bars, too, but Summit Energy Bars were like quick-drying cement. After a few of them, your insides turned to concrete. Better to stick with the liquid.

One more bottle. One last try.

Out of habit, he checked the recycling bin behind the store first, but it was empty except for a couple of soda cans. Inside, he grabbed a bottle of Fruit Medley. The flavors didn't matter with Summit Athletic Fuel; it all tasted the same — like weak, slightly salted lemonade backwash. He paid, walked out, and flopped down on the wooden bench next to the store.

Before popping the cap, he addressed the good-luck charm the way he'd seen his brother do it. "Find me a V and it's Everest or bust! I'll take you to the top of the world!"

Sheepishly, he looked around to make sure no one had overheard. When Chris talked to his little vial of sand, it always seemed cool. But in the

THE CONTEST

7-Eleven parking lot, it was just plain embarrassing.

He twisted the cap off and peeked underneath.

Another E.

Until the wave of disappointment washed over him, he hadn't realized how much faith he'd had that his brother's good-luck charm would deliver.

The leather strap slipped from his fingers, and the vial dropped to the pavement and began to bounce down the small strip mall's parking ramp. Horrified, Dominic stumbled after it. Losing a shot at Everest was nothing compared with what he'd have to face if he came home without Chris's Dead Sea sand.

He scrambled like a crab, but the bottle rolled ahead of him, just out of reach. As he ran across the garage entrance, a hulking SUV roared up suddenly. The driver slammed on the brakes, and the big vehicle squealed to a halt just inches from the boy.

"What's the matter with you, kid? Why don't you look where you're going?"

"Sorry." Dominic picked up the vial and scooted out of the way. Mom had continuous nightmares that climbing would kill at least one member of her family. *I'll bet she wasn't expect-*

ing it to happen like this, he reflected, a little shaken.

The SUV accelerated up the ramp, pausing at the top. The driver tossed a candy bar wrapper into the trash barrel and drove off.

It was a Summit Energy Bar. Dominic recognized the logo from where he stood, rooted to the spot. He had climbed towering cliffs, yet walking up this gentle slope to get that piece of paper seemed much, much harder.

He reached into the garbage and fished out the sticky wrapper. In a way, he almost knew what he would see before he turned it over.

A V!

It was a ticket to the top of the world.

THE CONTEST

CHAPTER TWO

Cap Cicero wasn't much of a worrier.

That time climbing Mount McKinley, when the boulder dropped from fifteen thousand feet and whizzed by so close that the wind almost knocked him off the fixed ropes, he didn't worry. His philosophy was, if it misses you, it didn't happen. And if it hits you, then you've *really* got nothing to worry about.

A worrier in the mountaineering business was like a surgeon who fainted at the sight of blood. Neither was likely to make it very far, and Cicero had been racking up death-defying feats and glorious triumphs for thirty-one of his forty-seven years.

But now, watching the twenty SummitQuest candidates, Cicero fretted that signing on as the team leader might have been a mistake.

"They're *children*," he told Tony Devlin, who ran Summit's Sports Training Facility in High Falls, Colorado. "A trip up Everest takes twenty-five pounds or more off the average adult. Half of these kids would fade to nothing."

EVEREST

"Relax," Devlin soothed. "Look at Ethan Zaph —"

"I know all about Ethan Zaph," Cicero interrupted. Several months before, Ethan had achieved fame by climbing Everest a few weeks shy of his sixteenth birthday — the youngest person ever to stand on top of the world. "So where is he?"

Devlin chuckled. "He knows he's got a spot guaranteed. Why should he suffer through a month of boot camp?"

Cicero harrumphed, but he knew Ethan Zaph wasn't the problem. At six foot one and 220 pounds, the kid was built like a lumberjack. Christian Alexis was also adult-sized. But Chris had brought his thirteen-year-old brother with him. Thirteen!

"That was a mistake," Cicero told Devlin. "Chris I understand. But the brother? Look at him. I don't think he's five feet tall."

Devlin shrugged. "We didn't pick him. He qualified as a wild card through the retail contest."

Cicero raised an eyebrow. "Lucky kid. Either that or he really likes Summit bars."

"Or maybe he just doesn't give up until he gets what he's after," suggested Devlin. "Not a

THE CONTEST

bad guy to have on an expedition. I hear he's an A-1 climber."

Cicero shook his head. "Too small. Can't use him."

"Do me a favor," said Devlin. "Don't cut him just yet. Summit got a lot of publicity out of that contest. We want to make it look like the wild cards have a real shot at the team."

Cicero nodded wisely. "And *then* we cut them."

"Not necessarily." Devlin reached out and pulled aside a sturdy runner with a mass of dark curls. "Here's one of our wild cards. Rob Barzini, meet Cap Cicero."

The boy turned shining eyes on the team leader. "It's an honor to meet you, Cap. I've read up on some of your expeditions." He grinned broadly, revealing an upper and lower set of gleaming braces.

Cicero regarded him in dismay. "When can you lose the iron?"

"The orthodontist says I've got another two years to go."

Cicero sighed. "Pack your bags, kid. I can't take that mouth into hundred-below windchill. The cold will bust your braces, and you'll be running around the Death Zone with a faceful of razor blades."

There were a few tears, but Rob accepted his fate and headed off to the office to arrange for an early flight home.

"You're a tough man," accused Devlin.

"It's a tough mountain." Cicero blew his whistle. All around the quarter-mile track, the candidates stopped running and turned to him for instructions. All except Dominic. He kept going, his twenty-pound pack whacking him between his narrow shoulders. The kid sure had stamina.

Cicero clapped his hands. "Okay, step it up! Double time. There's no dogging it on the mountain!"

The running resumed, faster this time. Dominic was practically sprinting now. The supreme effort only had the effect of making him look even smaller as he darted around the bigger kids.

One time, on K2, Cicero dropped his glove into a crevasse while securing a slipped ladder. He got stuck high on the Abruzzi ridge and had to bivouac — spend a forty-below-zero night in a cramped ice cave with his exposed hand jammed up the opposite sleeve clear to the armpit in order to prevent frostbite. He awoke to the agony of a dislocated shoulder, but he didn't panic.

Finding four climbers in this lot. *That* was a cause for panic.

Okay, he thought. Zaph and Chris Alexis. He needed only two more.

His eyes immediately traveled to Norman "Tilt" Crowley, who was lumbering steadily around the track. Tilt — great nickname for a climber — was younger than Ethan and Chris, but almost as big, with the same powerful build and easy athleticism. Plus, he was only fourteen. If Cicero could somehow get him to the top, it would smash Ethan's record by more than a year. SummitQuest would be on the front page of every newspaper on the planet — which was the whole idea. The purpose of this expedition was advertising, after all.

He watched as Tilt rounded the curve and came up behind Dominic. It happened so fast that the team leader wasn't really sure he had seen it. Tilt put his hands on Dominic's backpack and effortlessly leapfrogged over the smaller boy.

Terrific, Cicero groaned to himself. The last thing a high-altitude expedition needed was a hot dog.

His eyes shifted down the line. Sixteen-year-old Joey Tanuda was smaller and less impressive, but rock-solid, with a reputation as a great team player. Also, he had ice experience. Every winter, his parents took him to Alaska to climb frozen waterfalls.

He knew that Summit Athletic was also pushing to put at least one girl on the team. Bryn Fiedler was the obvious choice. The country's top-rated female alpinist under seventeen, she was known to be a smart climber. Tall — five foot nine — and blessed with great arm strength, she was also tough. She had to be. Mountaineering was a sport dominated by men. Women climbers had to be bulldogs to get the respect they deserved, and Cicero figured the young ones had to try even harder than that.

Bryn aside, there weren't any girls who caught his eye, except —

The team leader stepped out into the track and plucked a Walkman and sunglasses off Samantha Moon, a fifteen-year-old brunette in a No Fear T-shirt. She was not only keeping pace with the other kids, but also windmilling air guitar as she ran. As the headphones cleared her ears, the pantomine power chords stopped, and so did Sammi.

She stared at Cicero in surprise. "What's up?"

"This isn't a fun run," he informed her hotly.

"Who said it was?" she retorted, snatching the headphones from his hands.

"People *die* climbing Everest," Cicero said. "I'll wash you out right now if you're not going to train seriously."

"I *am* training seriously," she shot back. "This" — more air guitar — "is just my style."

"Not on my expedition," he told her.

"Well, why didn't you say so?" She set the Walkman and glasses down at the side of the track and rejoined the running group, leaving Cicero shaking his head.

Devlin tossed him an offhand shrug. "If you don't like her attitude, cut her."

Cicero was tempted, but he held himself back. The truth was he didn't know a single top-notch alpinist who didn't have a bit of a screw loose. Aloud he said, "I'm keeping my options open."

Devlin pointed to a fifteen-year-old who sported the brightest orange hair Cicero had ever seen. "What do you think of the redheaded kid?"

"Easy to rescue," the expedition leader laughed mirthlessly. "We'll be able to spot him on the summit ridge all the way from base camp."

"Seriously," Devlin persisted.

Cicero followed the bouncing shock of hair. He was very much an "in the middle" teenager. Not tall, not short. Not fat, not thin. The kind of kid who'd get overlooked a lot — if it weren't for that lighthouse beacon on his head.

"Lazy," he observed, noting the lackluster

stride. "Not a good sign. But like I said, it's early. What's the big interest?"

"That's Perry Noonan," Devlin replied.

Cicero snapped to attention. "*The* Perry Noonan? He's here?"

"That's him," Devlin affirmed.

"Aw, Tony, we talked about this! I'm not doing anybody a favor putting a climber on that mountain who's not prepared."

Devlin met his gaze, and it was Cicero who looked away first.

"This is *my* decision," the team leader insisted. "That's in the contract. I'm the boss, right?"

"You're the boss of the expedition," Devlin agreed. "But there's always another boss. A higher boss, with the power to say something like, 'Maybe we won't climb Everest this year.' You know?"

Cicero thought back to the time on the north wall of the Eiger, when an ice screw snapped in two. He dropped sixty vertical feet and swung back into the rock face, shattering one ankle and spraining the other. He didn't panic back then. Who had the time? It would take all his skill and concentration to get down alive.

After what he'd seen and heard today, Cap Cicero was officially worried.

THE CONTEST

CHAPTER THREE

The Summit Athletic Sports Training Facility in High Falls, Colorado, was nestled amid snow-capped peaks in the Rocky Mountains. Built on a plateau at eighty-five hundred feet above sea level, it was by far the highest such complex in the United States. At that, it was still nearly two vertical miles *lower* than Everest base camp, and more than four below the summit.

The facility had hosted some famous names from the world of sports — Tiger Woods, Michael Johnson, Kobe Bryant, Tony Hawk, and the entire U.S. Women's World Cup soccer team. But never had the place seen the kind of workouts that were going on as the nineteen remaining candidates fought to land spots on Cap Cicero's Summit-Quest team.

For three hours each morning, the class trained in the huge gymnasium. This included weight lifting, aerobic machines, calisthenics, and hours practicing rope techniques on the massive sixty-foot climbing wall built especially for this group. It was a grueling effort, but nothing compared with what was in store for the after-

EVEREST

noon. Cicero and his trainers would take them on six-hour hikes over some of the roughest and steepest terrain in North America.

"Cap, I gotta stop," gasped Cameron Mackie after nine miles under a thirty-pound pack. The trail they were following went up and down so often it had been dubbed the Toilet Seat. Climbers were notorious for nicknaming routes.

"What's the problem?" asked Cicero, barely breathing hard.

"The problem is we're dying back here," Tilt complained belligerently. "If we wrack ourselves up in boot camp, how are we supposed to climb Everest?"

Cicero nodded but never slackened the pace. "That's the rule for regular mountaineering. For high-altitude ascents in the Himalayas, you go till it hurts, and then work through it. You have to get used to carrying on when your body says quit."

Sammi looked out over a dizzying precipice. "Man, can you imagine hang gliding from here? What a rush!"

"A rush to the hospital," commented Bryn wryly. "Once they helicopter your broken carcass out of the trees."

"You'll never summit Big E watching your back like that," Sammi warned.

"I may not get to the top, but I guarantee I'll

THE CONTEST

make it back to the bottom," Bryn said seriously. "Climbing is about figuring the angles, predicting the hazards, and avoiding them."

"In some textbook," scoffed Sammi. "It's an extreme world out there. You've got to be extreme with it! My boyfriend and I tried bungee last week. Caleb liked it, but I say it's a little artificial. I mean, once you bottom out, you're just hanging there."

"And your folks let you do all this?" Bryn asked, amazed. Her own climbing career was a constant source of conflict between her mother and father. Not that Mom and Dad needed much help to fuel an argument.

She fought off a wave of guilt. They would have split up regardless of whether her hobby was climbing mountains or collecting stamps.

Sammi shrugged. "Dad thinks climbing E will calm me down. But what I really want to do is, there's this underwater cave off Australia where you can scuba with sleeping sharks."

Bryn had to laugh. "You never met a risk you didn't like, right?"

"Just one," said Sammi Moon. "Living a boring life."

Lenny Tkakzuk waved a video camera in their faces. He was the guide in charge of documenting the expedition for the SummitQuest Web site.

"Aw, come on!" Cameron rasped.

"You've all agreed to give interviews for the site," the cameraman/guide reminded him.

"You mean on E," said Sammi. "Who cares what we do in boot camp?"

"We think we can build up some interest in who's going to make the team. Let's see a little of that can-do attitude. Say something positive!"

"I'm positive I'm going to throw up," Cameron supplied.

Tkakzuk, Lenny's mind-boggling last name, was actually pronounced *ka-chook*, or, as he himself explained, "A sneeze between two k's." A few of the candidates started calling him Sneezy. Not only did the moniker stick, but it sparked a whole Seven Dwarfs nicknaming craze. The zombified kitchen manager became Sleepy. The Web designer, who never looked straight at anybody and whose best friends were probably all computers, was known as Bashful. Andrea Oberman, the expedition doctor, who was also a world-class climber, was Doc. No one was Dopey, or at least not yet. It was Dominic's opinion that the name was being held in reserve for whoever turned out to be dopey enough to claim it. Dominic felt that the smart money was on Tilt. Surely, the loudmouth was going to open his big yap one time too many and get himself

bounced. Others insisted he was such a lock for Grumpy that to call him anything else was almost a crime.

Then there was Happy. He was a fifteen-year-old climber from California who always seemed to be in a good mood. According to Joey, his roommate, he smiled in his sleep. No matter how high Cicero twisted the agony meter on the afternoon marathon, Happy always seemed pretty thrilled about it.

"You think this is hard?" he'd say cheerfully. "This is nothing!" And he'd launch into a story of a killer rock climb in Yosemite.

Happy loved the cafeteria food. He thought the small dorm-style rooms they shared were the ultimate in luxury. Each night he spent hours in the computer lab, E-mailing his hordes of friends back home about how thrilled, excited, rapturous, and generally pumped he was.

"He's like a ray of sunshine," commented Joey. "I can't stand him."

That left Snow White. By unanimous agreement, the title was awarded to team leader Cap Cicero, because, as Sammi put it, "He's the unfairest of them all."

Cicero never seemed to run out of new and exciting ways to take the group through torture. When they got used to the thirty-pound packs, he made them carry forty. When they mastered the rough terrain, he found rougher. One time he led them on mountain bikes thirty miles to the top of a cliff called the Edge of the Earth. There, he had them descend on ropes with the bicycles strapped on their backs.

"You think this is hard?" beamed Happy. "At least it's cool. One time I got lost in the Pinnacles, and it was one hundred five degrees!"

When the indoor climbing drills became automatic, Cicero had a wrinkle to add to that, too. He led them through the same maneuvers lugging another climber, who was designated injured and unable to help.

"You can forget about me doing this on the real climb," Tilt grunted, struggling with Todd Messner's deadweight. "If one of you losers wipes out on Everest, consider yourself lucky if I don't step on your face on my way to the summit."

"And if *you* wipe out?" challenged Bryn, lowering Perry on a rope.

"It'll never happen," Tilt replied.

And watching his strength and confidence on the climbing wall, Bryn figured he was probably right.

That afternoon, five hours into a six-hour hike, Happy passed out cold halfway up a rock scramble called the Devil's Staircase. "You think this is hard?" he began, and then disappeared down the granite wedge.

Joey reached for his receding roommate, but overbalanced and fell. The unconscious Californian slid past Sammi and right between Tilt's legs. He was just about to drop off the slab when Bryn managed to trap him by pressing her backpack against the rock.

Luckily, Dr. Oberman was right there. After some water and a short break with his head between his knees, Happy was able to finish the workout.

The scare did nothing to wipe the perma-grin off his face.

MEDICAL LOG — PSYCH PROFILES
Interview with Dominic Alexis

Dr. Oberman: *How did you feel when Happy fainted today?*
Dominic: *I was sorry for him.*
Dr. Oberman: *Anything else?*
Dominic: *What do you mean?*
Dr. Oberman: *Fear, maybe? That it could happen to you?*
Dominic: *My dad has been training Chris and*

me. We know all the warning signs — dehydration, exhaustion —

Dr. Oberman: *Some of the kids have been complaining that Cap is too hard on them.*

Dominic: *Cap Cicero is a legend! I've read all his books. I practically memorized his 1999 K2 expedition. I can't believe I got to meet him!*

Dr. Oberman: *Does it bother you that you're the youngest and the smallest?*

Dominic: *I'm used to it. I train with Chris all the time.*

Dr. Oberman: *Your brother has an excellent reputation. Is that why you were so obsessed with winning the contest? To keep up with him?*

Dominic: *I don't think I was obsessed.*

Dr. Oberman: *The contest people say you showed up with 145 drink caps and 36 energy bar wrappers. You had to know the chances were slim. What made you keep trying?*

Dominic: *I couldn't find a V.*

Cicero looked up from the folder at Dr. Oberman. "What did you interview him for? I told you he's not going."

"I was curious about him," the doctor admitted. "He's such an intense little guy."

"And what did you find out?"

She grinned. "That he's honest, decent, dedi-

cated, motivated, healthy as a horse — exactly the kind of person you'd want on an expedition."

"Yeah," Cicero snorted. "If he was a foot taller, two years older, and forty pounds heavier."

She laughed. "You might also be interested to know that he's a huge fan of yours."

"Good," said Cicero. "I'll give him an autographed copy of my memoirs. He'll need something to read while his brother is busy climbing Mount Everest."

The next morning, Lenny "Sneezy" Tkakzuk got up bright and early so he could film the Everest hopefuls coming downstairs for breakfast. He was the first to see the damage.

In the small lobby outside the cafeteria, someone had knocked over an end table, breaking two of its legs and smashing a crystal lamp.

Ten minutes later, Cicero stood beside him, wiping the sleep from bloodshot eyes. "You got me up at six in the morning to show me a pile of broken glass?"

Sneezy looked worried. "Think about our kids, Cap. They're used to walking knife-edge ridges over thousand-foot drops. They're not exactly the clumsy type."

"Don't talk to me in riddles. I'm not even

awake," complained Cicero. "Are you saying someone did this on purpose?"

"Either that or there was a big fight last night. We're driving these kids pretty hard, and there's a lot at stake here."

Cap sighed. "I could have taken those orthodontists up Nanga Parbat. But no. I had to play hall monitor to a gang of juvenile delinquents!" He ran his hand through his thick, uncombed hair. "All right. I'll talk to them."

THE CONTEST

CHAPTER FOUR

It was a blinding blizzard, the kind that hit the Colorado mountains in January. The snow began just after dark, and by two A.M., when Cicero hauled the nineteen candidates out of their beds, there were already six inches of new powder on the ground.

"What's going on, Cap?" asked Chris, half asleep.

"Ever spend a night on the South Col of Everest?" Cicero asked.

"No."

"Well, this is the next best thing. Grab the tents. Camp-out tonight."

Bundled into their deep winter gear, they stumbled bleary-eyed into the storm. The biting cold woke them up in a hurry, but the operation of setting up aluminum poles was almost impossible in the blowing squall.

"Let's move," called Cicero. "You'll need to do this after eleven hours on the mountain." He turned to Sammi, who was flat on her back, napping, using the folded tent as a pillow. "What's the matter, Moon? I thought you liked it extreme."

"Yeah, extreme snowboarding," came the groggy reply. "Not extreme snow."

The climbing brothers, Chris and Dominic, were used to working together. Theirs was the first shelter up.

"I said hold the flap, idiot!" Tilt roared at Perry.

"Okay, okay." The red-haired boy did his best to squeeze into what little space was left by Tilt's bulk.

"What a waste of time!" Tilt raged.

Cicero overheard him. "No, it isn't," he said seriously. "Where do you think you're going, summer camp? Training for hard work and miserable conditions is hard and miserable."

"So where's *your* tent?" challenged Tilt.

"I've already done this part of the training," Cicero replied.

"Easy for you to say," Tilt muttered under his breath.

"You want to see my diploma?"

Tilt glared back in defiance.

"Fine!" The expedition leader ripped off his left boot and then the sock. "Annapurna, 1989. My helmet lamp malfunctioned, and I had to spend a night at twenty-five thousand feet. The

THE CONTEST

thing about frostbite is, there isn't any pain. You just feel numb. But it's worse than pain because you know what's happening to you."

The candidates gawked. The two smallest toes were missing from Cicero's foot. It was a cruel truth of high-altitude climbing. There was only one treatment for the worst kind of frostbite — amputation.

For the Everest hopefuls it was a reality check. They were all accomplished alpinists, but were they ready for the brutal toll that the great mountains could impose? Even Tilt was struck dumb.

"This is Honolulu compared with where we'll be in a couple of months," Cicero informed them harshly. "Aloha." It would have been an ideal moment to stride dramatically away. But since his boot was off, he had to hop, muttering under his breath as he disappeared into the storm.

"There goes one of the all-time legends," Dominic said admiringly.

"There goes one of the all-time crackpots," Tilt amended. "Like I need to look at his freak-show foot."

Chris glared at him. "You may be a good climber, Crowley. But it's going to take a long time before you've got the experience of that man."

Tilt spread his arms wide. "Forgive me for

thinking it's stupid to freeze out here for nothing."

"This is exactly the kind of camping we'll have to do on Everest," Dominic argued.

"And on Everest, I won't mind doing it!" Tilt roared. "But not when I've got a nice comfortable bed on the other side of that door!"

The tents offered protection from the wind and snow, but not the cold. The candidates snuggled deep in their sleeping bags and tried to stay warm. The space was so confined that they found themselves pressed together like sardines. It made sleep impossible.

"If you don't get your elbow out of my back, you're never leaving this tent alive," Tilt promised Perry.

"I can hardly move," Perry complained. He tried to get comfortable, but Tilt's bulk kept him pinned against the sidewall. "Hey —"

"What's the problem, rich boy? Accommodations not to your liking?"

Perry stared at him. "What are you talking about?"

"Look at your stuff. Titanium crampons. The best ice ax money can buy. Gore-Tex everything." He tweaked the fabric of Perry's jacket. "Heat panels, right? You're toasty warm while the rest of us freeze."

"It was a present —"

"You're loaded."

"My dad works at the post office," Perry insisted stubbornly.

"You mean he *owns* it."

Perry sighed. "I've got a rich uncle, okay? He's the one who pays for all my stuff."

"You should get him to buy you some talent," the big boy taunted. "You climb like my grandmother."

Perry wasn't even insulted. The fact was, he reflected unhappily, if it were possible to purchase mountaineering ability, Uncle Joe probably would have given him that, too, along with the lessons, and the equipment, and the clothes. Money was no object for Uncle Joe.

It was great and terrible at the same time.

And now it was starting to get out of control.

CHAPTER FIVE

For Perry Noonan, having a billionaire uncle was a lot like playing Twister with an elephant. No matter how well-meaning the animal is, you can't help but get pushed around a lot. Joe Sullivan's own alpine dreams were replaced by high blood pressure and a business that took up twenty-five hours of every day. That was when the bachelor CEO had traded in his ice ax and high-altitude gear for weekend climbs with his only nephew in the foothills outside Boulder.

And Perry had said yes. Of course it was yes. What kid would turn down a chance to spend time with the family legend? A man who was constantly in the paper or on TV? Never mind that Perry might have preferred to go to a hockey game with his uncle, or even take him on in a spirited chess match. (Chess — that was something Perry was good at.) But this was *Joe Sullivan*. If he wanted to hang out with you, out was where you hung. And if that meant climbing, so be it.

Climbing — Perry shuddered. He could do it. He even got pretty good at it. But the unnaturalness of it — the feeling that he was where he wasn't supposed to be — that never went away.

If God wanted me to get up that rock face, he would have installed stairs. It was an old joke, but Perry truly believed it. To him, there was something in a steep cliff or a rough crag that plainly said: *You don't belong here. Stay away.*

Over the years, he had learned to control the uneasiness. Something as simple as not looking down helped a lot. And the rope work kept his mind engaged. Belaying — the placement of bolts, anchors, and cams so that a climber can be secured by a companion in the event of a slip — took a lot of concentration. Because it kept his mind off of where he was and what he was doing, Perry had become a great belayer.

It made Uncle Joe proud. "I love watching you handle those ropes, kid. You're a natural!"

Uncle Joe never quite figured it out: Perry Noonan was good with ropes precisely because he *wasn't* a natural. He had been faking it all these years — up all those crags, all those gorges and cliffs. Now he was going to try to fake his way up the tallest mountain on Earth, twenty-nine thousand feet of not looking down. And just because he didn't have the guts to disappoint Uncle Joe.

His reverie popped like a bubble, and Perry was back in the tent.

He rolled over in the tight space. "It doesn't matter how I got here," he muttered in the darkness. "I'm not going to make the team anyway."

"You got that right," snorted Tilt.

It was Perry's one consolation. There was no way an expert like Cap Cicero could fail to notice that Perry didn't exactly measure up to his fellow candidates. For starters, Ethan Zaph would be coming soon. He was as good as 90 percent of the adult alpinists in the world and had summited Everest already. Then there were guys like Chris and Joey — *and* Tilt, who was a loudmouth and a bully, but athletically, a Mack truck. Even a couple of the girls seemed miles ahead of Perry. He thought of Bryn's confident efficiency and Sammi's fearlessness. This was more than a hobby to them. It was a way of life. Half the kids spent their free time bouldering. Nine hours of workouts a day, and these guys choked down lunch so they could race outside the complex and find a twenty-foot rock to scale. For *fun*.

Perry didn't belong on the same mountain with them. They were the kind of people who looked down.

He peered through the tent flap. All was quiet except for a shadowy figure about fifty feet away, barely visible in the storm. As he squinted

THE CONTEST

through the blowing snow, whoever it was tumbled over the rise and disappeared down the slope.

"Hey!" He grabbed Tilt's sleeping bag. "Somebody fell!"

"Not my problem," the big boy mumbled, turning over.

Perry burst out of the tent in a full sprint — or at least as much of a sprint as was possible plowing through snow. He peered down the hill. There was very little light, but he could hear distant screaming and could make out a dark shape plunging into the valley at unnatural speed.

He scrambled down the slope, breathing a silent prayer that he wasn't in hot pursuit of some kind of wolf, or worse, a bear. At the bottom, there was a shower of white and the figure disappeared. Perry rushed over.

"Hello?" he called. "Hello, are you all right?"

The snow shifted, and a frosted Sammi Moon sprang up, eyes shining. "Not bad!" She reached down into the drift and came up with a plastic garbage can lid. "I wonder if there's some way I could get this waxed."

Perry stared at her. "It's two-thirty in the morning! I thought you'd fallen over the edge!"

"I couldn't sleep," Sammi said innocently. She held out the lid. "Want to try?"

Correction, Perry reflected, amending his thought from before. He didn't belong on the same *planet* as these people.

The next morning, the camp awoke to clear blue skies gleaming off a foot of fresh snow. The storm was over. Dominic rushed to unzip the tent, eager for his first blast of warming sun. Instead, he found himself staring into the weathered face of Cap Cicero.

"All right, vacation's over!" the team leader bawled. "Everybody into the gym! We've got a mountain to get ready for!"

Tilt was belligerent. "I can't believe you made us do this!"

Cicero winced. "Change of plan, everybody. First mouthwash, *then* into the gym."

By the end of the day, two more SummitQuest candidates had quit and were on their way to the airport in Denver. Happy was one of them, smiling no longer. His parting words were: "It's too hard. It's the hardest thing I've ever done."

Perry had never even learned his real name.

THE CONTEST

CHAPTER SIX

The first round of official cuts was scheduled for the end of that week. Everybody realized it was coming, but nobody knew exactly what to expect. Would Cicero pull you aside and give you the bad news? Or maybe Sneezy, or Dr. Oberman? Would it be public? Would you be yanked away from the dinner table and marched off in disgrace? Maybe it would be the opposite of that: You'd wake up in the morning, and a whole bunch of kids would be just plain gone. And, of course, the million-dollar question: Who?

One thing was certain. As the time approached, the tension rose so high that you could almost hear a hum throughout the complex.

Tilt thought he might be the most nervous of the lot. It was crazy. What did he have to worry about? He was the best climber in the group, except maybe for Ethan Zaph, who still hadn't shown up. But Tilt was worried about all the mouthing off he'd done to Cicero. Not that the dictator didn't deserve it. The guy was on some kind of power trip and got his jollies by bossing

EVEREST

around a bunch of kids. But maybe it was stupid to bug the person who was in charge of picking the team. Tilt would have only himself to blame if he washed out.

And he needed this more than the others. *Tilt Crowley, the youngest kid to climb Everest. Buy this breakfast cereal; it helped Tilt Crowley reach the top of the world. Oh, Harvard needs a man like Tilt Crowley.* How else was he going to get to the Ivy League? Was he supposed to pay the tuition by working himself to death on a triple paper route, the way he'd bought his secondhand crampons? And the ice ax with the slightly warped handle? The other kids here all had state-of-the-art stuff. That was Tilt's definition of rich people. He didn't mean mansions and private jets, like Perry's uncle probably had. Rich was anyone who could climb as a hobby — a hobby that wasn't attached to a second career, seven miles a day, lugging the *Cincinnati Inquirer* through sleet or hundred-degree heat. If he made it to the summit, only he would know that the mountain had been the easy part of the ascent.

Sure, he realized the others didn't like him. They climbed on ropes; he climbed on attitude. If he had their advantages, he could be a nice guy,

THE CONTEST

too. Maybe he *should* have been nicer. Maybe he was going to be cut now for getting on people's nerves — on Cicero's nerves.

Come on, Cap, don't wash me out! I'm the best you've got. And I need this!

It finally happened after a thirty-mile hike with full gear through the snow. Seven lockers in the equipment room were tagged with yellow Post-it notes. *See Cap* was all they said. But everyone knew instantly. The ax had taken its first swing.

Four boys and three girls were headed home. Their Everest dreams were over.

Astonishingly, Joey Tanuda was one of them.

"But you've been eating Cap's workouts for lunch!" exclaimed Bryn.

Joey could only shake his head miserably.

Sammi was also surprised. "I mean, *Perry* made it, and you're twice the climber he is!"

"Hey!" Perry said feelingly.

"No offense, but it's true," Sammi persisted. "Why cut him and not you?"

Joey was so devastated that he could barely raise his gaze from the floor tiles. "A couple of years ago, I broke my nose bouldering, and the surgeon offered to do a nose job while he was in there anyway. I figured I might as well be beautiful, right? Now Andrea says my nasal passages are too tight for easy breathing when the air gets thin high on the mountain."

"Won't the bottled oxygen help?" asked Chris, feeling the other boy's pain.

"Not enough," said Joey. "I'm done."

"And after all that, you're still ugly," observed Tilt, kicking his climbing boots into his locker.

"I love you, too," Joey mumbled miserably.

Chris turned on Tilt. "The guy just washed out for something that's not even his fault. Think maybe now isn't the time for jokes?"

Tilt shrugged nonchalantly. "Who's joking?"

Joey glared at him. "You know what would make this okay? If you're next."

"Dream on, nose job," sneered Tilt. "I'm the best climber in this dump."

"Maybe so," said Joey. "But you're a self-centered jerk. There's no place for that on a climbing team." He shouldered his duffel and stood up.

"Sure, go ahead and hate me," invited Tilt. "But I'm the only honest one here. These guys all act like your best friends. But they don't want to admit that, deep down, they're celebrating. With you gone, one more spot on the team is up for grabs."

There was an awkward, embarrassed silence

THE CONTEST

as the truth of Tilt's words sunk in. Joey had been a favorite to make the chosen four. Sad as it was, his departure meant better chances for the remaining climbers.

"Hey," Joey said in a subdued tone. "I've got no hard feelings. I'll be following along on the Web site, pulling for you guys. *Most* of you," he added with a dirty look at Tilt.

Sneezy entered to record the parting on video. He was almost as disconsolate as Joey. "Sorry, kid. I know it's hard, but I've got to shoot this for the site."

Joey smiled halfheartedly. "Don't worry, Sneezy. We all knew the rules before we got here." With the camera running, he turned to Chris. "This is my Cub Scout mountaineering badge," he said, holding out a tattered piece of felt. "It's the first climbing thing I ever won. I want you to leave it on the summit for me."

Chris accepted the token. "If I get there, you get there," he promised.

And then there were ten Everest hopefuls left in the Summit Athletic Sports Training Facility.

What none of them knew was that, during the hike, Cap Cicero had actually affixed eight Post-it notes, not seven. The extra cut had been Dominic Alexis. Cicero had made the decision with regret.

The boy was a talented climber with incredible stamina and unfailing courage. But Cicero had felt from the start that the kid was too young and too small. So Dominic was out.

Later, Cicero was in Dr. Oberman's office, examining the candidates' chest X rays, which were all lined up across a wide viewing box. It was important for kids especially to have good lung capacity on Everest, where there was so little oxygen in the air.

He was looking with approval at an assortment of healthy chests when Tony Devlin ran up, all atwitter. "You have to change the cut."

Cicero looked surprised. "Why? Perry's still alive — not that you can tell from his effort level."

"This isn't about Perry," Devlin explained. "You've sent home all the wild-card kids."

Cicero adjusted the backlight. "Yeah, and I wonder why. Everest isn't a theme park, you know. You don't take tourists up there."

"The retail contest focused a huge amount of attention on SummitQuest," Devlin argued. "Already the newspapers and wire services are running updates from our Web site. It's like *Survivor*. People want to know who's going to make it. It looks bad if all the contest kids wash out by the first cut."

THE CONTEST

"It looks worse if we leave them dead in the Khumbu Icefall," Cicero said shortly.

"I'm not saying they have to end up on the team," Devlin reasoned. "Just keep one of them in the running a little longer so we can play it up on the site. Make it seem like the contest wasn't totally bogus — you know, like this kid really has a chance to go."

"It's not fair to the kid, either," Cicero noted. "These workouts aren't exactly patty-cake."

"Just do it," coaxed Devlin. "You of all people know how important it is to keep the sponsor happy."

It was true. Star alpinists would be stopped in their tracks if a disgruntled sponsor cut off the shipments of food and equipment.

"Fine." The team leader's eyes scanned the X rays and came to rest on the scrawny body that could belong only to one person. He blinked. Dominic Alexis was half the size of the others, but he had a chest full of dark, expanded lung tissue that would be the envy of anyone there. *He may be small,* Cicero reflected, *but he has the respiratory system of a six-foot-five bodybuilder.*

"We'll keep the little guy," he said suddenly. "Just till the next round. Then he's history."

"Thanks, Cap." A satisfied Devlin headed off to remove the Post-it from Dominic's locker.

MEDICAL LOG — PSYCH PROFILES
Interview with Perry Noonan

Dr. Oberman: *You seem surprised that you survived the first cut.*
Perry: *No, I'm not. I'm as good as anybody here, right?*
Dr. Oberman: *What do you think?*
Perry: *I've been climbing since I was nine.*
Dr. Oberman: *With your uncle?*
Perry: *Right.*
Dr. Oberman: *Do you want to climb Mount Everest?*
Perry: *Every mountaineer —*
Dr. Oberman: *Not every mountaineer. You. Do you want to climb Everest?*
Perry: *Yes.*
Dr. Oberman: *You're sure about that?*
Perry: *What do you want me to tell you? That it's less than useless? That if you're going to spend zillions of dollars on something that's practically impossible, you might as well be curing cancer, or stopping wars, or feeding the hungry? Well, forget it. People climb mountains, period. And the biggest one is the one they want to climb most.*
Dr. Oberman: *And that includes you?*
Perry: *Yeah, sure. Why not?*

THE CONTEST

Dr. Oberman: *I'm not hearing any straight answers.*
Perry: *I'm not hearing any straight questions.*

The kitchen manager, aka Sleepy, escorted Cicero around the wreckage of the crockery cabinet. The breakfront itself was tipped over on the floor. Around it were a million shards of broken glass and dishware.

The team leader was appalled. "My guys did this?"

"Unless we have a poltergeist," Sleepy said grimly.

Dr. Oberman spoke up. "I've been doing psych evaluations on all the kids. I could be wrong, but nobody jumps out at me as a vandal."

"Psych, my butt!" seethed Cicero. "It's Tilt Crowley! He's gone, first thing tomorrow morning."

The doctor was shocked. "You can't do that. You have absolutely no proof!"

"The Supreme Court needs proof!" Cicero raged. "I'm instant law! Ask any of the kids, and they'll tell you Tilt's the one."

"He has a lot of anger," Dr. Oberman agreed. "And there may be good reasons to send him home. But this isn't one of them. For starters, I don't think he did it. And if I'm right, the real culprit would still be here, and might even end up on the team."

"What about my dishes?" Sleepy demanded.

Cicero could only shake his head. "Charge them to the expedition, I guess." To the doctor he said, "I don't care about the money. It's the distraction that worries me. We can't lose our focus. Not on Everest. Not when we're facing the Death Zone."

THE CONTEST

CHAPTER SEVEN

The cuts brought a change in the atmosphere at the Summit complex. When the Everest hopefuls had been twenty in number, the final team had seemed very remote. Now they were ten, vying for four spots. And even though the top place was being held for Ethan Zaph, the odds were improving. The candidates could almost feel their crampons biting into the blue ice of Everest's glaciers. The biggest prize in mountaineering was slowly coming within reach.

A new sport was born, one that was almost as popular as climbing: figuring the angles.

Cameron Mackie was an expert at it. "Z-man takes the number-one spot; Chris gets number two — that's pretty definite."

"And one of the girls," put in Dominic. There were three left.

"Bryn," mused Cameron. "Then again, you can't write off Sammi. She's crazy, but she's good."

Dominic did the math. "That leaves only one spot for the rest of us. Probably Tilt."

"Tilt's too dumb," Cameron said seriously.

"He'll give Cap a wedgie and get himself cut. So, depending on the Perry factor, if I keep my nose clean, maybe I can sneak in the back door."

The Perry factor was the question of why Perry was still standing after much stronger climbers had been packed off to the airport.

"Maybe Cap thinks I'm good," was Perry's explanation. "Maybe you guys are wrong about me." But he didn't sound convinced.

"Maybe Cap's your rich uncle," sneered Tilt.

Perry said nothing. He had often thought of having a different uncle, but in his imagination it was always a nonclimber who thought the Himalayas was a chain of doughnut shops.

"It's getting weird," Bryn admitted to Sneezy in an on-camera interview for the Web site. "Normally, climbers are the friendliest people on the planet. You take six total strangers scaling El Capitán, and by lunch you've got six best buddies. Here you want to be nice to people. But part of you says that, if they do well, it could cost you *your* chance."

Nowhere was that more true than with Bryn and Sammi. Both were convinced that only one female would advance to the final team. So their competition, they felt, was solely between them and the other girl, who wasn't really a threat. Their growing friendship cooled. They weren't enemies, but they became afraid to trust each other.

Tombstone IV was a black crag, not enormous, but steep and awkwardly shaped — the toughest piece of technical mountaineering the candidates had tackled so far. The route required them to get over a rocky spur called the Club, and while they were climbing up the underside, they would be hanging exposed over a hundred-foot drop.

"Extreme," breathed Sammi reverently.

"I'm really starting to hate that word," groaned Bryn.

Bryn inserted a spring-loaded CAM in a crack on the bottom of the spur and watched the unit expand to secure the protection point. Sammi passed a rope through the ring and then wiggled out to place a second piece of hardware. But as she tried to scramble around to the top, the tangle of lines imprisoned her ankle. Bryn climbed out and reached to free her partner's leg.

And froze.

High up the crag, the two girls' eyes locked, and the message passed between them as if by radar: *If I leave you here and go for help, Cap could cut you for a beginner's mistake and then I've got a guaranteed spot on the team.*

The moment was over as quickly as it had unfolded. Bryn broke out of her inaction and undid the snarl of rope around Sammi's ankle. The two clambered atop the Club and rested, eyeing each other suspiciously.

"Was that what I think it was?" panted Sammi.

And Bryn could only shrug miserably. Helping a fellow climber should be as automatic a response as a dog chasing a stick. What was this competition doing to them?

"This is so bogus," Sammi complained to Dominic that night. "No mountain is worth it."

"This one is," Dominic said simply. He couldn't help noticing that, as his fellow climbers became cagier with one another, they were growing more open with him. That meant no one, not even his own brother, felt he had a shot at making the team.

Dominic himself didn't really expect to last much longer.

The cold air of the Rockies was rife with competition. Six-hour workouts now took five. Everything was speeded up as the candidates competed for Cap Cicero's attention.

Even leisure time was turning into a tournament. Bouldering after lunch had become an ex-

tension of boot camp, despite the fact that Cicero and his guides weren't even watching. It was now a full-blown obsession.

Dominic scrambled up a twenty-foot rock, scanning for handholds the way a chess master seeks out weaknesses in an opponent's defenses. On the other side of the craggy diorite outcropping, Tilt raced against him with strong, steady moves. Dominic couldn't see his adversary, but he had a good idea of his progress because Tilt climbed with his mouth as much as he did with his hands and feet.

"Getting tired, shrimp? You can't beat me. If you're looking for the top, just follow the soles of my boots. . . ."

"Tilt Crowley," Perry said with a sigh, watching from below. "The only climber who uses trash talk."

In a mammoth burst of energy, Tilt scrambled to the crown of the boulder and stood there, beating his chest and howling like Tarzan.

From below, Dominic snaked out a hand and began to feel for a handhold on the top. Tilt stuck out his boot and applied gentle pressure to the searching fingers. "No way, shrimp. This is *my* rock."

Dominic gave no answer, but it was not in his nature to retreat.

The boot pushed a little harder.

"Geez, Tilt," coaxed Perry, looking up at the two, "leave him alone."

Tilt nodded. "As soon as he gives." The foot bore down.

Dominic gritted his teeth against the pain. Because of the angle of the rock, he couldn't see his tormentor. But he could picture Tilt's expression of nasty triumph. It made him more determined than ever to hang on.

Perry searched the group and spotted Chris. He caught the older boy's attention and redirected it with a nod to the standoff atop the boulder.

Chris loped over. "Come on, Tilt. Let him up."

"No chance," said Tilt. "My summit, my record."

"What are you talking about?" asked Perry. "Half the kids have been up that thing."

"I'm the youngest, and that's what counts," Tilt said stubbornly. "The shrimp's younger than me, so he's not going."

"Is that how it's going to be on Everest, too?" challenged Chris.

A derisive snort. "No one's taking this runt to Everest." Now Tilt was leaning on the fingers. Dominic saw stars.

Chris established one handhold and one

foothold. "If I have to come up there, your descent is going to be fast and headfirst!"

"You think?" Tilt snarled defiantly.

Todd Messner came running down the path, waving a copy of the *National Daily.* "Hey, guys! Check it out! We're in the paper!"

Tilt stepped off Dominic's hand. "You're lucky, shrimp. My public awaits." He climbed effortlessly down and joined the crowds around Todd.

The article was a double-page spread in the sports section under the headline:

FROM DAY CAMP TO BASE CAMP

In a few weeks, the youngest expedition ever
will set out for the world's highest mountain.
But will their adolescent hang-ups prove to be
a bigger obstacle than Everest?

"Hey, wait a minute —" began Chris in protest.

The article was very different from the kind of information Sneezy was posting on their Web site. It said almost nothing about the SummitQuest training or the upcoming climb. Instead, it was written like a reality-TV episode, focusing on personal habits, embarrassing details, and petty squabbles. And the general tone of it seemed to ask, *How can these kids form a team to survive the Death Zone when they can't even agree who gets to use the bathroom first?*

"Hey, that only happened once!" exclaimed Perry.

Chris's face was carved from stone. "There's no way they could know this stuff about us!"

Somehow, the *National Daily* reporter had found out that Bryn's parents were filing for divorce, and the argument over sending their daughter to Everest had been the final blow to a shaky marriage. It was also stated that Chris was on academic probation at school, and the expedition would probably cost him a year. The fact that Sammi was E-mailing her boyfriend back home was blown out of proportion. According to the article, every other sentence out of her mouth was "Caleb did this" or "Caleb said that." The gutsy, in-your-face athlete came across as a love-struck ditz.

It went on: Cameron was in phone contact with his psychiatrist. Tilt was unpopular. Perry wasn't good enough. Dominic was too young and skinny. And Cap Cicero, famous alpinist and guide, was an inflexible bully who lived by the adage *My way or no way.*

"I don't get it!" exclaimed Todd. "I mean, it's all true, but — how did *they* find out?"

THE CONTEST

"Obviously," said Chris, "there's a rat around here. The question is who."

Tilt shrugged. "Simple. One of the guys who washed out got mad and squealed to the newspaper. It's no big deal."

"That's easy for you to say," put in Todd. "You're just unpopular. But Sammi's going to have a heart attack when she sees this."

"Not to mention Cap," added Perry.

"Cap's a big boy," put in Chris.

"Cap's a big jerk," Tilt amended. "But he's used to the media." Out of the corner of his eye, he spotted Dominic sitting cross-legged atop the mass of diorite. The younger boy's face radiated defiance.

"Your brother's spooky," Tilt informed Chris.

"Tell me something I don't know."

Bryn sprinted through the trees, all breathless excitement. "Sammi's found a monster problem down in the valley!"

In bouldering, a "problem" was a large, technically difficult rock. Climbing it was referred to as "solving."

They all raced after Bryn, including Dominic, who had to rush to catch up after descending the disputed boulder.

In a broad valley, almost hidden by a grove

of pines, stood the ultimate rock formation. It was three stories high and resembled a mammoth mushroom sitting atop a lopsided pedestal. As they watched, Sammi Moon scrambled up on the base and began to work her way onto the stem of the mushroom.

Perry waved. "Way to go, Sammi!"

"Shhh!" The others glared him into silence. No true climber would ever distract a fellow alpinist who was in the middle of taking on a tough problem.

Sammi reached the "ceiling" and clung there in the shadow of the enormous slab that made up the mushroom crown. It stretched at least seven feet around her in all directions. She reached up and ran her hand over the smooth limestone. She managed to get a finger lock in a small fissure and hung, twenty-five feet above them, searching for another hold. But there was nothing.

She paused for a moment, taking stock, then began to sway back and forth in an effort to swing her legs over the edge of the mushroom and find purchase on the top.

"Don't do it," urged Chris under his breath.

"Of course she'll do it," whispered Tilt. "Somebody get a mop."

But Sammi didn't like her chances and pulled

her lithe body back to the stem for a descent.

Tilt passed her on the way up. "Not very extreme," he commented cheerfully.

"You won't make it, either," she promised, tight-lipped.

She was right. First Tilt, then Bryn, then Todd were unable to get to the top of the mushroom. Chris, who was tallest, managed to get a foot over the edge of the crown, but couldn't find anything to latch onto up there and had to retreat. Dominic had the least success of all. His reach was too short to make it to the first finger lock, so he never got off the stem.

Cameron was smiling as he dipped his hands in the chalk bag. "Watch," he grinned, "and take notes." He had noticed a different hold, this one closer to the edge. The fissure was even narrower, but he succeeded in hooking two fingers into it.

There was no warning. A small shower of dust rained down at the same time the handhold crumbled.

CHAPTER EIGHT

Legs windmilling wildly, Cameron dropped fifteen feet straight down and bounced off the pedestal. He hit the ground like a ton of bricks and lay there, unconscious.

Chris got to the fallen climber first. "Find Cap!" he barked at the others. He looked at the trickle of blood coming from the corner of Cameron's mouth. "And Andrea!"

Bryn, who was the fastest runner, took off for the complex.

Sammi stepped toward Cameron, but Dominic held her back. "We can't move him," he warned. "He could have a broken neck."

There was no panic. The candidates fidgeted in grim acceptance. In their sport, the thrills were many, but the mishaps were often deadly.

Todd removed his glasses and held them in front of Cameron's nose. The lenses fogged. "He's still breathing."

The roar of a motor shattered the mountain quiet. The SummitQuest candidates watched as an all-terrain vehicle plowed down into the valley in a shower of powdery snow. As it drew closer, they could make out Cicero at the wheel. Beside him rode Dr. Oberman, with Sneezy and Bryn in the back.

The doctor leaped off the still-moving ATV and rushed to Cameron's side. Shedding her gloves, she lifted his eyelids and examined his pupils. Then she checked his pulse.

She addressed the nine candidates who were hovering around. "Don't look so tragic. He's not dead, you know. Concussion, I figure." She scanned her patient from head to toe. "And I don't like the look of that ankle."

All eyes followed her gaze to Cameron's right foot. No one had noticed it before, but the boot was twisted at an unnatural angle.

Cicero winced. "It's broken, all right. He's on his way home."

Somehow, that pronouncement percolated down to Cameron, who came awake with a howl. "No-o!"

"Just lie still," the doctor soothed. "I've got a splint in the ATV."

Cameron wept bitter tears of disappointment as the three guides immobilized his leg and placed him in the back of the vehicle.

"I blew it," he mourned. "Everest was so close I could see it in my sleep."

"It wasn't that close," Tilt told him mildly. "You were going in the next cut anyway."

"Hey, Crowley," Sneezy growled. "Ever consider a career in diplomacy?"

"I'm so stupid," moaned Cameron, covering his face with both hands.

"No!" Sammi exclaimed urgently. "Don't you get it? This is exactly how it's supposed to go! You went out in a blaze of glory, making a move nobody else saw! It's *poetry!*" She leaned over and kissed him on the forehead.

"It doesn't rhyme," was Tilt's comment.

Cicero regarded his nine remaining climbers. "Everybody's okay with this, right? Accidents happen."

Perry's mind screamed what his mouth didn't dare say: *Of course we're not okay with it! If this happens on Everest, it's going to mean a lot more than a broken ankle and a little concussion! It's going to be a four-thousand-foot drop down the Lhotse face!*

But aloud, he just murmured his assent along with the others.

Chris spoke up. "Cap, I know this is the wrong time to ask, but have you seen this?" He held out Todd's copy of the *National Daily.*

"I've read it," said Cicero, throwing a blanket

THE CONTEST

over Cameron. "I'm hoping it's just a one-time thing. But the fact is, we had a spy who might still be with us. So think twice before sharing your life story. Remember — Summit Athletic is sponsoring this expedition because it's good publicity. If they start getting more bad publicity than good, they could pull their funding and cancel the whole thing. Then nobody goes."

"And for God's sake tell them to stay off these boulders," added Dr. Oberman. "Especially this one!"

Cap started up the ATV, drowning out the doctor's suggestion.

Two words he would never say to a climber: *Stop climbing.*

MEDICAL LOG — PSYCH PROFILES
Interview with Samantha Moon

Dr. Oberman: *When you told Cameron his accident was like poetry, did you mean it?*
Sammi: *When you're a climber, that's what you are. To go down tackling a tough problem is as natural a thing as breathing. If you have to wash out, fine. But it shouldn't be because of a runny nose.*
Dr. Oberman: *If Cameron had fallen on his*

head, he could be dead right now. Would that be as natural as breathing?

Sammi: Why worry about something that didn't happen?

Dr. Oberman: People have died on Everest. 150 of them.

Sammi: That's what makes it extreme.

Dr. Oberman: You're not afraid of dying?

Sammi: I'm not going to die.

Dr. Oberman: How can you be so sure?

Sammi: Don't worry about me.

Dr. Oberman: If the possibility of dying is what makes it extreme, and you know for sure you're not going to die, then it's not really extreme, is it?

Sammi: Are we going to look at inkblots, or what?

THE CONTEST

CHAPTER NINE

It happened just before midnight.

The quiet of the slumbering sports complex was shattered by a deafening clatter. It woke every sleeper.

Cap Cicero, still hopping into a pair of sweatpants, exploded into the hall with every ounce of the determination that had propelled him up the Matterhorn during the famous blizzard of 1998.

Perry appeared at the doorway of the room he shared with Tilt. "What was that?"

"Go back to bed!" roared Cicero, pounding down the hall. He wheeled around the corner, narrowly avoiding a collision with Sneezy.

"Calm down!" the cameraman/guide exclaimed. "Nobody's hurt."

Cicero looked past him to the utility closet. The door was open, and mops, brooms, and pails were scattered everywhere, along with bottles of detergent, floor wax, and bleach.

Cicero picked up a deck mop and stormed up and down the corridor, banging on doors.

"Maybe you're used to cushy guidance counselors and child psychologists who think that busting up people's property is a cry for help. *I* work in a place where there isn't any vandalism because every ounce of energy has to go to keeping yourself and your teammates alive! If Summit came to me today and asked, 'Is your team ready to go?' I'd have to say no. Because any idiot who thinks it's fun to trash a broom closet has no place on that mountain. And two weeks from now I'll say the same thing and scrap this expedition. Don't think I won't!"

He tossed the mop back into the closet and stormed off.

"I'll wake up Maintenance," Sneezy called after him.

In the gloom of her dorm room, Sammi Moon's face wore an oddly stricken expression. It was not Cap's speech that had upset her; nor was it even the grim prospect of having SummitQuest canceled.

She gazed across the sparsely furnished space at Bryn's bed.

Her roommate was not there.

Dominic lay for a long time after the disturbance, trying to empty his mind and will himself back to sleep. This was weakness — on an expedition, the ability to rest was as important as a good ice ax. Look at Chris. In the other bed, his brother was out like a light — and had been since thirty seconds after his head had hit the pillow.

The dim red glow of the digital clock on the nightstand read 2:11.

Resolutely, he got out of bed, pulled on jeans and a sweatshirt, and shrugged into a down ski jacket. Carrying his boots, he tiptoed out the door and down the hall to the darkened equipment room. He didn't risk a light — the locker room was directly across the courtyard from the security desk by reception. He felt around behind the door until his hand closed on a helmet lamp. He pulled it from its wall peg, then sat down on the floor, laced on his boots, and let himself out the side entrance into the frigid night.

Had Dominic turned on the light in the equipment room, he would have seen that there were Post-it notes — washout notes, they now called them — on four lockers. One of them was his.

He made his way over the rise and, when he was out of sight of the building, switched on the lamp. Light flooded the snowy terrain ahead of him. The trees cast unnaturally long shadows, like eerie pointers, showing the way down into the valley where the great mushroom stood. That had been his destination all along. When Dominic was restless, the answer was always the same: *Go climb something.*

All at once, he halted in his tracks and switched off the torch. Ahead of him, the mushroom was bathed in light. Someone was up there!

Staying in the cover of the trees, Dominic moved slowly forward.

The ATV was parked thirty feet away. On the back of it was a portable floodlight, its bright beam illuminating the "problem." Suspended there, dangling from the handhold on the underside of the crown, was Cap Cicero.

Dominic's first impulse was to turn on his heels and run for the complex. Instead, he stayed riveted to the spot. This was one of America's top alpinists, *climbing!*

He watched in awe as Cicero managed to gain a boot in the fissure. Then, hanging upside down, he literally created a hold out of thin air by wedging the side of his hand up against a quarter-inch ridge in the rock.

Dominic let out his breath and realized he'd been holding it. It was a brilliant move that required amazing wrist strength. Maybe one climber in a hundred could even have seen it was possible, let alone pulled it off. But, he noted, Cicero was still too far from the edge of the mushroom to have a shot at the top. Spectacular as it was, this wasn't the move that would solve the problem.

Cicero retreated to the stem and began to climb down. Suddenly, he froze.

"Who's out there?"

Escape crossed Dominic's mind only briefly. Surely, he had no right to be here in the middle of the night. But somehow he had the feeling that a true climber would understand.

He stepped out into the light.

Cicero was surprised, and not pleasantly. "Alexis, are you crazy? It's two-thirty in the morning — " Then it occurred to him that there might be a confession coming. He descended the sloped pedestal and leaned against it to catch his breath. Dominic approached him, squinting against the powerful beam of the floodlight.

"So what's on your mind, kid?" Cicero prompted.

"I couldn't get back to sleep," Dominic admitted. "Sometimes my brain just goes wild, and I think about a million things one after the other. Tonight it kept coming back to this rock. So I thought I could — I don't know — study it or something."

Cicero flushed with anger. "Not on my watch! You're supposed to be in training, Mister, and — "

He stopped himself. Dominic *wasn't* in training anymore. Cicero himself had placed the Post-it on the kid's locker. What was the point of being mad at him? Even if it turned out that Dominic was the SummitQuest vandal *and* responsible for leaking information to the *National Daily*, he was leaving tomorrow. It didn't matter if he was guilty of insomnia or a whole lot more; he was *gone*.

Cicero inclined his head toward the boulder. "It's a tough one," he agreed. "But to tackle it solo, in the dark — "

In answer, Dominic clicked on his helmet lamp. "And *you* came here alone," he pointed out.

Cicero had to laugh. "What, you don't think I've got the credentials?"

Dominic quoted from memory. *"Summer, 1998. Cap Cicero climbs every important peak in the Alps in six weeks."*

"I had good weather," the team leader said, embarrassed.

Dominic clambered up the pedestal and worked his way over to the stem of the mushroom.

Cicero looked at the sky in exasperation. "I thought I was speaking English. It must have been Cantonese." Yet he couldn't help but watch as the young climber moved efficiently up the problem. "You won't make that handhold," he predicted. "You haven't got the wingspan. Here — " He shinnied up the stem to Dominic and positioned himself to provide a platform to get the boy within reach of the fissure.

With a grunt of thanks, Dominic was able to make it to the cleft in the rock, using Cicero's knees as a stepping-off point. Then, carefully but with confidence, he duplicated the team leader's move. As he hung there, upside down, the helmet lamp fell off his head and shattered on the pedestal below.

"See?" said Cicero. "If it wasn't for my light, you'd be in the dark right now. Alone. Wait a second, and I'll give you a hand getting down."

"I can do it." The voice was not even strained. Slowly, exhibiting remarkable muscle control, Dominic reversed the move. But instead of swinging back down to the artificial ledge provided by Cicero's knees, he launched himself directly at the stem, catching on and sticking, Spiderman-style.

Cicero replayed the reverse move and dismount with wide eyes. Of course it wasn't impossible; he had just witnessed it. But someone of Dominic's size should not have that kind of strength, not to mention the guts to try something like that.

"Get in the car!" he said gruffly.

As they drove off in the ATV, Cicero noticed that Dominic didn't face front until the boulder was out of sight.

Cicero fretted over the steering wheel. Dominic was cut, finished, gone. And yet the team leader couldn't get the kid out of his head.

He thought, *Is it wrong to let this boy stay in boot camp when he has absolutely no chance of making the team? Is it fair to keep him around just because I like him and I want to see what he'll do next?*

The next morning, the nine candidates awoke to find only three Post-it notes in the equipment room. Three more Everest hopefuls were going home.

Dominic Alexis was not one of them.

THE CONTEST

CHAPTER TEN

Chris, Bryn, Tilt, Sammi, Perry, and Dominic were still standing. Somewhere, Ethan Zaph made seven. By the end of the month, three of them would be gone.

The Summit complex, scene of budding friendships, excited chatter, and screaming arguments, became as silent as a tomb. As Everest moved within reach, the candidates retreated inside themselves and focused on their training with the concentration and tunnel vision only athletes understand.

Sammi explained it in an interview for the Web site. "Last week, we were supporting one another to get this far. Now, all of a sudden, it's me me me."

"There's too much at stake to be nice to people," Tilt agreed.

"Like he'd know anything about being nice to people," Chris muttered under his breath.

But as the front-runner, confident, affable Chris was feeling the pressure more than anyone. He had watched Ethan Zaph become a star by summiting Everest. Now it was finally his turn. His

Dead Sea sand could be headed for the top of the world. A SummitQuest spot was his for the taking — but also his for the losing if he slacked off.

"My brother hasn't talked to me in three days," Dominic said on camera. "But that's okay. He hasn't talked to anybody else, either."

Even the normally boisterous Tilt seemed subdued. In part, it was an effort to avoid angering Cap this close to the moment of decision. But it was also from just plain nervousness. To him, this was more than an expedition; it was his future. Mess up, and it was back home, back to the paper routes, back to his life as a nobody. Who knew when he'd get another chance like this? Maybe never.

So he kept his mouth shut while Cicero ran everybody ragged. A speed climb? Great idea, Cap. Of course the slave driver didn't mention that they'd be doing it on Amethyst Peak, a full sprint up a thirteen-thousand-foot mountain. Eight grueling hours on the ascent, plus three more going down — get this — in the *dark*. No helmet lamps. No ropes. Nothing. A guy could break a leg and cost himself a chance at the summit that *really* counted.

"Congratulations," Cicero told them as they lay gasping at the end. "You've just put in a typical day's work in the Himalayas." Never mind that the whole Everest route was fixed with ropes, and the closest thing to free climbing they'd be doing was the walk along the yak trail into base camp. Biggest challenge — not stepping in the yak doo. Sure, Cap. Anything you say.

And when they had to wait an hour for Perry to catch up, Tilt didn't say a word about that, either. Only Cicero knew why Perry was still alive in this thing when he wasn't fit to carry Tilt's crampons.

Mealtimes were the worst. With none of the candidates saying much, there were plenty of empty spaces for Cicero to fill with boring memories of his alpine career: "Did I ever tell you about the time on Gasherbrum . . . ?" "Once, I was climbing in the Andes and there was this avalanche. . . ." "I'll never forget the night I was trapped in a crevasse on the Vinson Massif in Antarctica. . . ."

The others actually seemed to like those stupid climbing stories, Dominic especially. The runt's eyes lit up every time Cicero opened his mouth. And even Tilt had to admit that Cicero's Greatest Hits was still better than having to listen to Sneezy's dumb jokes or Dr. Oberman's probing questions: "And how does that make you *feel?*"

It makes me feel like I want you to shut up.

To minimize his chances of combusting in front of Cicero or his guides, Tilt had thrown himself into his schoolwork. The complex had a computer lab where the Everest hopefuls could keep up with their classes via the Internet. These days, all of them were clocking major time there. It was a way to avoid conversation. Even Chris, the flunk-out champion of the group, was a student all of a sudden. Not that Chris was going to have any trouble getting a full ride to any college in the country. Cicero loved him. He was going up Everest no matter what. But he wouldn't be the youngest. Not if Tilt Crowley had anything to say about it!

Tilt slipped up only once in front of Cicero. It happened on yesterday's ascent. Low on the mountain, there was a steep rock scramble that led through a narrow limestone crevice — almost like a vertical tunnel in the route. It was simple enough for a real alpinist, but Perry was obsessed with his lines and bolts and pitons. The guy would top rope a flight of stairs. Free climbing spooked him.

He made it up the tunnel part okay, but at the opening he just froze. Either he couldn't find the foothold, or he just couldn't compel his body to heave itself out into the open.

THE CONTEST

Cicero was about twenty feet away, talking to Sneezy, who was shooting for the Web site. Tilt could have reached out and hauled Perry up by the collar, but didn't it make sense to show Cicero that he had a climber who was either too uncoordinated or too chicken to execute a maneuver straight out of Mountaineering 101?

Cicero quickly took in the situation. "Give him a hand, Crowley."

Tilt could have done it, *should* have done it, and the incident would have passed unnoticed. But then came the frustration, the anger that some person, some *force* was protecting this mediocre climber from the washout that should have happened weeks ago. And Tilt couldn't hold back: "Maybe you should ask his *guardian angel* to come save him!"

The expedition leader glared at him. "I told you to help him out!"

Tilt yanked Perry up beside him. The red-haired boy brushed himself off. "Thanks."

Tilt didn't answer. He was in equal measure enraged and terrified by the expression on Cicero's face — the I'm-writing-it-all-down-and-this-is-going-to-cost-you look he had seen so many times before.

That night, to stay out of Cicero's face, he studied so hard for a science test that he scored

100 percent. If he didn't get to go to Everest, he reflected, at least he was turning himself into a genius in the process. And a hermit.

That was the plan. Keep quiet. Speak only when spoken to.

And pray.

MEDICAL LOG — PSYCH PROFILES
Interview with Norman Crowley

Dr. Oberman: *Tilt — is that a climbing nickname?*

Tilt: *No, ma'am. It's a name I got because I used to love playing old-fashioned pinball machines.*

Dr. Oberman: *Is mountaineering a Crowley family sport?*

Tilt: *My parents aren't into sports.*

Dr. Oberman: *But you are?*

Tilt: *Just climbing. It's everything to me. I'm nothing without it.*

Dr. Oberman: *What about Everest? Think you'll make the team?*

Tilt: *Hope so. I'm really counting on it.*

Dr. Oberman: *What's your attitude toward your fellow climbers here at boot camp?*

Tilt: *Everybody's great. I want to make it, but I wish them all luck.*

THE CONTEST

Dr. Oberman: *And I'm talking to the real Tilt Crowley?*

Tilt: *What do you mean?*

Dr. Oberman: *The word around here is that you're abusive, unfriendly, uncooperative —*

Tilt: *I understand. Really, I do. Climbing is very intense, and to be up against a competitive group like this — who wouldn't be scared of guys like Chris Alexis and Ethan Zaph? I guess I come on a little strong. . . . Do you think I should apologize to the others?*

CHAPTER ELEVEN

Crash!

Bryn came awake in the usual way, the way she had come to dread. First, a murky semiconsciousness, and then dawning horror. Horror that it had happened again.

There she stood, pajama-clad and barefoot in the TV lounge, surrounded by shattered glass. The trophy case — destroyed. The soapstone Eskimo sculpture — broken in half where it had been thrown through the doors. Where *she* had thrown it —

"What's going on out there?"

Cicero's voice galvanized her into action. She ran out of the lounge, avoiding the shards of glass with high-stepping feet.

A commotion in the dormitory hall. Doors opening. Voices. She began to panic. She would never get back to her room without being seen.

Don't let me get caught now! Not when I'm so close!

The laundry room! She ducked through the door.

That was stupid. They might look in here.

THE CONTEST

Feeling like she was losing control of an already absurd situation, she climbed into an industrial-sized dryer and pulled the door almost closed.

The sounds that followed had become familiar: footsteps and groggy voices; Cicero's tirade. She couldn't make out all his words, but the message was obvious: If he ever found out who was behind this vandalism . . .

But it isn't vandalism!

The timing was everything. She had to hit the gap — the lull after the SummitQuest people had gone back to bed but before Maintenance arrived to clean up the mess. What a skill to become expert at!

Just be grateful nobody decided to throw in a midnight load of laundry.

She crept down the hall, her feet barely touching the floor. Her eyes were focused like laser beams on the door to the room she shared with Sammi. Climber's habit. You never take your eyes off the destination — the next pitch, the next ledge, the next camp.

She let herself in and paused, calming her racing heart as she waited for her eyes to get used to the dark. She had made it. She had pulled it off. Again.

The light clicked on, and there was Sammi, watching her intently. "We need to talk."

"Somebody threw the black igloo into the trophy case," Bryn explained, struggling to keep the panic out of her voice. "It's smashed."

"I know," said Sammi. "You'd better get your brush. There's still some glass in your hair."

As soon as she heard the words, Bryn knew it was over. That sculpture had shattered her Everest dream as surely as it had the glass of the trophy case. She was going home. But what was home, anyway? A place to watch Mom and Dad snipe at each other through their lawyers instead of directly? To witness them dividing up the assets, the last of which would be *her*? The irony was that her parents, who had fought so hard over SummitQuest, weren't going to live happily ever after just because she was the next washout.

Sammi picked up the phone on the nightstand. "This is Sammi Moon. Could you ask Cap to come to room fourteen? Thanks." She faced Bryn. "Before he gets here, answer this one question: What's your payoff? What are you getting out of this? I mean, I'm good, but you're better. That spot was all sewn up for you. Why would you throw it away just to smash a little glass?"

Bryn was so downcast that she couldn't even look at her roommate. Her entire reply was addressed to the weave of the carpet.

"I was five years old when I started sleepwalk-

THE CONTEST

ing. I don't even remember it. Just the stuff that happened because of it — the window I broke, the stairs I fell down, the special doctor I had to see. I'm not even sure when it stopped, just that it did. It was ancient history — until I came here. Honest, I'm in bed, and then suddenly I'm in the middle of a demolition derby — busted dishes, the ruins of a lamp, a tangle of mops and pails. And I can't remember how I got there."

Sammi was wide-eyed. "You have to tell Cap! A sleepwalking climber! Here it's a broken trophy case; on E it's a ten-thousand-foot drop!"

Bryn tried to explain. "You don't understand! This isn't a part of my life. It's just boot camp. It's like living in a pressure cooker. I know once I get away from here the sleepwalking will stop!"

"But what if it doesn't?"

"It will! There's something freaky about this place — the stress, the competition, the feeling that your every move is being watched. You make friends and then you have to stomp all over them before they stomp all over you."

"I love climbing," Sammi agreed, "but this is no way to live. By the time it's over, we're all going to be like Tilt."

"But once the team is set, everything will be back to normal," Bryn persisted. "And I *know* I won't be sleepwalking anymore!"

Sammi was silent for a long time. "I want to win that spot," she said finally. "But not like this."

"We can both make it," Bryn enthused. "It's a long shot, but it's *possible*. Or maybe you'll get picked over me. Cap's unpredictable. Who knows what's in his mind? Perry and Dominic are still here. Who would have believed that?"

There was a sharp rap at the door. "What's going on in there?" came Cicero's gruff voice. "Are you guys okay?"

Sammi and Bryn locked eyes. The decision was made in that instant.

"Is everything all right, Cap?" Sammi called.

"You couldn't ask me that over the phone?" was the roared reply.

"Sorry," Sammi apologized. "Did you find out who broke the case?"

"And stop the fun so soon?" snarled the team leader. "No, I want to give the person a chance to spray-paint graffiti on the Khumbu Icefall! Go back to sleep!"

They listened to him stomp away.

Bryn's eyes filled with tears. "I can't believe you did that for me."

"I can hardly believe it myself," said Sammi Moon.

THE CONTEST

CHAPTER TWELVE

Cicero: *Come on, Andrea, is this really necessary? I'm not one of the kids.*
Dr. Oberman: *I heard you on that three-hour conference call. They could hear you in Denver.*
Cicero: *Sometimes I say things with emphasis.*
Dr. Oberman: *The final cut is Friday. I'm guessing you were making a last-ditch effort to unload a certain climber.*
Cicero: *You'll never know how hard I tried. I don't want him. Even the kid doesn't want to go. I was as good as told that the whole expedition depends on it.*
Dr. Oberman: *So that's it, then. You did all you could.*
Cicero: *I always said I'd never put an unqualified climber on that mountain. I'd scrap the whole thing first. Do you think it's easy to admit to yourself that you're not as honorable as you thought you were?*
Dr. Oberman: *What do you mean?*

EVEREST

Cicero: *A fifteen-year-old boy might die half a world away from his family and everything he knows. I could prevent that. But apparently, all I care about is having another crack at Everest.*

Dr. Oberman: *Aren't you forgetting something? That fifteen-year-old is going to have a guide who's the best in the business. If anyone can get Perry to the top, it's you.*

Cicero: *A guide can't stop altitude sickness or a falling chunk of ice.*

Dr. Oberman: *Those things are acts of God. They'd have the same effect on the most skilled climber in the world. Summit picked you because you're number one, because they know that their kids will be as safe as it's possible to be on a Himalayan peak.*

Cicero: *Okay, but just don't ask how it makes me feel.*

Dr. Oberman: *If anything, this does your job for you. That's one less spot you have to pick. Will you be ready to announce the team on Friday?*

Cicero: *I'm ready now.*

The final team was unveiled late Wednesday afternoon, two days early. Ethan Zaph, Christian Alexis, Bryn Fiedler, and Perry Noonan would be

THE CONTEST

traveling to Nepal as Cap Cicero's SummitQuest expedition. Sammi Moon, Tilt Crowley, and Dominic Alexis were going home.

It was never easy to tell a climber, young or old, that he or she didn't measure up. But Cicero was actually looking forward to his meeting with Tilt. He had even prepared a speech: *You're a great climber but a lousy person. I wouldn't put you on my team if you were the last kid on Earth.*

And when the moment came, the Tilt Crowley who sat across the desk from him wasn't the brash, selfish bully Cicero had come to know and dislike. He was just a heartbroken fourteen-year-old who was having his life's dream snatched away.

"Crowley, you've got some growing up to do," was all Cicero could manage. "Sorry it didn't work out."

Tilt stumbled out of the office, stunned and devastated, and managed to fumble his way into his room to pack.

It was too late to make it to Denver to catch flights home, so Sammi, Tilt, and Dominic were not scheduled to leave until morning. The last night at the Summit complex was not going to be a pleasant one for them.

Tilt didn't show up at dinner. Sammi and Dominic were there, but without much appetite. Neither had expected to make it, but the disappointment was still keenly felt.

"I'm sleeping in the TV lounge tonight," Perry said feelingly. "Tilt's going to strangle me in my bed."

In truth, if there was anyone more shaken than Tilt, it was Perry. The news that he had made the Everest team had shocked him to the core. Oh, sure, it had been obvious, as he survived cut after cut, that there was something more than talent keeping him in the running. But never had he expected it to go this far. Like the moment in a bad dream where you're conscious enough to know you're going to wake up before the really hideous part, he had always relied on Cicero to put an end to this. And now he was on his way to climb a killer mountain.

That night, he sat in the lounge, surfing old reruns on TV until around midnight, when Dr. Oberman caught him there.

"You're in training, Perry. You know you should be in bed."

"Right," said Perry. "I was just on my way."

She regarded him intently. "And congratulations."

For a moment, he looked at her as if she were speaking Greek. Then, "Thanks, Andrea. Thanks."

THE CONTEST

She paused. "You know, no one can make you do something you don't want to do."

Perry nodded slowly. "Good night." She had obviously never met Uncle Joe.

If Perry had expected rage, bullying, and abuse, it was not to be. In fact, Tilt was already in bed and did not address a single word to him.

All night, Perry could hear muffled sobs coming from the other side of the room. And if Tilt had not been so wrapped up in his own misery, he would have been able to detect similar sounds coming from Perry.

It was a curious paradox that one roommate should be crying because he wasn't going, and the other because he was.

Dominic zipped up his duffel bag and swung it over his shoulder. "I'll see you in a few days," he said to his brother.

Tomorrow, the team would be flying up to the Alaskan panhandle for a practice ascent. After that, they would return home for three weeks of rest and preparation for the trip to Kathmandu and the ultimate adventure.

Chris put an arm around his younger brother's slender shoulders. "You know, Dom, I thought it was crazy, you saving all those wrappers and caps. But I'm really glad you were here with me.

Is there anything you want me to take to the summit?"

Dominic grinned ruefully. "Yeah — me."

"You'll get your shot," Chris promised. "You're a great climber. There's nothing wrong with you that time won't take care of. Try not to hold it against Cap."

Dominic looked surprised. "It's been the greatest thing in my life, training with Cap Cicero. I'll never forget this month." He opened the door. "I've got a plane to catch."

Outside, Bryn was helping Sammi load her luggage into the Summit van.

"It's called cliff jumping," Sammi was explaining brightly. "Caleb did it last year in the Canadian Rockies. You're on skis, but it's not a real run, so you have to jump from snow patch to snow patch. If you hit rock, the wipeouts can be nasty. It's pretty extreme."

Bryn was all choked up. "I'll never forget what you did for me."

Sammi shrugged. "You climbers are too obsessed with mountains, mountains, mountains. There's plenty of adventure out there. I'll find something cool to do." She embraced her roommate. "Sleep tight," she said meaningfully.

"I will," Bryn promised.

Tilt was already in the van, eyes staring

THE CONTEST

straight forward, his face a thundercloud. He said good-bye to no one, and no one said good-bye to him.

Sneezy's video camera rolled on as Sammi and Dominic pulled the door shut. The footage was shaky and of low quality. The cameraman was having his usual hard time watching candidates on their way home. To make matters worse, Lenny Tkakzuk would be driving the van into Denver. So he would be seeing the three disappointed climbers all the way to their airplanes. It was extra agony for a tenderhearted guide.

The drive was shattering — two hours of nothing but mountains, the last thing a failed climber wanted to think about. Dominic tried to envision the scenery of Kansas or maybe Nebraska. But the winding Colorado highway offered up snowcapped peak after snowcapped peak, stinging reminders of what had been so close, but had slipped away from them.

He listened to the never-ending scores and analysis from the all-sports station that the radio was tuned to, mingled with the tinny whine escaping from Sammi's headphones. The only other sound in the van was Tilt's breathing, steady, but too heavy, like a bull about to charge.

Tilt's temper snapped about an hour into the drive. In a single motion, he had the tape out of the player and out the window before Sammi could exclaim, "Hey! That was Garbage!"

"Now it's roadkill," muttered Tilt.

Dominic slipped out of his belt and positioned himself between the two of them on the bench seat.

"You're going to pay for that!" Sammi raged.

"Who's going to make me?" sneered Tilt. "The shrimp?"

"Come on, guys," pleaded Sneezy, trying to watch the road and keep an eye on his charges at the same time. "I know this isn't an easy trip —"

Sammi fixed her furious gaze on Tilt. "You think because I'm a girl, I'm not going to put you through that back window?"

Tilt seemed to relish the chance to blow off steam. "You think because you're a girl, I'm not going to hope you try?"

"Leave her alone," ordered Dominic.

"Shut up!" chorused the combatants.

Sneezy pulled the van over to the shoulder, stopping in a spray of gravel. He turned in his seat. *"Cut it out!!"*

They were momentarily shocked into silence. No one had ever heard the affable Sneezy raise his voice in anger. It was in that lull that the announcement came over the Sports Report:

"It was learned today that Ethan Zaph, the

teen who conquered Everest last year, has pulled out of Summit Athletic's SummitQuest expedition. In a case of 'Been there, done that,' Zaph has signed on with This Way Up, a team that's planning a double ascent of Everest and nearby Lhotse. Zaph, the youngest ever to bag the world's tallest peak, promises this year's climb will be made without the help of supplemental oxygen."

Everybody froze. The news was so stunning that it brought on a disorientation. The four occupants of the van couldn't even remember what they had been fighting about scant seconds before. The whole world had shifted. The final team was no longer locked in.

Sneezy's cell phone rang, but he made no move for it. It rang again.

"Answer it," breathed Tilt.

The conversation was brief. "Got it, Cap." Sneezy threw the van into a U-turn, squealing across four lanes of highway. They were already doing seventy when the left front tire flattened and pulverized Sammi's Garbage tape.

CHAPTER THIRTEEN

Cap Cicero was screaming now. "You want me to do *what*?"

Tony Devlin tried to be calm. "When Ethan Zaph quit the expedition, we lost our star, the guy who was going to draw attention to our team. The only way to regain that spotlight is to break his record — to summit a kid even younger. Or the youngest girl. Or both."

"All right," said Cicero. "If anybody has a chance, Bryn does. She's Himalayan quality."

"We need a sure thing," Devlin insisted. "Or as close to it as we can get. We have to pack that team with home runs."

"I'll take Sammi Moon in Zaph's spot," agreed Cicero. "I didn't really want to cut her anyway."

"What about Tilt Crowley?" asked Devlin. "He's like a guaranteed record."

"He's like a guaranteed head case," Cicero shot back. "We live in close quarters up there. A disruption can be death — and I'm not speaking figuratively."

THE CONTEST

"The board of directors thinks you should give him another look."

"All right, I'll take him," Cicero said defiantly. "In Perry Noonan's spot."

Devlin didn't blink. "Perry goes, no matter what."

"Well, I'm not taking Crowley over Moon."

"You don't have to," said Devlin. "You're going to take him over Chris Alexis."

Cicero stood up so violently that his chair went flying. "Chris Alexis is the best climber I've got! I *need* him. He'll be like an extra guide on Everest."

Devlin was firm. "He's too old to break the record. We can't put our resources behind a kid who isn't going to get us the attention we need. As Ethan Zaph's teammate, he was fine. But now the rules have changed. He's no use to us."

Cicero took a deep breath as Devlin's words sank in. Part of him wanted to lash out for the expedition's sake and poor Chris's, too. But Cicero had been climbing far too long not to understand the way things worked. It took a lot of money to put an alpinist atop Everest. A sponsor didn't ante up that kind of cash for the love of mountaineering. They did it for the glory, the prestige, and mostly for the advertising. If Summit wanted a record, Cicero had to try to deliver, even if he thought the whole business stank.

"I'm surprised you're not asking me to take Dominic," he muttered resentfully. "The kid's barely out of diapers."

"We considered it," said Devlin in all seriousness. "To put a thirteen-year-old on the summit would be an unbelievable coup. But we decided he's just too small. He wouldn't have a real chance to get to the top. Not like Tilt."

But even then Cicero couldn't commit. Devlin was still protesting as the team leader showed him out of the office.

"Don't worry," Cicero assured him. "We'll be ready for Alaska tomorrow."

"Taking which kids?" probed Devlin.

"You'll know that as soon as I do."

Cicero went through the day as if in a daze. He had led dozens of expeditions before, full of rich and powerful clients who had paid tens of thousands of dollars to have a crack at Everest or one of the other eight-thousand-meter peaks. The infighting! The egos! The one-upmanship! But none of those trips had created the kind of headaches he was having over this one.

It came down to this: All his instincts told him to avoid Perry Noonan and Tilt Crowley. He was

already stuck with Perry. And now it looked as if he would have to take Tilt, too. He thought back to the kids who had disappeared in the prior rounds of cuts. Surely there was someone in there who was young enough and able enough to take instead of Crowley!

After twenty-seven days of nonstop training, the Summit complex suddenly saw leisure time, and lots of it. The van with the former washouts returned to find no climbing exercises, no hikes, no drills — just confusion. The final team was set — or was it? What was going on?

The returnees filled them in — the famous Ethan Zaph was a scratch.

The six waited for news at first, but Cicero's office door remained shut. Eventually, Sneezy and Dr. Oberman shooed them away. But no one chose to visit the gym or the indoor climbing wall. No one could concentrate on anything but the suspense of the moment. They wandered the building like tourists, rubbernecking as though they were seeing the complex for the first time.

Except Dominic.

Cicero was still in his office when he spied the boy trudging through the snow down into the valley. He could have been going anywhere, but Cicero knew his destination instantly. It was where he would have been going in Dominic's place, where any bred-in-the-bone climber would go — the mushroom boulder, the unsolved problem.

With a sense of urgency, Cicero raced up to the observation lounge on the top floor of the building. The plush suite, used for receptions and high-level corporate meetings, had telescopes mounted all around the panoramic windows. The westernmost had a clear view of that valley.

He peered into the eyepiece and fiddled with the knob until the Mushroom came into focus. Then he zoomed in. Sure enough, there was Dominic, right on schedule.

The boy didn't climb right away, but sat there, leaning against the lopsided pedestal at the base, three times his height. He was looking up, studying the problem. At last, he rose, rubbing his hands together — a rock climber's gesture. He ascended the pedestal and then the stem, searching for handholds on the underside of the massive top slab.

Once again, the team leader found himself completely absorbed. "Come down, kid," he murmured aloud. "It's just not there."

And Dominic did come down. But only as far as the pedestal. He paused for a second, took three running steps, and launched himself off the highest point of the base, up and out — a dyno, the ultimate rock climber's move. For a split second, his slim body hung in midair, twenty-five feet off the ground. Then, his hands came out of nowhere and clamped onto a small knob on the side of the mushroom cap. An instant later, he was on the top.

Cicero very nearly cheered. The move was as daring as it was brilliant. If Dominic hadn't stuck that hold, he'd be on the way to the hospital right now! The kid had solved the unsolvable. And he did it just because he refused to let it beat him.

Too young. Too small. These things would disqualify other climbers. But not Dominic, because Dominic always found a way. And if the boy didn't deserve Everest yet, maybe Everest deserved him.

The team came together in his mind: Bryn Fiedler, Sammi Moon, Perry Noonan, and Dominic Alexis.

No Ethan Zaph, no Chris Alexis, two girls, a guy who didn't even want to go, and a middle-school kid.

The gods must be crazy!

The farewell scene was replicated in the Alexis brothers' room, but this time it was Chris who was packing to leave.

Dominic was distraught. "I can't believe Cap

did this to you, Chris. I should tell him to stuff it!"

"Are you crazy?" Chris exclaimed. "You don't owe me that much loyalty! When he cut you, I never said boo."

"I deserved to get cut!" Dominic insisted. "Not you. You're the best of all of us!"

"But I'm over the hill," Chris said bitterly. "I'll be sixteen soon."

"Cap's a jerk!" Dominic raged. "I'll never respect him again. Tilt wasn't right about much, but he was right about Cap."

His brother almost managed a smile. "If there's one consolation in all this, it's seeing Tilt Crowley get cut for the second time in two days."

"You watch out for him," Dominic warned. "When he gets mad, he's nastier than usual."

Chris undid the leather strap from around his neck and pressed the small vial of Dead Sea sand into his brother's hand. "It's all up to you now, Dom. I want this left on the summit. From the bottom of the world to the top. That hasn't changed."

"It's changed because you're not going to be there." Dominic was close to tears.

"You make sure you get there," Chris said bravely. "And back down again. Remember — summiting is optional, but coming home is mandatory."

THE CONTEST

CHAPTER FOURTEEN

For the past month, the Summit complex had been their universe. Now, suddenly, jarringly, the SummitQuest team was on the move.

Harried preparation. Pack your personal gear. Hurry up. No, you don't need sunblock; you're going to Alaska in February. Ice ax — check. Crampons — check. Helmet lamp — check. Inner gloves, outer mitts. Everybody into the van. We're late! Drive to Denver. Fly to Juneau. Load all the gear into the helicopter. And off into the air again.

Through the window of the chopper, Dominic watched the Juneau airport fall away. Even at one o'clock in the afternoon, it was dusk this far north. Not that you could see the sky. A heavy overcast was dropping a fine, hazy mist. A few miles inland and that turned to snow — not heavy, but steady. After the spectacular blue cloudlessness of the Colorado mountains, this place seemed as alien as outer space.

"When's the weather going to clear?" Perry asked nervously.

EVEREST

Cicero laughed. "People have gotten old waiting for the weather to clear up here."

Sneezy had his face pressed against the glass. "Look! There it is — Lucifer's Claw!"

"All I see is snow," commented Bryn.

Then, like a 3-D Pixelgram, it appeared out of the squall — a tall, misshapen, ice-covered spike, stark and massive.

"Extreme," breathed Sammi. It was the highest compliment she could pay.

The helicopter began to descend.

At 9,500 feet, Lucifer's Claw was less than a third the height of Everest. It wasn't even as tall as some of the peaks they had tackled in the Colorado training ground. But with a base just short of four thousand feet above sea level, it represented more than a vertical mile of ascent. Most important of all, they would encounter many of the same obstacles that the expedition would face in the Himalayas — glaciers, crevasses, ice walls, cornices, and all the bad weather a mountaineer could hope to use as preparation for the top of the world.

It was three degrees below zero when the pilot unloaded the team and their gear onto the Atkinson Glacier at the base of Lucifer's Claw.

"I guess you bring a lot of climbers out here," Perry commented.

THE CONTEST

The pilot shrugged. "There were these three Germans back in the early 1990s. Never did find out what happened to them." And he clambered back into the chopper and disappeared into the murky sky.

Dr. Oberman put a hand on Perry's shoulder. "Don't look so terrified. He was kidding."

But away from the comforts and conveniences of the Summit complex, there was no time to be scared. First priority was shelter; then food.

All at once, Dominic was grateful for their forced camp-out during the snowstorm at boot camp. The tents went up efficiently, the propane stoves were assembled and burning. It was now pitch-black outside. Dominic's watch read two-thirty.

They ate by the light of a small campfire — a luxury. At the high camp the next night, there would be nothing to burn. Cicero went over the plan.

"If you climb your whole life, you're never going to have a tougher day than the one we've got tomorrow. We're going to get up that wall, and it's all or nothing, because there's nowhere to stop until we hit the south shoulder at eight thousand feet. We'll sleep there, summit the next morning, and shoot straight down to meet the helicopter to take us out of here. We'll be in the dark a lot of the time, so guard your helmet lamp with your life."

As Dominic concentrated on the team leader's words, he became aware of a wetness on his cheeks. He sat there, expressionless, the tears pouring from his eyes. He'd been on the move for over ten hours, yet it was only now starting to sink in that he'd made it. His disbelief and his sympathy for Chris's pain had left no room for him to feel joy. Here, in the dark and blowing snow of a remote Alaskan glacier, he finally had the chance to celebrate himself. The journey that had begun with him chasing his brother's vial of Dead Sea sand down the parking ramp at the 7-Eleven had brought him here.

And the next stop was Everest.

Perry Noonan's climber's Rolex, another gift from Uncle Joe, read 2:15 A.M. when he raced out of the tent he shared with Dominic to answer nature's call. Of all the things he hated about climbing — and there were many — the bathroom situation was the worst.

With the fire out, it was dark. No, that wasn't strong enough. It was inky, suffocating black. There might have been moonlight somewhere, but behind fourteen layers of overcast it wasn't doing him much good.

He took a careful step, then a few more. In this visibility, to stray too far from camp was suicide. Another step — and suddenly he was down and sliding.

It was like no terror he had ever experienced to be falling, out of control, when he was completely blind. Then it was over. With a whump at the base of his spine, he came up against hard rock or ice.

A quick inventory. No broken bones, everything still attached. He got on all fours and began to crawl. He was out of the hole in a few seconds — at least he was enough of a climber to accomplish that. He was lucky. As near as he could tell, he had fallen into the gap between two chunks of glacial ice, each about the size of a refrigerator. If that had been a crevasse on Everest, he'd be dead already. Or worse — trapped alive and waiting for death. It had happened many times before, to amateurs and top climbers alike. It would no doubt happen many times again.

It took him twenty-five minutes to locate the tent in the dark. He had been a grand total of twelve feet away. Shaking with relief, he crawled into his sleeping bag and huddled there, trying not to wake Dominic with his ragged breathing.

It was then that he realized there was something he had forgotten to do. But another bathroom trek was out of the question.

CHAPTER FIFTEEN

Five A.M., when Cap Cicero woke the team, was no different from the dead of night — pitch-black, ice-cold, and snowing.

By a meager fire, the climbers melted snow for a breakfast of hot chocolate and instant oatmeal. No one had much of an appetite. After four weeks of preparation, there was climbing to be done, and this was not a drill.

They struck down the camp. All gear — tents, stoves, sleeping bags — was to be carried on their backs to be reused at their next stop, nearly a vertical mile above them. It was time to don wind suits and Gore-Tex face masks and mitts, and to strap on crampons — boot attachments featuring twelve sharp prongs. The metal spikes bit into blue glacial ice as they shouldered their packs.

The mission could not have been simpler. First, a half-mile hike to the base of Lucifer's Claw, skirting dangerous crevasses. It made the hair stand up on the back of Perry's neck. If last night's tumble had been into any of these, there would be no Perry Noonan today.

THE CONTEST

Once they reached the mountain, they were vertical almost immediately, ascending the steep wall.

The front points of their crampons jabbed into the frozen shell covering the rock. Then a swing each from ice axes in both hands. Pull yourself up and start over again. *Kick. Kick. Thunk. Thunk.* To Dominic, the rhythm became almost as familiar as his own heartbeat.

They climbed, roped together in pairs: Dominic and Bryn, Sammi and Dr. Oberman, Cicero and Perry. The expedition leader figured it would take all his talent as a guide to keep Perry from falling behind. The red-haired boy was nervously securing himself with ice screws every few feet.

"For God's sake, Noonan," Cicero called impatiently, "if you put one more piece of hardware in that ice, you're going to magnetize the whole mountain!"

Sneezy was the odd man out. He climbed solo, taking miles of video of the ghosts cast by helmet lamps on the icy south wall of Lucifer's Claw.

The sun rose at around ten o'clock, or at least, as Bryn put it, "It's bright enough to watch the snow blow in our faces."

They celebrated with water and Summit bars.

The ice was thick and strong, and between the bite of ice screws and the front points of their crampons, the climbers were able to pause for a break while hanging off the wall. It felt something like comfort. Cicero and Sneezy changed positions. Now the expedition leader was solo.

By that time, Dominic had lost track of how many pitches they'd climbed. It had to be at least a dozen. But they were not yet even halfway up.

Within a few hours, it was dark again.

The month of training held fatigue at bay for a long time. But when it finally came, it was crushing. All at once, the effort of swinging an ax seemed to call for superhuman strength. Kicking crampon points into the ice felt like blasting through armor plating. Their feet weighed sixty tons. Even Perry's boundless energy to stud the mountain with screws disappeared. Sneezy had to remind him to place a belay station every thirty feet.

Conversation dwindled down to the bare essentials — "almost there," "hold this," "tired." Then even the essentials were no longer essential. After that, the only sounds were wind, grunts of effort, and the crunch of ice axes and crampons.

When their helmet lamps illuminated the rounding of the wall that marked the start of the

THE CONTEST

shoulder, Dominic and Bryn sped up, a new vitality coursing through them at the sight of their goal.

"We're there?" puffed Sammi off to their left. "We're close?"

"Slow down," ordered Dr. Oberman. "The angle of the shoulder has a foreshortening effect. It looks closer than it really is."

Sure enough, an hour of backbreaking work later, the shoulder appeared no nearer.

They slogged on until Cicero front-pointed past them in a show of speed and stamina that was breathtaking. Above them, he disappeared over the rounding of the icy rock face. Once on level ground, he slung a top rope around a boulder and dropped it down the wall. Sidestepping with their crampons, the climbers converged on it. One by one, they ascended the line and joined the expedition leader on the shoulder.

Bryn, Sammi, Perry, and Dominic collapsed in an untidy heap. But the guides soon had them up again.

"Now's the time you *don't* rest," barked Cicero. "Not until the tents are up and dinner's on."

Their bodies had been pushed to the limit for eleven and a half hours. The altitude gauge on Perry's watch read 8,063 feet. The air temperature was thirty-seven degrees below zero.

Their destination was an unnatural-looking place, even in the forbidding environs of Lucifer's Claw. The mountain's towering walls were gray-white with frost and snow. But the shoulder was naked black rock, swept clean by a relentless wind.

From the center of this obsidian moonscape rose the summit cone, more than a quarter mile up — tomorrow's project.

It was there that the four tents were placed, sheltered from the wind. Dinner was hot tea, hot soup, and a lot of instant pasta for carbohydrate energy.

The adults went to their bedrolls early, extracting a promise from their teenage charges that this would not be a late night.

"Remember what you did today," said Dr. Oberman, "and what you still have to do tomorrow. Five A.M. wake-up." She slipped into her tent, leaving them in the glow of a single helmet lamp.

"Five A.M., five P.M.," said Bryn wearily. "It's all night here, unless you're talking about high noon."

"Aw, come on," countered Sammi, eyes gleaming. "Think about where we are — up a freak of nature that's halfway to the North Pole, hanging on by our toenails —"

"If you say it's extreme," Bryn interrupted, "you're eating the tent."

"Well, it is," Sammi insisted. "We're thumbing our noses at gravity. I love this place! And if you're a real climber, you should, too."

"I'm a climber," Bryn retorted. "I just don't delude myself into thinking this is beautiful. Because even if you could see it, it would still be the armpit of the universe."

"I suppose you're going to dis E, too," Sammi said scornfully.

"It's not *what* you climb; it's that you're *climbing*," Bryn tried to explain. "The physical demands, the personal challenge — "

"Yawn," put in Sammi. "How about you, Dominic? You climb for the rush, right? Or are you searching for your true self like Oprah over here?"

Dominic seemed surprised to be consulted. Then he said slowly, "When I look at something, I automatically try to think of a way to get to the top of it. I don't know why. Maybe because Chris does it. And he got it from my dad. It's like when George Mallory was asked why he was climbing Everest, and he said, 'Because it's there.' "

"He was joking," Perry broke in.

The others looked at him.

"No, really. It was in a book my uncle gave

me. There was a press conference, and one reporter kept asking, 'Why do you want to climb Everest? Why? Why? Why?' And just to shut the guy up, Mallory told him, 'Because it's there.' It was a put-down. It's nothing to base your life on!" He had started off softly, but now he was speaking sharply, his voice full of scorn.

"I read you loud and clear," said Sammi. "You hate this. So why are you here?"

"I made it up that wall, same as you," Perry defended himself.

"Agreed," said Bryn. "You did fine today. But it's pretty obvious to the three of us that you're just not into it. And if we can see it, Cap can see it, too. Why didn't he wash you out?"

"Maybe Cap is a better judge than you guys."

"Or maybe Tilt was right," challenged Sammi, "and your uncle bought you onto this expedition."

Perry smoldered silently in the dim light.

"Is it true?" prompted Bryn.

The flush began in his cheeks, spreading until his many freckles melted together to create a complexion of fire.

"Well, is it?"

And then the dam burst. "You don't know what you're talking about," he said tersely. "My

THE CONTEST

uncle didn't buy me onto this expedition. My uncle bought the whole expedition! He's Joe Sullivan — does that name ring a bell?"

"The founder of Summit Athletic," breathed Dominic, impressed.

"And president, and chairman of the board," Perry finished. "Cap didn't cut me, and I didn't quit for exactly the same reason — because Joe Sullivan always gets what he wants!" He was up, in the tent, and crawling into his sleeping bag before any of them could say a word. As upset as he was, he felt a certain measure of relief that this was finally out in the open. And if the others hated him, then so be it. They'd probably expected something like this anyway. Perry knew that speculation about him had been flying around boot camp. At least that was over.

He snuggled in his bedroll and covered his ears in an attempt not to listen to their conversation. But the quarters were close, and he couldn't help overhearing snippets here and there. Like Bryn's comment: "You know what's really Looney Toons about all this? He's got the guts to take on Everest, but not to tell his uncle that he doesn't want to go."

Or Dominic: "What bugs me is that he's here, and Chris is sitting at home."

"Don't even go there," groaned Sammi.

"Chris had no chance. They needed youth. If Perry wasn't here, ten to one we'd be stuck with Tilt."

Perry was never sure what time he dozed off. But when he awoke, he could hear Dominic's even breathing in the sleeping bag next to him. The glowing face of his watch told him it was after three. He lay there, bone weary, yet wired at the same time.

Come on, Perry, go back to sleep! Wake-up is less than two hours away.

Sleep would not come. He tossed and turned for a while, but the air mattress did little to soften the rock floor. His bones, already achy from the climb, began to protest in earnest.

He crept out of the tiny tent, struggling into his jacket and boots as he moved. He stood motionless in the light snow, unwilling to risk even a step in the total darkness. If last night's little episode was repeated up here, he could find himself four thousand feet below, permanently impacted in the glacier. Almost in self-defense, he located the helmet lamp and switched it on.

"Oh." For the first time, he realized he was not alone. Bryn Fiedler stood there facing him. "Couldn't sleep, either?" he asked.

She gave him no answer and began to saunter slowly away.

THE CONTEST

Great, he thought. *Either she just plain hates my guts, or she thinks I'm trying to spy on her trip to the bathroom.*

And then he noticed something peculiar. The girl wore no coat and was bootless.

"Hey, aren't you cold?"

Still no answer, not even any indication that she had heard him. She kept on walking toward — what? There was nothing up here. If you went far enough, you'd just —

"No-o-o-o!"

CHAPTER SIXTEEN

His heart in his throat, Perry charged across the camp. He grabbed Bryn right at the rim of the shoulder, but she shrugged him off. Her strength and his momentum took the two of them over the edge.

At the last possible second, his fingertips felt rock, and he clamped on in desperation. Sobbing in shock and terror, he tried to scream *"Cap!"* but no sound came out. All of his life force was channeled into the effort to pull himself back onto the shoulder. It was only a few feet — a single chin-up — but it seemed to take a very long time, and even more effort than the entire day's climb.

And then he found himself lying on level terrain. Bryn was gone. Gone as if she had never been there.

"Cap! Ca-a-ap!"

His cries brought everyone running.

"What's wrong?" roared the team leader.

"She's gone!" Perry howled, beyond hysteria.

"Who?"

THE CONTEST

"Bryn! Bryn! She just walked over the side! She killed herself!"

"Where?"

"Over there!" Still on his hands and knees, Perry led the team to the spot where Bryn had fallen from sight.

Cicero switched on his helmet lamp and shone it into the blackness of the void below. Time ground to a halt in tense agony. If Bryn had plummeted all the way to the glacier, there was no chance that she would be alive.

Here on the southwest face, the ice wall had come away from the rock of the mountain, creating a narrow envelope beginning about thirty feet below them.

There, lying motionless in the bottom of that impossibly thin gap, lay Bryn. The whole party shouted down to her, but she did not respond.

Cicero turned to Perry. "She walked over the side? Just like that?"

"Yeah!"

"That's not it!" Sammi countered, shrill with hysteria. "She was sleepwalking!"

Cicero stared at her. "What?"

"She sleepwalks!" the girl exclaimed. "She did it at boot camp. That's how all the stuff got busted up. It wasn't vandalism. She couldn't help it!"

The team leader was furious. "And you didn't see fit to tell me?"

"And watch a good climber get cut?"

"That girl could be home in bed instead of dead or dying!" snapped Cicero.

The terrible reality crystallized in his gut and radiated outward, freezing his entire body. Sure, he had lost team members before — more than he cared to think about. It was the nature of this dangerous game. But he knew in an instant that this was *different*. Bryn Fiedler was sixteen years old. She should be preparing for the junior prom.

"Bryn!" he roared. "Bryn, can you hear me?"

The form below them was still.

Now Sammi was crying. "She said she'd be okay once the pressure was off! I believed her. I'm so sorry. . . ."

Cap Cicero had no time for tearful apologies. He was a veteran climber in an emergency. Blame was irrelevant now. There were no *should haves*, only *have tos*. Nothing mattered except extricating Bryn from the envelope of ice and, if she was alive, getting her off the mountain and to medical attention.

As panic overtook the others, a calm professionalism descended over him, and he began to bark orders. "Andrea, get on the horn and

THE CONTEST

see when the rangers can get us a helicopter. Lenny, I need crampons, a harness, and some rope."

Perry was wide-eyed as the guides sprang into action. "You're not climbing down there?"

"If you can think of a better way to get her out, I'm all ears."

Sneezy reappeared, his arms laden with gear. As the team leader affixed a top rope to a sturdy boulder, Dr. Oberman returned to the scene, the long-range cell phone at her ear. "They'll give us a chopper, but the pilot won't go close to the mountain until sunup. Around ten o'clock."

"Tell them we'll be waiting," confirmed Cicero, clipping his harness onto the fixed line.

The doctor relayed the information and then called, "They also want to know if we need a medical team for the injured climber."

"I'll let you know in a minute," Cicero replied grimly, and was gone.

Dominic watched in awe as the renowned alpinist rappelled expertly from the top of the shoulder. Cicero covered the distance in a few seconds and stood on the lip. Easing himself into the narrow gap, he began to descend to Bryn.

From above, the others looked on breathlessly. Cicero's lower body disappeared into the opening. But he went no farther.

"Why's he stopping?" asked Sammi.

It was Dr. Oberman who put two and two together. "He's stuck! The gap is too small."

And with that, Dominic was pounding across the shoulder to camp. At the tent, he grabbed his helmet lamp, shrugged into his climbing harness, and strapped on crampons. The sharp points grated jarringly against the naked black rock, but he barely noticed, running as fast as his awkward footwear would allow. There was an unwritten rule of climbing: *The job falls to whoever can get it done.* Right here, right now, thirteen-year-old Dominic Alexis had an advantage that even the great Cap Cicero couldn't match.

"Dominic — come back!" Dr. Oberman cried.

She ran to stop him, but he clipped onto the rope and lowered himself over the side.

Free fall. He swung himself into the cliff face, pushed off with his feet, and dropped some more. The feeling of gravity on his body gave him confidence. The axis of motion was vertical, and Dominic was in his element.

He dropped to the lip to find Cicero chipping at the thick ice with his ax.

He gawked at his youngest team member.

THE CONTEST

"Get out of here, Alexis! I've lost one climber already! No way I'm going to risk a double whammy!"

"I can get down there!" Dominic panted, catching his breath. "I'm smaller than you!"

"Forget it!" roared Cicero. But he examined Dominic's slight frame and mentally pasted it into the narrow passage of uneven ice that stood between Bryn and any chance of rescue. It would take hours to widen the opening with ice tools alone. Bryn — if she was alive at all — would fall victim to shock, hypothermia, frostbite. The only chance was to get her out *fast*.

"All right," he conceded. "But be careful. The last thing I need is two of you trapped down there."

It was like spelunking in an ice cave, only straight down, Dominic reflected. Pressed hard against the rough rock of the mountain's granite core, he squeezed past jagged chunks of ice. The painful, awkward movements were almost comforting to him. It was the style of the Alexis brothers to take the ordinary and turn it vertical. Only this time, there was no Chris to help him, and Bryn's life hung in the balance.

As he descended, the rope that tethered him to Cicero wrapped around his legs. Untangling himself in the unbearably confined space was an arduous task that ate up his two most precious assets — strength and time. Finally, he reached the bottom of the chasm where Bryn lay on her side, battered and bleeding.

The moment of truth: He bent an ear to her slightly open mouth.

CHAPTER SEVENTEEN

Warm breath, faint but regular.

"She's alive!" he howled out.

"How about *you*?" asked Cicero from twenty feet above.

"I'm fine!" Dominic gulped air. "What now?"

The team leader lowered a warm blanket to Dominic, who wrapped it around Bryn's unmoving form. Next, Dominic secured her with three slings — one at her shoulders, one supporting her back, and one at her knees. Cicero tied the tops of these lines onto a single rope dropped from the shoulder above. There, using a rounded rock as a pulley, Dr. Oberman, Sneezy, Sammi, and Perry began to haul her up.

Bryn rose about seven feet before snagging in the jagged ice.

"Stop! Stop!" cried Dominic. "She's stuck! You're crushing her!"

He scrambled up his own rope and tried without success to maneuver Bryn around the protruding chunk of ice. Then he pulled out his ax and began hacking at the obstruction.

EVEREST

"How does it look?" Cicero called down to him.

"Bad." Dominic could hear the panic edging into his voice. "This could take hours."

"We've got hours," he soothed. "Six before the chopper gets here. I'll start cutting a path from the top."

Dominic had been climbing since he was four years old, but this was something he never could have imagined — trapped in the ice on a hostile mountain, chopping away at a two-foot-thick outcropping in a race against the elements and the clock. Each strike of the ax chipped a millimeter or two away. Barely a hair. Dust.

An hour passed. Then two. The repetitive motion of swinging the tool made his shoulder socket throb with pain. He shivered in the forty-below cold as he worked, and ice fragments from Cicero's efforts rained down on him from above.

And then, a voice from a place buried so deep inside him he wasn't even sure it really existed: *Rest.*

"Never!" he seethed, enraged that he would entertain such a thought when Bryn's life was at stake. He began to flail his ax wildly. *Thunk! Thunk! Thunk!* The teeth bit repeatedly into the ice until he realized that the passage was clear and he was exhausting himself for nothing.

THE CONTEST

"Okay!" he rasped, his voice barely audible. Louder: "Okay! Ready to lift!"

Cicero echoed the call, and a moment later, Bryn began to ascend once more. Dominic followed beneath her, kicking his crampons into the ice wall for leverage as he guided his unconscious teammate up through the narrow pathway.

They were getting close. He could see flashes of Cicero's helmet lamp in the thin strip of dark sky above. Then, just a few feet below the lip, Bryn got hung up again. Dominic tried every which way to finesse her around a protruding ice boulder, but it was no use.

The news was grim from above as well.

"I just talked to the ranger station," Dr. Oberman called down to Cicero. "Bad weather on the way!"

Sammi was right beside her. "Well, duh! It hasn't stopped snowing for five seconds since we got here!"

"They grounded the chopper?" Cicero asked in dismay.

"We've got a helicopter window from ten to ten-thirty!" Sneezy supplied. "After that, the high winds come, and we're on our own. The National Weather Service is calling for a foot of snow."

Cicero checked his watch. It was seven-forty. "Take the kids and get down."

Perry was appalled. "But what about Bryn?"

"Don't worry about her," Sneezy said seriously. "She'll be riding in a nice warm chopper while we bust our butts on that wall!"

Sammi was uncertain. "If there's a chopper!"

The cameraman grabbed her by the arm and began dragging her back toward camp. "If you're still hanging off that cliff face when the storm hits, you're going to learn the true meaning of extreme!"

That was enough for Perry. "Let's get out of here!"

But Sammi dug in her heels. "What about Dominic?"

On the lip thirty feet below, that was the very subject under discussion. "Kid, there's a storm coming, and I'm sending everybody down," Cicero called down through the ice. "That includes you."

Dominic was horrified. "You're going to *leave* her?"

"I can get her out myself," Cicero assured him. "The chopper's giving us till ten-thirty."

"You won't make it! We've got four feet of ice to cut through!" He swung his ax harder, faster.

"Forget it, Alexis, I'm not risking you!"

"No!" A whirlwind of activity beneath the ice. *Thunk! Thunk!*

"You little snot, where do you get off telling me how to run my expedition? I was soloing mountains before you were in diapers!"

Thunk! Thunk! Thunk!

The expedition leader's face flamed red. "If you disobey this order, you're *history* on this team! You're not going anywhere with me! Not Everest. Not around the corner to buy a stick of gum. Got it?"

Dominic barely even heard him as he hacked away. His universe, at that moment, was a four-foot mass of ice that had to be cut away in less than three hours. Compared to that, Cap Cicero, SummitQuest, even Dominic's own safety seemed as insignificant as the price of peanuts in Peru.

Cicero was powerless to stop him. He couldn't reach Dominic through the narrow opening in the ice. All he could do was take out his own ax and work at the obstruction from the top. Now the chipping sound had a double rhythm — *thunk-thunk! Thunk-thunk!*

Dr. Oberman lowered the long-range cell phone to Cicero, and the team on the shoulder began the long descent. There was no talk of a summit bid — not with a climber unconscious and a blizzard on the way. The video camera remained in Sneezy's pack. This was one part of

SummitQuest that the general public would never see.

Dominic had no watch. He measured the hours by the burning fire in his arm and the numbing cold that gripped the rest of his body. His fatigue went far beyond what he had felt after ascending the four-thousand-foot wall. This was a single motion — the swing of an ice tool — repeated without rest for countless hours. Doubt and dread plagued him. Was he tiring to the point where he'd have no strength left to get *himself* out of this frozen tomb? And even if he could make it back to the shoulder, would he have the energy and the will to front-point nearly a vertical mile down to the glacier?

Doesn't matter. Not important. Keep working. Don't stop.

He was aware of a brightening in the sky. Sunrise, or the closest thing to it in the permanent gloomy overcast. The sound came soon after the light, low but audible, even from under the ice. Almost like a slow-motion drumroll.

A helicopter!

THE CONTEST

CHAPTER EIGHTEEN

"*Ten o'clock!*" Cicero bellowed the time check.

Dominic sized up the foot-thick obstruction that still imprisoned Bryn and took it apart mentally blow by blow. They had half an hour. Would there be enough time?

There has to be!

Brandishing the ax with both hands, he hacked with an unbridled ferocity that surprised even him. He could hear Cicero begging him to calm down, to budget his energy, but Dominic knew that right now fever pitch was the only speed for him. He didn't dare slacken the pace for even a second for fear that his whole body would shut down.

Thunk! Thunk!

"*Ten-fifteen!*"

It seemed to go on forever. Hours — no, they didn't have hours. But minutes felt like hours in this endless motion, endless exhaustion, endless ice. The edges of his vision began to blur.

Don't faint on me now!

EVEREST

"Ten-twenty-five!"

Thunk! Thunk!

Above him, Cicero was barking into the phone, "Give us five more minutes! *Two* more minutes!"

Thunk! Thunk!

And then: "Heads up!"

Cicero's boot broke through the obstruction, raining ice and snow down on Dominic's head. Marshaling every ounce of strength he had left, the boy dug in his crampons and put his full weight under Bryn in an attempt to push her up to Cicero. The team leader grabbed the injured climber and hauled her onto the lip. "Now!" he bawled into the phone.

Barely conscious, Dominic crawled out of the envelope after being entombed for seven hours. Wobbling on unsteady feet beside Cicero, he noted that the weather had already changed. Howling wind blew snow in their faces. Surely, the full force of the storm could not be far behind.

When the helicopter became visible, it was a lot closer than Dominic expected. It seemed to explode out of the gray-white squall sixty feet in front of them, coming up fast.

"He's too low!" shouted Dominic.

At the last minute, the pilot veered off, looping

THE CONTEST

up and away from the mountain, vanishing once more. When the chopper reappeared, it was higher, descending gradually toward them.

Cicero put an iron grip on Dominic's shoulders and eased him to his knees to keep him clear of the spinning rotor blades. There wasn't enough room to land on the lip, so the pilot set the nose wheel down on the rim of ice and hovered — a difficult and treacherous piece of flying. The helicopter was "parked," but it couldn't stay that way forever.

Cicero climbed into the chopper, grabbed Bryn under the arms, and hauled her aboard. Then he reached out a hand to Dominic.

A powerful gust of wind buffeted the mountain, plastering Dominic against the rock face. The nose wheel slipped off the lip, and the helicopter seemed to bounce in the air, the deadly rotors dipping toward him.

"*Duck!*" howled Cicero.

With no time to think or even breathe, Dominic dove back into the opening.

The lethal blades shaved the ice at the top of the lip before the pilot yanked on the control and drew the chopper up and away from the mountain.

Falling. Dominic kicked out with both legs. Crampon points dug into the walls and he lurched to a stop. Hand over hand, he climbed back into the wind and snow. A desperate scan of his surroundings. The helicopter was gone.

"Cap!"

No answer. The panic began in his stomach, leaping up the back of his throat. All their lines, bolts, and ice screws had descended with the rest of the team. Could he make it down that wall of ice, alone, unroped, through a howling blizzard?

Chris should be here. He's the better climber. He'd find a way out of this.

He reached inside his jacket and clutched at his brother's vial of Dead Sea sand, which was never going to Everest. Which might not even make it off Lucifer's Claw . . .

"Dominic!!"

The cry was so faint that he would have missed it if not for the frantic urgency in the voice. With a roar of machinery, the helicopter burst out of the driving gray snow. Cicero crouched at the hatch, dangling a rope that blew every which way.

A screaming fight was in progress between the team leader and the pilot. How close to Dominic did they dare go?

"If the wind currents blow us into the mountain, then none of us make it home!" the pilot argued.

THE CONTEST

"That's a thirteen-year-old kid out there!" Cicero shouted back. "If you land this bird without him, you're gonna *wish* you'd crashed into a mountain!"

I'm lost, Dominic thought to himself. *They can't get close enough. Not in this wind.*

No sooner had the idea crossed his mind than the wind died and there was a moment of sudden, unexpected calm. All at once, the snow was falling directly downward, and the rope hung straight and unmoving from the chopper.

"Get him! *Get him!*" roared Cicero.

Slow motion — that's how it seemed to Dominic. Waiting for the helicopter to approach was the longest few seconds of his life. Thirty feet away . . . then twenty . . . then ten . . .

As he unclipped his harness from the rope, he was struck by a flash of foresight. There was no explanation for it. Call it climber's instinct. He just *knew.*

The wind's coming back.

Dominic Alexis took two powerful steps and hurled himself into the thin air — a spectacular dyno more than a mile above the Atkinson Glacier.

"No-o-o!" cried Cicero in horror.

And there, in midleap, Dominic found a strange serenity. He wasn't in Alaska at all. In his mind he was in the valley outside the Summit complex in Colorado, making the jump that would solve the Mushroom. It was madness to spring off a mountain, but no climber could resist the move that would unravel a tough problem.

He felt the jolt of the returning wind in the small of his back, driving him onward. When his mitts first touched the rope, he was startled for a moment, as if he hadn't expected to make it. Then he grabbed on for dear life and hung there as the team leader hauled him aboard.

Cap Cicero, veteran of a hundred expeditions and every tragedy and rescue in the book, threw his arms around his youngest climber and squeezed until Dominic could barely breathe. "I thought we lost you, kid!" he panted again and again. "I thought we lost you!"

"I'm right here, Cap," Dominic managed. "I'm fine."

The pilot pulled back on the controls, and the chopper swung away from Lucifer's Claw. "Let's get out of here," he said, his face white. "We've already used up eight of our nine lives."

THE CONTEST

CHAPTER NINETEEN

Bryn Fiedler suffered a broken arm and ankle, four cracked ribs, and a severe concussion. She also had mild frostbite on her fingers and toes, but the doctors said she would make a full recovery.

"Doctors in Alaska see a lot of frostbite," Cicero informed her. "So they know what they're talking about."

Sammi, Perry, and Dominic visited her the next day in the hospital in Juneau. She was propped up in bed, her arm in a cast, bandages on her head, hands, and feet.

She started when she saw them. "Oh, it's you guys. I thought you were my parents."

"They're coming up from Chicago?" asked Sammi.

She nodded. "Separate planes, separate rent-a-cars. I guess that's how things are going to be in my family from now on — separate." She shifted in bed to face Dominic. "Cap told me how you saved my life."

"Anybody would have done it," Dominic mumbled uncomfortably.

"No," she said seriously. "If Cap had chosen

your brother instead of you like everybody thought, I'd be dead right now. Do you honestly think Chris could have made it into that tiny chasm to get me out? He's almost as big as Cap." She regarded the slight boy, shamefaced. "I'm sorry I didn't have more faith in you. You deserve to go to Everest."

"I don't think anybody's going to E anymore," Sammi put in sadly. "Cap's on the phone with Tony Devlin right now. Word is they're going to scrap the expedition."

All eyes turned to Perry.

"What's everybody looking at me for? You think my uncle calls to ask how to run Summit?" He added, "But my guess is they'll cancel."

"You're relieved," Bryn accused.

"You bet I am," Perry said feelingly. "If all this stuff could happen on Lucifer's Claw, how could we go up three times as high?"

"It's my fault," Bryn mourned. "I thought my sleepwalking would stop when we got out of boot camp. And now I'm lucky to be alive." She sighed. "I ruined it for everybody."

Sammi put a hand on her shoulder. "I guess this means cliff jumping is back in the plan. Caleb will be happy."

And then, a gruff but familiar voice: "Caleb is out of luck."

THE CONTEST

Cap Cicero strode into the room. "I just got off the phone with Tony Devlin. SummitQuest is still on!"

Perry was wide-eyed. "But what about yesterday?"

"If you kids can get out of a jam like that, then you're ready for Everest," the team leader said positively. "Even you, Noonan. You held it together up there."

Perry didn't know whether to be horrified or flattered.

"But not me, right?" Dominic ventured sadly.

"What are you talking about?" asked Bryn.

"I disobeyed a direct order," Dominic explained, "and Cap washed me out."

Cicero put an arm around his narrow shoulders. "Kid, after what I saw yesterday, I'm amazed I ever climbed anything *without* you. Yeah, you wouldn't listen, and I was mad. But we saved a team member because of it, and that trumps everything." His smile vanished as suddenly as it had appeared. "So no cheeseburgers when you get home — you're in training! We leave for Nepal in three weeks."

"I'll have a cheeseburger for you," Bryn volunteered wanly. "It's the least I can do."

"One more thing," Cicero added. "Nobody talks to the press about what happened, got it?

That comes straight from the Summit board. If a reporter asks why Bryn isn't going, just say she turned an ankle on the test climb."

"I didn't turn it; I *broke* it," Bryn reminded him. "Along with every other bone in my body."

"You broke it because you turned it," the expedition leader explained glibly.

"Yeah," Perry winced at the mere memory, "at the bottom of a fifty-foot fall."

"What about her replacement?" asked Sammi. "Who's going to be the fourth team member?"

Dominic snapped to eager attention. "It's my brother, right? We're taking Chris?"

Cicero shook his head sadly. "I'm afraid not."

EPILOGUE

E-mail message
To: BU@national-daily.com
Subject: SummitQuest

Good news! Summit made Cap put me back on the team. At least somebody knows a real climber when they see one.

We leave for Nepal on March 15. Now I can continue to E-mail your newspaper more dirt about the SummitQuest boneheads. Don't worry, Cap doesn't suspect a thing. He still thinks it's sour grapes from some loser who washed out.

Tilt Crowley

P.S. Remember, when I summit Everest, I'm doubling my usual fee. The next time you see me, I'll be a star!

EVEREST

BOOK TWO: THE CLIMB

EVEREST

For Mark Wise, M.D.,
expert on what ails you
at twenty-nine thousand feet

PROLOGUE

Dominic Alexis was waiting his turn to use the airplane bathroom when he got his first glimpse of Mount Everest.

Standing there in the narrow aisle of the 747, he froze, gawking out the porthole in the emergency door. To the north rose the jagged, icy spires of the Himalayas, the highest mountain range on the face of the earth. And right in the heart of it, the giant among giants — barely lower than the cruising altitude of the plane — Everest.

There should be trumpets, he thought reverently. *A fanfare. Fireworks.*

Norman "Tilt" Crowley came up behind Dominic and hip-checked him out of the way. "Man, this airline stinks! What do you have to do to get a bag of peanuts?"

Wordlessly, Dominic pointed out the window at the unmistakable silhouette.

Tilt peered through the porthole. "Big deal — Mount Everest. What, you thought they were going to move it before we got here?"

But for all his attitude, Tilt stayed riveted to the

spot, fascinated by the sight of the big mountain that the Nepalese called *Jongmalungma* — "Goddess, Mother of the World."

An announcement came from the cockpit. "On our left, we see Mount Everest." It was repeated in several other languages.

There was a rush for the left side of the plane. For most of the passengers, this was the closest they would come to the top of the world. But Dominic and Tilt were part of SummitQuest, the youngest expedition ever to attempt the planet's highest peak. For them, the massive profile of Everest was the shape of things to come.

Sammi Moon shut off her Walkman and rushed over to join them at the porthole. "How is it? Extreme, right?" She spotted the mountain. "It's beautiful!"

"You paint it; I'll climb it," put in Tilt. "That lump of rock is going to make me famous."

"We have to wake Perry," said Dominic. "He should see this."

The fourth member of their team, Perry Noonan, was in his seat, fast asleep.

"Are you kidding?" snorted Tilt. "He's so scared of Everest that he can't even face the picture in the in-flight magazine. He'd take one look out the window and wet his pants!"

Dominic's eyes never left the mountain. "You're crazy if you're not a little bit scared."

"I'm just amped," said Sammi. "I can't believe we're really on our way!"

They squinted through the clouds, trying to discern the summit — the object of years of climbing and months of preparation.

What Dominic, Tilt, Sammi, and Perry could not know was that the mist-obscured peak was more than a goal. For one of the four team members, it would be a final resting place.

THE CLIMB

CHAPTER ONE

Kathmandu Airport, Nepal. Passports, permits, and paperwork.

The arrivals line stretched from gate 1 to gate B76.

Cap Cicero, legendary mountaineer and expedition leader, marched his team straight through in five minutes.

No one questioned this. Their sponsor was Summit Athletic, one of the richest corporations in the world. Big money opened a lot of doors and smoothed a lot of paths.

"So long, suckers," Tilt tossed over his shoulder at the milling, exasperated crowd they'd left behind in the passport queue. He awarded Perry a slap on the back of the head. "Tell your uncle I said thanks."

Perry's uncle Joe Sullivan was the president and founder of Summit Athletic. Although Cicero would never admit it publicly, that was the only reason Perry was on the team. No one believed this more strongly than Perry himself.

The red-haired boy sighed, wishing he was al-

EVEREST

most anywhere else in the world than Nepal. "Yeah, when Summit does something, they do it right."

"You think they'll have limos for us?" Tilt asked hopefully.

But when the group passed through the gate, their welcome consisted of a hand-lettered sign scribbled in Magic Marker on the flap of a corrugated box:

SUMIT

Dominic regarded the short, squat man holding up the cardboard. "Is that a Sherpa?" he whispered to Cicero. Sherpas are the inhabitants of the Khumbu region around Everest.

Cicero roared like a bull moose and rushed forward to throw his arms around the man with the sign.

"This isn't a Sherpa!" he cried. "It's *the* Sherpa! I want you to meet Babu Pemba, the greatest climbing Sherpa the mountain has ever seen!"

"*Climbing* Sherpa?" Tilt stared at the chubby Babu, who was taking bites out of a large sandwich clenched in his free hand. "Isn't he a little, you know, out of shape?"

THE CLIMB

Babu surprised him by replying in perfect English with only a slight accent, "Oh, no. I'm just short for my weight."

Sammi giggled until she had the hiccups. Even Perry cracked a smile.

"I've heard of you," Dominic said with respect. "You saved Cap's life on Annapurna." He indicated the sandwich. "Is that a traditional Sherpa delicacy?"

"Philly cheese steak," mumbled Babu, his mouth full. He looked meaningfully from Dominic to Cicero. The message was clear. Tilt, while only fourteen years old, was built like a lumberjack and radiated power and physical ability. Perry and Sammi, at fifteen, were both solidly put together. But Dominic Alexis looked like a fifth grader. He'd just turned thirteen and was small for his age. Who in his right mind would bring him on an Everest ascent?

Cicero answered the unspoken question. "He climbs bigger than he looks."

It was a measure of their respect for each other that the Sherpa accepted this completely and without comment.

Babu Pemba drove them to their hotel in a rented Volkswagen bus so ancient that pieces were flaking off as they rattled over the cobblestones and rutted pavement. The chaos on the streets was total. There were cars and trucks that made the VW look like a brand-new Ferrari. Motorcycles and mopeds whizzed everywhere. Further down the food chain, bicycles and rickshaws did their best to compete against the motorized vehicles. Yaks and other beasts of burden meandered along like they owned the place. Flocks of geese were driven in all directions. There seemed to be no traffic regulations. The rule was every yak for itself.

To four teenagers who had never left the United States, Kathmandu was an eye-opener. Dilapidated hovels stood next to modern hotels and Buddhist temples. The air reeked of car exhaust, incense, and manure. The food smells were positively bizarre. The general din was a mixture of unmuffled motors, religious chants, animal lowing, and rock music. Orange-clad monks walked the streets side by side with businessmen, panhandlers, and Western tourists.

At the hotel, the SummitQuest group met up with Andrea Oberman, the expedition doctor, and Lenny "Sneezy" Tkakzuk, the cameraman who would be recording the ascent for the Summit Athletic Web site. Both were top-notch climbing guides.

That completed the team — four adults and four teens. If one of the young climbers succeeded in reaching the summit, he or she would break the record currently held by the Z-man, Ethan Zaph, and become the youngest human ever to conquer Everest.

CHAPTER TWO

An expedition survives on its supplies. That was Cicero's job while in Kathmandu — to make sure SummitQuest had all its material and personnel in place when the climbers arrived at Base Camp eleven days later. Everest Base Camp had nothing — no year-round inhabitants, no stores, no conveniences. Everything there was shipped from home, sent by yak train from Kathmandu, or purchased in one of the villages on the trek.

As the guides set about seeing to the arrangements, Cicero had this warning for his young team: "I'm not going to be a hypocrite about this. If I can trust you to take on Everest, I can trust you to kill a few hours in Kathmandu. Don't talk to strangers, stay close to the hotel, and keep out of trouble."

Sammi sprung up from the lumpy couch in the hotel lobby. "Time to see the world."

Cicero looked disgusted. "Can you at least wait till I'm out of the building before you completely disregard everything I say?"

"Come on, who's with me?" Sammi persisted.

"There's nothing to see in Kathmandu," Tilt as-

THE CLIMB

sured her. "This town is a sewer." And he headed for the hotel's seedy basement rec room to play video games.

In the end, Sammi headed out alone. Dominic left, too, but in a different direction. He wandered for a long time, barely noticing the wild and noisy activity of the city streets. He saw only the footsteps of legendary climbers on the worn cobblestones. Most of the great Himalayan expeditions had started right here.

His reverie was interrupted by a half-demented scream. "Get out of the way! *Get out of the way!*"

Sammi flashed into his field of vision and right out again, a blur on rented Rollerblades. He could follow her progress down the sloped street, not by watching her, but by noting the pattern made by people jumping out of her path.

Dominic allowed himself a small smile. That was Sammi. She was not so much a pure climber as an all-purpose daredevil. Everest appealed to her because it was, as she put it, "extreme."

He found what he was looking for right where the guidebook said it would be — a small Buddhist temple sandwiched between a dry cleaner and a shop that sold junky souvenirs to tourists. He stepped into the tiny courtyard, and the sounds of the city seemed to fade away. Himalayan climbers had great respect for the traditions of Buddhism, the religion of their Sherpa guides.

This was not a large temple or even an important one. But it was close to the hotel district and had been mentioned in some of the books Dominic had read. Cap Cicero had come here before his first Everest ascent. So had Sir Edmund Hillary.

He slipped off his shoes and approached the prayer wheels. Spinning them was thought to release the blessings heavenward. He hesitated, unsure of what was expected of him. He didn't want to do something stupid and offend an ancient religion.

A quiet voice behind him said, "You just turn them. There's no right way or wrong way." A tall figure came into view and stood beside him.

Dominic recognized the face instantly. "You're Ethan Zaph!"

The young man looked surprised. "Do I know you?"

"I followed your climb last year inch by inch on the Internet! I kept a scrapbook with all the pictures from the paper. When you hit the summit, my brother and I were going nuts!"

Ethan grinned. "Me, too. You guys climbers?"

"Big-time!" Dominic exclaimed. "My brother's climbed with you. Chris Alexis?"

THE CLIMB

Ethan nodded. "Oh, sure, I know Chris. He's here, right? With the Cap Cicero expedition? I was almost on that team."

"Chris isn't here," said Dominic in a subdued tone. "He didn't make the cut."

Ethan was shocked. "Chris Alexis is the best climber I know! Why would Cap cut him?"

"When you quit SummitQuest," Dominic explained, "Summit decided to go for your record. Chris is too old to beat your mark, so they filled the team with younger kids — like me." He held out his hand. "I'm Dominic."

Ethan made no move to take it. "Like you? You're going up that mountain? How old are you — ten?"

"Thirteen," replied Dominic, a little defensively.

"Has Cap gone crazy? Is everybody on the team like you?"

"I'm the youngest," Dominic admitted. "And the smallest. But Cap knows what he's doing."

"Does he?" Ethan challenged. "That's a mean mountain! When I summited, I came back twenty-three pounds lighter, dehydrated, and with three separated ribs from coughing!"

Dominic took a half-step back, his shoulder brushing up against the prayer wheels. "It's really nice meeting you. I hope we get the chance to climb together someday."

It was Ethan's turn to retreat. "Listen, I'm sure you've got talent. It runs in the family. Just do me one favor, okay? Go slow, and be honest with yourself about when it's time to quit. There are a lot of dead people up there. You don't want to be one of them."

CHAPTER THREE

At six o'clock the next morning, the Summit-Quest team piled themselves and their luggage inside the Volkswagen bus.

"Hold it." Dr. Oberman took a close look at Sammi. She had a swollen lip and a nasty scratch across her chin. "What happened to you?"

Sammi shrugged sheepishly. "You should see the other guy."

Cicero jumped on this. "You got into a fight in Kathmandu?"

"I was Rollerblading and I hit a yak," Sammi confessed.

"Those things are tougher than they look," put in Babu, who was munching on an Egg McMuffin and holding two more in reserve.

Soon they arrived at a small military airfield outside of town. There, waiting on the tarmac, was a decrepit-looking army surplus helicopter from the Korean War. Parts of it were held together with duct tape.

"That," said Tilt, "is never going to get off the ground."

It did, though, promptly at seven, with a roar that threatened to jar Tilt's back teeth loose. The pilot, who spoke no English, had handed out cotton balls for them to use as earplugs. No one had bothered. They were bothering now.

There were no seats. Tilt perched on his duffel bag, hanging on to a frayed leather strap on the wall.

God, this country is a sinkhole, he raged inwardly. And this had to be first class, because Summit always paid for the very best. Pity the poor saps who were doing this on the cheap.

But you're here, he reminded himself. *And every day takes you closer to the summit.*

The chance to conquer Everest had become the center of Tilt's universe. The others were hobby climbers; for Tilt this was serious business. Ethan Zaph was famous, with six figures in his college account, thanks to last year's expedition. Well, if Ethan could get rich from an ascent at fifteen, then it stood to reason that Tilt could get even richer at fourteen. He'd endorse ice axes and crampons in climbing magazines. His face would appear on cereal boxes. His future was sitting there, just waiting to be claimed. All he had to do was get up one mountain.

Not that he was going to get any help from his teammates. Cicero had a big name, but he was past his prime. And anyway, it would take all his talents just to keep the others from killing themselves. Dr. Oberman was all doctor, no climber. Sneezy cared about his video camera, period. And Babu? Hah! Baboon would be more like it. The guy was 90 percent lard. He couldn't get up Everest unless someone told him there was a pizza waiting at the top!

The country they were passing over was green and hilly and dotted with tiny villages. To Tilt, they all looked like a few miserable shacks arranged around a gas station that had long since gone out of business.

The farther they got from Kathmandu, the more primitive the construction became — mud huts. This place was like something out of *The Flintstones!*

While the helicopter always seemed to be the same distance from the ground, it was pretty clear that the general direction was up. Tilt could tell from the popping of his ears and by glances at Perry's three-thousand-dollar climber's watch — another gift from his rich uncle, along with his place on this team. They had started at 4,120 feet, and now the altimeter was approaching nine thousand.

The flight lasted two earsplitting hours. Their destination was indistinguishable from all the miles they had passed over — a depressing, dingy, dirt-poor village amid acres of terraced barley fields.

Five minutes later, they were standing with their knapsacks, holding their ears as the chopper roared away. Sneezy videotaped it disappearing over the bleak horizon.

Perry looked around. "Where's Mount Everest?"

Cicero laughed in his face. "Fourteen hours on a plane, but I guess nobody had any time to read the material I handed out. Everest is like Disneyland, Noonan. This is where we wait for the courtesy van to take us to Base Camp."

Perry kept his mouth shut. How had it come to this? He was on the wrong side of the globe and soon he would be on Everest itself! And all because he didn't have the guts to disappoint Uncle Joe.

Joe Sullivan. Was it that the man always got what he wanted because he was a billionaire? Or was he a billionaire because he always got what he wanted? It didn't matter. Right now he wanted his favorite nephew up Mount Everest. What that nephew wanted was apparently much less important.

Perry sighed. He hadn't expected to make this team, so he had done no Himalayan research at all. The Disneyland explanation was clearly not the truth, but he had no way of knowing what was.

Dominic, who had read every word he could get his hands on about Everest, pointed to the northeast. "If this village is Lukla, then Base Camp should be about thirty-five miles that way."

"But how do we get there?" asked Perry.

"We walk," Cicero replied.

Perry just stared.

Dr. Oberman took pity on him and explained. "The problem isn't the thirty-five miles; it's the altitude. We're now at nine thousand feet, and Base Camp is almost twice that. If you go up too fast, the changes in atmospheric pressure and the thinning of the air could make you sick and even kill you. At minimum, it would scuttle your chances of ever attempting the mountain."

"It's called acclimatization," Sneezy supplied. "If you could beam somebody from sea level to the summit of Everest, he'd be dead in three minutes. The air there has two-thirds less oxygen. That's why we have to go up slowly."

"How slowly?" Tilt asked suspiciously.

"Ten days," said Cicero. "That's to Base Camp at seventeen thousand six hundred feet. Acclimatizing on the mountain is a little trickier."

"Ten days?" Sammi was distraught. "Ten days

around *here?* I mean, it's okay, but there's not exactly a ton of excitement."

Babu brayed a laugh right into her face. "Sure there is," the stout Sherpa guffawed. "Wait until you see the bathrooms!"

CHAPTER FOUR

http://www.summathletic.com/everest/trek

Day 3: Trekking north along the *Dudh Kosi*, or "Milky River," the four youngest Everesters of all time have traveled for a week, including three rest days to get used to the altitude. Each step takes them farther into the land of the giants.

The names defy pronunciation: Kangtega, Thomserku, Ama Dablam. **CLICK HERE** to see the climbers hiking before the immense granite wall of Nuptse, a Himalayan Hoover Dam, four miles in the sky. It is from behind these multipeaked ramparts that Everest will finally reveal itself, the titan among titans.

This is the payoff for their arduous journey: multicolored strings of Buddhist prayer flags, carved Mani stones, and the most spectacular peaks on the planet. Nothing could be so exhilarating.

EVEREST

"I'm *bored*," Sammi complained. "What say we find a flat log and shoot some of those rapids on the Dudh Kosi?"

Dr. Oberman was horrified. "That's glacial runoff! If you fall in that frigid water, you'll be dead faster than the passengers on the *Titanic!*"

"Well, how about we jog for a while?" she suggested. "Get to Base Camp a couple of days early."

The doctor shook her head. "We have to take it slow. If we ascend too fast, we'll risk altitude sickness."

"If we stay here, we'll risk lapsing into a coma," Sammi countered.

The guides struggled to dig up some entertainment. It was a lost cause. Their "hotels" were little more than dormitory-style huts. Shopping was out because there was virtually nothing to buy. They toured villages that could be experienced in thirty seconds. Monasteries took longer, but Perry turned out to be allergic to the incense. It was brutal.

Sammi had always craved adrenaline — even before she was old enough to understand the word. At age four she had leaped a line of wastebaskets while riding a bicycle that still had training wheels. Broken her ankle, too, taking the pain without so much as a single tear.

Along with Caleb, her boyfriend and partner in crime, she had tried it all — extreme rock climbing, extreme skateboarding, extreme ski jumping, and much, much more. But this was the toughest of them all.

Extreme boredom.

Tilt crouched in the tiny foyer, pounding the keyboard of his laptop computer, which was hooked up to E-mail via SummitQuest's satellite phone.

E-mail Message
TO: bv@national-daily.com
SUBJECT: Arrived in Dingboche

We've been running into a lot of climbers from other expeditions on the trek, and everybody says the same thing: Dominic Alexis is too young and too small to take on Everest. Sure, I'm only a year and a half older, but I'm a foot taller and almost double his weight. Ask anybody here — Cap should have his head examined for picking a shrimp like that for the team. . . .

Tilt was under secret contract to provide inside details of the SummitQuest expedition to the *National Daily*. It was a dangerous arrangement, no doubt about it. If Cicero found out, he'd kick Tilt off the team in a heartbeat. But how else was a guy supposed to pay for his ice ax and crampons and climbing harness? For state-of-the-art Gore-Tex clothing? He couldn't take on Everest with secondhand junk financed by a paper route. He felt a little guilty about spying on everybody, but he needed the money. Not everybody had a billionaire uncle, after all.

His reports were basically just a lot of gossip. Sammi E-mailed her boyfriend back home every three seconds. Perry was only here because of his uncle. Cicero was a control freak with a short fuse.

But lately Tilt's attention had settled on one teammate and one only — Dominic.

His thinking was simple. Tilt's entire future depended on making it to the top of Everest. Only two things could spoil that plan. 1) He might not get there, and 2) Dominic might get there with him.

The problem was that Dominic was younger than Tilt. If the shrimp summited, *he*, and not Tilt, would become the new Ethan Zaph. The record

THE CLIMB

— and fame and fortune — would go to Dominic.

Of course, there was no way a ninety-pound runt was going to climb the highest peak on the planet. But why take the chance? If the *National Daily* kept printing articles about how unsafe it was for Dominic to be on the mountain, there could be a public outcry to ground him. Who knows — Dominic's own parents might even yank him.

Tilt continued to type:

If Dominic gets into trouble up there, it'll risk all our chances for the summit. And if he gets killed, it'll be a black eye for the whole country of Nepal, who will look like idiots for letting Cap put a little kid on his climbing permit. . . .

"There you are," came a voice.

Shocked, Tilt jumped to his feet to find Dominic in the tiny entranceway. "Get out of here, shrimp!"

Dominic peered at the screen. "What are you writing?"

In a single motion, Tilt slammed the laptop shut and swung it like a battle-ax, smacking

Dominic in the chin. "None of your business!"

The impact sent Dominic staggering backward. His small knapsack dropped from his shoulder and hit the floor. He stood there, coughing into his fist. The Khumbu cough, Dr. Oberman called it. Caused by the altitude and the thin, dry air. Sneezy and Perry had it, too.

"I was E-mailing my dad," Tilt lied. The kid was likely to run crying to Cicero. That would mean trouble. "It was private. Sorry."

"Cap says we're ready to roll," Dominic managed between spasms.

"Gotcha." Tilt stuffed the laptop into his own pack. "You sound lousy, shrimp. It's hard enough to sleep around here with Sneezy and Perry barking up a storm. Now it's going to be like feeding time at the dog pound."

"I'm okay," said Dominic.

But he did not feel okay. The cough had come with a scatterbrained, spacey feeling. It had taken him fifteen minutes to stuff a couple of T-shirts and a few toiletries into his knapsack. It should have been a thirty-second operation. Yet for some reason, it had seemed as complicated as defusing a bomb.

Tilt tucked the laptop under his arm. "Let's go."

His pack forgotten, Dominic followed.

THE CLIMB

"Hey, stupid — " The big boy soccer-kicked the knapsack out of the hut, and the two hurried after it.

The true monsters revealed themselves during the day's trek. Lhotse was first, the fourth-highest mountain on Earth, towering in mighty profile behind the Nuptse wall. Another quarter mile up the trail, the pinnacle of Everest came into view.

It was a view Dominic had been waiting for his entire life. But now, slogging along in a half-daze, he just couldn't seem to bring himself to care.

As the trail wound higher, the air was becoming increasingly thin. He found himself gasping for breath on a path he would have had no problem sprinting back home near sea level.

His cough was getting worse. It was no longer the dry hacking of the others. Each bronchitis-like spasm seemed to be coming from deep in his chest.

By noon, they had reached the heap of stones that marked the Khumbu glacier's terminal moraine.

"Terminal," Perry repeated aloud. Around here, even the innocent words sounded deadly.

"Moraine means any debris pushed by the glacier," Cicero explained. "It's just a whole lot of rocks and dirt, because, at sixteen thousand feet, there are no trees or anything green. We're on the moon, guys. Or as close as you can get without a rocket."

Dominic forged on, choking and wheezing. He found himself looking down in intense concentration as he trudged over the rocks and chunks of glacial ice that littered the snow-packed trail.

In the back of his mind, alarm bells were going off: *You've made it up every crag and cliff in the East! This shouldn't be so hard!*

Late in the afternoon, the group turned off the trail to the tiny village of Lobuche. Cicero sent Babu to secure the team sleeping accommodations for the next two nights.

"Two more nights?" Sammi was distraught. "But Base Camp is only a few miles away!"

"Last stop," the expedition leader promised. "A couple of nights above sixteen thousand and you'll be ready for base."

"We're ready *now*," Tilt argued. "We've been on this dumb trail forever. . . ."

He fell silent, realizing that no one was paying attention. All eyes were on Dominic, who was still trudging along the path. If the boy had any idea that he was alone, he gave no indication.

"Hey, kid!" called Cicero. Louder: "Dominic, come back!"

His youngest climber did not even look up.

Sammi rushed over and got Dominic turned around. He took three steps and collapsed, sinking to a sitting position on the trekking route.

Cicero was there in a heartbeat, posing the questions that decades of Himalayan experience had made automatic: "Feeling dizzy, kid? Can't get your act together? Do the simplest little things seem like rocket science?"

Dr. Oberman clued in. "You think he's got HAPE?" she asked in alarm.

"But we're not even in Base Camp!" Dominic managed to protest.

"Listen to his lungs," ordered Cicero.

She produced a stethoscope from the medical pack and held the bell to Dominic's chest. There was a breathless silence.

"What's HAPE?" Perry whispered to Sneezy.

"High Altitude Pulmonary Edema," the guide replied grimly. "Altitude sickness."

The doctor exhaled nervously. "Fluid on the lungs. It's HAPE, all right."

CHAPTER FIVE

It's like being dead, thought Dominic.

He was lying flat on his back in a Gamow bag at the Himalayan Rescue Association clinic in the village of Pheriche, several miles south and two thousand feet below Lobuche. The vinyl bag billowed around him as Dr. Drake of the clinic pumped air inside — the thing was a cross between a coffin and an inflatable life raft. Through the clear plastic window, he could see Cicero and Dr. Oberman peering in at him in concern. He felt like a lab rat.

No, that was wrong. The indignity of the bag paled before larger, more disturbing truths: *I am halfway around the world from my home and family. I have a potentially life-threatening illness. . . .*

That was probably a little too dramatic. Most people recovered from HAPE. A few of them even went on to climb the mountain. It was unlikely, but not impossible. He could be one of those.

If Cap and Andrea will even let me try.

The letdown hurt worse than the edema. He

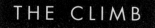

THE CLIMB

couldn't shake the feeling that his Everest dreams were over.

Was the bag working? He couldn't tell. The pumped-in air increased atmospheric pressure, which simulated lower altitude. The clinic was at fourteen thousand feet, but the altimeter on his watch read 7,487. He certainly felt clearer-headed. But he was still coughing.

The discomfort and claustrophobia were nothing compared to the agony of not knowing.

Come on, Cap! Don't send me home.

Finally, he was allowed to crawl out of the bag. He was examined by Dr. Drake and then by Dr. Oberman. Cicero sent him outside to await his fate.

"He's okay, right?" Dr. Oberman asked the other doctor. "Full recovery?"

"You caught the illness early enough," Dr. Drake confirmed. "I'd say full recovery, but who knows? I've never treated a thirteen-year-old before."

"You're kidding," said Cicero.

"The Sherpa children are born to the altitude, and none of the expeditions ever bring kids along." He looked at Cicero. "Why did *you?*"

"That kid is one of the toughest climbers I've ever seen," Cicero said readily.

Dr. Drake was appalled. "He's a *climber?* An *Everest* climber?"

"He looks little — " Cicero shrugged. "Okay, he *is* little. But he's got a mixture of spirit and ability this mountain hasn't seen in twenty years. In Alaska, I watched him save a teammate on nothing but guts."

"Physically he's still a child," Dr. Drake insisted. "He was taking two steps to everyone else's one on the trek."

"My mistake, not his," Cicero conceded.

"And mine," Dr. Oberman added.

"He should go home," Dr. Drake said decisively "No, that's not strong enough. He never should have been here in the first place."

On the way out, Dr. Oberman drew a deep breath. "It's not going to be easy to break the news to Dominic."

The team leader grabbed her arm. "Don't say a word," he ordered. "If he asks, just say you're treating his HAPE, that's it. I don't want him to know he might still climb."

She gawked at him. "Climb? But Dr. Drake said — "

"Three times I tried to wash that kid out," Cicero interrupted. "And three times he proved me wrong. I'm not underestimating him again."

Base Camp was the biggest town the Sum- mitQuest team had seen in a week. More than three hundred tents, big and small, dotted the boulder-strewn ice, and at least that many people — foreigners and Sherpas alike — bustled around, talking, laughing, testing equipment, and unloading shipments from an armada of laden yaks lumbering up the glacier.

The altitude was 17,600 feet, higher by half a mile than any peak in the lower forty-eight U.S. states.

Perry couldn't take his eyes off the beehive of activity. "I think we're going to need a bigger mountain."

"Don't worry," laughed Sneezy, who was filming the spectacle. "Most of these people are porters and Base Camp staff. We won't all be on the summit ridge at the same time."

"Don't forget cooks," added Babu, who had already helped himself to a cinnamon bun from the mess.

Under a huge banner strung across a boulder the size of a cement mixer, the Summit camp consisted of an enormous bright orange tent surrounded by four smaller two-person rigs for sleeping. The central structure was called the kitchen, but in reality, it was the living room, dining room, rec room, communications facility, and sleeping quarters for the Sherpas. Cicero had employed eight of them — four climbing Sherpas and four camp staff.

"Now, this is more like it!" exclaimed Tilt, dropping his pack and tossing himself onto an air mattress. After staying in a string of villages in which light and heat came from lamps and stoves fueled by burning dried yak droppings, the Summit encampment had all the comforts of home. Thanks to a solar generator, electricity powered lamps, a stereo, and even a TV and VCR.

By the time Sammi appeared at the flap, he had popped in a tape and was lost in the depths of *The Terminator*.

"Come on," she beckoned. "Let's take a look around."

"I'm busy."

Sammi rolled her eyes. "Tilt, you've got the greatest adventure on Earth right outside this tent."

He glared at her. "I've been living with the baboons for a week and a half. Go away. I want to watch Arnold Schwarzenegger shoot somebody!"

"Jerk," she muttered, and disappeared

The staccato chime of a telephone interrupted one of the movie's better killing sprees. He searched the cavernous tent, his eyes falling

on the communications table — really a board propped on rocks.

He picked up the satellite phone. "Hello?"

"Who is this?" Cicero's voice. "Larry?"

"It's Tilt."

"Oh." The distaste was evident in the team leader's voice. Cicero didn't much care for Tilt, and the feeling was mutual. "Listen, tell Larry or Babu I'll be up there late tomorrow. Andrea's staying with Dominic. They'll be a few days behind me."

Tilt froze. "You mean Andrea will."

"And Dominic. They're taking it slow to make sure the HAPE doesn't come back."

"But — " Tilt had been privately celebrating Dominic's departure. "He's okay?"

"If he isn't, we'll just climb without him. You've got to be flexible in the Himalayas." A pause, then, "Tilt, this call costs five bucks a minute. If you've got something to say, say it."

"Well — isn't that kind of — you know — dangerous?"

Laughter brayed over the satellite phone. "Take a look out the tent flap, kid. That's Everest, not Gymboree."

"I mean extra dangerous for Dominic," Tilt stammered, "because he's so young — "

There was irritation on the other end of the

line. "Just tell Larry and Babu I'm on my way. Think you can handle that?"

Tilt bristled. "Yeah, I'll tell Sneezy — and Baboon." He slammed down the phone.

The cold sweat came almost immediately. Why did he do that? He had nothing to gain and everything to lose by getting on Cicero's nerves. Back in the States, his attitude had almost cost him a spot on the team.

He relaxed a little. The satellite connection was lousy and crackled with static. The team leader probably hadn't even heard. He had nothing to worry about.

Besides, thought Tilt, *I've got more important things to do.*

Twenty million *National Daily* readers needed to hear the story of how climbing legend Cap Cicero was recklessly risking the life of a thirteen-year-old.

He pulled out his laptop and booted it up.

CHAPTER SIX

Base Camp was a land of logos — Summit, Nike, Coca-Cola, Starbucks. There were national expeditions, too, under bedsheet-sized flags. These ranged from a Japanese team twenty climbers strong to two affable brothers hoping to become the first Guamanians ever to scale the world's tallest peak.

Guam. The beach. Sea level. It sounded good to Perry.

Loud crashing from below made him jump. "What was that?"

Sammi laughed with delight. "We're on a glacier. It's a frozen river — always shifting and breaking apart." She did a dance to the beat of a series of aftershocks. "It's like Rice Krispies — snap, crackle, pop — "

"More like snap, crackle, heart attack," Perry said feelingly.

"It *is* pretty extreme," she chortled. "I can't believe Dominic's missing this."

Dominic. As soon as the news had come in that Dominic's life was no longer in danger,

Perry's jealousy had begun. The boy now had a built-in excuse not to climb.

"Look." Sammi pointed. "Ethan Zaph's team."

The famous Ethan was climbing with an expedition called This Way Up, which boasted the boldest plan on the mountain that year. After a punishing ascent of the 27,920-foot Lhotse, they would traverse to Everest via the South Col. Even more impressive, Ethan would be summiting both peaks without oxygen. All but the most elite mountaineers breathed bottled gas in the infamous Death Zone above twenty-five thousand feet. Yet Ethan, who was not yet seventeen, would be climbing without it — up not just one mountain, but two.

This Way Up's camp was even larger and more elaborate than SummitQuest's, sporting a library and even a makeshift shower. There was no sign of Ethan, but a tall, thin, olive-skinned young man with thick glasses was outside one of the smaller tents. He was painting a wooden sign that hung just above the flap:

> **NESTOR ALI**
> **FIRST-EVER NEARSIGHTED**
> **PUERTO RICAN/PAKISTANI**
> **DOUBLE ASCENT & YETI RECONNAISSANCE**

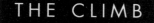

THE CLIMB

Perry frowned. "What's a 'yeti'?"

"Haven't you heard of the abominable snowman?" Nestor asked pleasantly. "It's a local legend — kind of the Bigfoot of the Himalayas. He's got to be up there somewhere."

Sammi gave him a skeptical once-over. "Who else do you expect to find? The Tooth Fairy?"

It turned out that Nestor was a journalist who had been hired by an Internet magazine to write humorous articles about Everest. His job, essentially, was to make fun of everything. He had already dubbed the sea of corporate logos "McBase Camp." The expedition leaders were "Everest cruise directors."

"Where does the abominable snowman fit in?" asked Perry.

"Look around you," said Nestor. "Everybody has a gimmick. There's a guy on the Australian team who plans to be the first garbage collector to stand on the summit. The Peruvians are taking a lab rat up there — the first rodent on top of the world. On the other side of camp, there's a lady who wants to be the first great-grandmother to make it through the Khumbu Icefall. Why can't I be the yeti guy?"

"Watch it, Nestor," came a voice behind him. "I think you're talking to one of those gimmicks right now."

Ethan Zaph stepped through the tent flap, unfolding his six-foot-two-inch frame. He faced Sammi. "SummitQuest, right? And you want to be the youngest girl?"

"I don't care about records," Sammi told him. "I climb for the rush." She held out her hand. "Sammi Moon. I'm a fan — but that doesn't mean I won't smoke your butt on the mountain. Carrot-top here is Perry Noonan."

There were handshakes all around.

"So you're after my record," Ethan said to Perry. "No, wait — what happened to Chris Alexis's brother?"

"He had to turn back," Sammi informed him solemnly. "HAPE at sixteen thousand."

"Is he all right?" Ethan asked in concern.

She shrugged. "He coughed a lot."

Ethan shook his head. "It makes you question Cap's judgment."

"Hey," Sammi said sharply. "You're talking about Cap Cicero. He stood on this summit and twenty others before we were even born."

"I *met* this kid," Ethan persisted. "Back in Kathmandu. He looks like he's in grade school."

"You've never climbed with him," she countered with more bravado than facts. "He's tough. He'll be back."

"That's what worries me," Ethan told her.

THE CLIMB

"You worry about your climb," Sammi suggested, "and we'll worry about ours. Right, Perry?"

"Right." Deep down, Perry knew he was worried enough for every expedition in Base Camp.

CHAPTER SEVEN

http://www.summathletic.com/everest/
icefall

A mountain the size of Everest must be tackled in pieces and ascended slowly, traveling up to and then down from a series of camps. The first challenge is the perilous Khumbu Icefall, which stretches from Base Camp to Camp One at 19,500 feet.

If the glacier can be thought of as a frozen river moving at four feet per day, the Icefall is its Niagara. Here, it drops precipitously. But instead of a rush of cascading water, in the Icefall this means collapsing seracs — massive blocks of ice, some of them one hundred feet tall.

If the Icefall has become the most feared part of the route up Everest, it is also the most strikingly beautiful. **CLICK HERE** to see the SummitQuest climbers taking on the vertical minefield of the Khumbu Icefall.

The crevasse was thirty feet wide and so deep that no bottom was visible, only a steely blue-gray darkening to black. Sammi Moon balanced precariously on an aluminum ladder — one of four lashed together to span the gap.

She turned back to her teammates, her face wreathed in smiles. "This is the coolest thing I've ever done — and I've done a lot of cool things!"

Cicero rolled his eyes. "Sometime this year, please."

She scampered to the other side, and then it was Perry's turn. His crampons scraped against the first aluminum rung, and he froze.

"Hurry up," grumbled Tilt.

"Come on, Perry," Sammi encouraged, so close, yet so far away. "Don't look down."

But down was the only place to look. Tiptoeing across the metal rungs in cramponed boots was as tricky as it was terrifying. His first glimpse of the chasm's yawning maw nearly caused him to lose his breakfast.

No, he thought. *No, Uncle Joe, I can't do this. I've gone on your rock scrambles and climbed your crags, but I won't walk a tightrope over a bottomless pit!*

There was a low rumble, and the ladder began to vibrate. Suddenly, a quarter mile away, a huge section of the Icefall disintegrated with an earsplitting roar, sending seracs the size of houses tumbling like tenpins.

Perry was glued to the spot, waiting out the earthquake. Trembling along with the tremors.

Cicero himself had said it best three hours before as the team was strapping on crampons and harnesses in the predawn chill: "You're walking into the last great democracy in the world. The Icefall doesn't care if you're the best climber in the world or the worst. If you're unlucky up there, you're dead, and there's nothing anybody can do about it. So I guess the rule is: Don't be unlucky."

Not exactly reassuring words.

Perry lifted his left foot and placed it ahead of the right. It was a tiny step, but it brought him twelve inches closer to being done with this. Then came the right and another twelve inches. The others were cheering like this was a triumph, but Perry knew it was really a form of surrender — surrender to Uncle Joe, nine thousand miles away. As his crampons crunched the ice beside Sammi, it occurred to him that, on the other side of the world, Uncle Joe was probably asleep right now, unaware of his victory.

In a remarkable show of skill and courage, Sneezy lowered himself on a rope several feet down into the crevasse so he could film Tilt's

THE CLIMB

crossing from below. As he passed over the camera, Tilt looked down and mouthed the words, "Hi, Mom."

"Watch," he whispered to Sammi on the other side. "Twenty bucks says Baboon bends the ladder."

"Climbing with your mouth again, huh?" Sammi observed. "How do you keep your teeth from getting stuck in the glacier?"

"It has to bug you, too," Tilt persisted. "We break our necks getting in shape, and then Cap hires a waterbed to be our Sirdar." The Sirdar was the leader of the Sherpas.

At last, the six were reunited beyond the crevasse. Dr. Oberman and Dominic were not there. They remained in the valley, awaiting the boy's recovery from HAPE.

Passage through the Icefall was nerve-wracking and difficult, but at least the trail was set. Each year, two Sherpas were hired as "Icefall doctors." So the SummitQuest team was following an established route with fixed ropes and ladders.

Perry never got used to it. His one strength as a climber was his ropework. It was a product of his nervousness, really. He was always so afraid of falling that he had become an expert at securing himself with safety lines bolted or screwed into the mountain. But here on Everest, the ropes were all fixed, rendering his talent useless. In the Icefall, an alpinist relied not on technical skill, but on a mixture of courage, blind faith, and pure stubbornness that bordered on insanity. Every time he set foot on a ladder, the terror was so immediate that his abdomen ached from clenching his stomach. In his school chess club back home, he was renowned as the guy who wasn't afraid to take risks. *Risks!* he thought bitterly. No chess player ever knew the meaning of the word. *In chess, the worst that can happen is getting checkmated. Here, a bad risk can send you plummeting to an icy grave!*

Fatigue was also a major factor. They were climbing two thousand feet higher than Base Camp, and the air was thinning as they rose. Every few steps, Perry had to stop and gasp for breath. Although the temperature was barely above zero, he was bathed in perspiration. His one consolation was that Tilt, with the physique of a rhino and twice the strength, was also puffing and sweating. The grin was gone from Sammi's face, replaced by a grimace of effort. Even Himalayan legend Cap Cicero slowed a little. Only Babu, born and raised at altitude, waddled along with no loss of speed.

"You're right," Sammi panted sarcastically to Tilt. "He's going to collapse any minute."

THE CLIMB

"Shut up."

The percussive drumrolls caused by splintering ice never stopped for a second. It was a chilling reminder that anything — even the ground beneath your feet — could crumble at any moment.

They had been in the Icefall nearly six hours when the fixed ropes angled sharply upward. It was by no means the steepest part of the route, but this time they were climbing a single colossal serac. Shaped like a shark's tooth the size of the Statue of Liberty, it towered over them, lord of the Icefall, leaning ominously forward.

Cicero sucked air between his teeth. "I don't like the look of that."

For Perry, who hadn't liked the look of anything since Base Camp, the pronouncement was a 9-1-1 call to every nerve ending in his body. "We're turning around, right?" he babbled. "We'll head down and find the Icefall doctors, and they'll rework the route — "

"I'll go first," Sammi interrupted.

One by one, they ascended the shark's tooth. With every heart-stopping footfall, Perry tried to beam his terror and misery across continents and oceans to Joe Sullivan's safe, warm bed in Boulder, Colorado. *I hope you're having a nightmare, Uncle Joe!* he thought bitterly. *I'm having one in broad daylight.*

Forty-five minutes later, the six stood at Camp One — a ragtag assortment of tents that stood at the entrance to the Western Cwm, the highest canyon on the planet.

Cicero was pleased. "Nice work. A little slow, but that'll improve as we get used to the thin air." Then he dropped the bombshell. "Ten minutes break, and we go back down."

"Down?!" protested Tilt. "You mean we're not staying at Camp One?"

"We're not ready for this altitude. Climb high, sleep low — that's the rule." He chuckled. "Don't worry, the descent is the fun part. It isn't any easier, but it takes half the time."

And double the stomach lining, reflected Perry, who felt his guts churning again.

So they turned around and headed back into the Icefall.

It happened just as Sammi was clipping her harness onto the fixed line to descend the massive shark's tooth. All at once, there was a crack as loud as a gunshot, followed by a mournful groaning sound, and the 150-foot serac began to topple forward.

"Jump!" bellowed Cicero.

CHAPTER EIGHT

Sammi leaped, swinging her legs up and clear, as the mountain of ice rolled over on its face, bringing with it the destructive power of a small nuclear bomb. The climbers below ran for cover as shattering ice flew every which way. The screw at the bottom anchoring the fixed rope snapped like a toothpick, and the line popped loose and hung there. With a cry of terror, Sammi plummeted 150 feet straight down, still harnessed to the useless rope.

In a spectacular display of speed for someone his size, Babu Pemba sprang into action. It was technically impossible to run in crampons, but he came close, hurling himself forward like an NFL linebacker making a highlight-film tackle.

He hit the ice a split second before Sammi hit him. He couldn't catch her — from that height, the impact would have crushed him. Instead, he redirected the free-falling climber to strike the glacier at an angle, and they rolled, somersaulting one over the other. They would have kept on going, tumbling and sliding until a crevasse swal-

EVEREST

lowed them, if they hadn't smacked into a glacial chunk the size of a small truck — a fragment of the former shark's tooth.

"*Sammi!*" With the route gone, Cicero was front-pointing down a 150-foot drop with a single ax. "*Babu!*"

"I'm okay!" called Sammi. Babu sat up beside her, and she clamped her arms around his hefty frame, mumbling, "At least I *think* I'm okay . . . I can't believe I'm okay."

Sneezy rushed up, Tilt and Perry hot on his heels. The guide set down the camera and examined Sammi and Babu inch by inch. Only then did he flash Cicero a thumbs-up.

"Thank God!" But the team leader didn't relax until he himself had made it down to stand with his Sirdar and his teenage charge.

"Take some time," he told Sammi. "As much as you need. I don't want you climbing again until you're one-hundred-percent comfortable."

"Are you kidding?" she scoffed. "You know me, Cap. I like it like that. Gets the blood pumping."

"That was almost prom night, your wedding — the rest of your life," he said seriously. "Be a strong, silent type if you like. But we're not moving until you admit what almost happened."

"Silly," she chided sweetly. "Sophomores don't go to prom."

But Cicero knew her bravado was just an act. Three hours later, when the exhausted team staggered back into Base Camp, Sammi Moon was still shaking.

The monotonous chanting seemed to float on the thin air as easily as the low overcast.

It was Dominic's second visit to the famous monastery at Thyangboche. Ten days before he had come eagerly to this rambling collection of temples, almost as much of a landmark on the mountaineering map as Everest itself.

Now the place merely reminded him of where he was not.

Patience, he told himself.

After five days at lower altitude, he had made a complete recovery from HAPE. It was astounding, Dr. Oberman assured him. Normally it took close to two weeks for the effects of altitude sickness to disappear.

He believed her. He could see it in her eyes as she poked and prodded him with her stethoscope. Yes, his chest was clear, although the dry Khumbu cough still plagued him. She kept raving about his healing power, but when he asked when they would start back up the valley, the answer was always the same.

"It's not time yet."

Will it ever be time?

"What does Cap say?" he would ask every night. "Did you talk to him?"

"Cap hired a doctor for his expedition. If he had medical training, he wouldn't need me."

He sat in the temple, with a *kata* — a white silk prayer scarf — draped around his neck. He was glumly sipping sweet tea when he spied an emaciated elderly lama. The man was so weak that he had to be carried in by several of his colleagues. All at once, the monk pointed at Dominic and began speaking in such agitation that he had to be restrained by his bearers.

Dominic and Dr. Oberman left soon after — they didn't want to be the cause of any disturbance. But as they made their way to the door, one of the younger lamas rushed up and addressed them in broken English. He apologized for the elderly monk frightening them. The man was coming off a three-week fast.

"But what was he saying about me?" asked Dominic

"He say, look this boy, he have shiny coils all around," the young lama informed him.

THE CLIMB

"Shiny coils?" repeated Dominic. "You mean like climbing ropes? They can look kind of shiny in bright sun."

The doctor shook her head. "It was just a hallucination."

The young monk was offended. "No hallucinate! *Vision!* Very important. Always remember."

"I — I will," Dominic managed as Dr. Oberman led him outside.

When they had reached their lodge in the nearby village, she turned to him. "Tomorrow," she said, "we'll start back up toward Base Camp. No guarantees, okay? We'll take it one day at a time."

Her cautious tone did nothing to dampen his celebration.

That night, he lay on his lumpy mattress, looking up at a small glass vial on a leather string. It held sand from the Dead Sea — the lowest point on Earth. The keepsake belonged to his brother, Chris, a gift from their grandmother before Dominic was even born. Chris had been planning to leave it on the summit of Everest. "From the bottom of the world to the top." That was his motto. And when Chris had been cut from the team, he had passed it on to Dominic.

Hang on, Chris. We're still in this thing.

Despite his exhilaration, he was strangely

troubled. The incident at the monastery was still very much on his mind.

Shiny coils. Did it mean ropes? Could the holy man actually have seen a vision of Dominic ascending the mountain?

More likely it's a scam, he thought. *They say it to every climber who goes in there.*

But there was another possible explanation for the shiny coils: Medical tubes and wires, snaking in and around his body.

In a hospital.

THE CLIMB

CHAPTER NINE

SummitQuest's next foray onto the shanks of Everest was a climb to Camp One for a two-day acclimatization stay.

If boredom had been an annoyance at Base Camp, here at 19,500 feet it was a full-fledged epidemic. There was absolutely nothing to do except read and melt snow into drinking water.

Perry looked into the pot. "The fire's broken," he complained, stirring a mound of slush that seemed determined to stay slush forever.

Sneezy laughed. "Fire burns cooler at altitude. Wait till Camp Four. You can spend a whole night trying to make a cup of soup."

Tilt headed for the tent flap. "I'm not thirsty."

The cameraman grabbed him by the arm. "If you get dehydrated on Everest, you're dead. Make yourself comfortable. We're going to be here a long time."

In contrast to the chill of the Icefall, the Western Cwm was like a giant solar oven. They were sandwiched between the Nuptse wall and the west shoulder of Everest. The sun's rays baked

EVEREST

the snow valley, raising the temperature well into the nineties.

"This is bizarre," complained Sammi. "I'm going to fry on a sheet of ice."

Stripping off layers of clothing was the only way to stay comfortable. But this far up into the atmosphere, there was practically zero protection from the sun's rays. Unprotected skin burned in minutes. They slathered on sunscreen, but in less than an hour they were forced to flee to the unmoving hot air of the tents.

"It beats being broiled," said Perry.

"So much nicer to be slow-roasted," growled Tilt.

At that moment, Cicero burst in, brandishing his walkie-talkie like a club. "Base Camp just patched me through to the satellite phone so I could take a call from Summit headquarters back in the States. They're getting flak because maybe Dominic isn't up to this climb."

"But how could they know anything's wrong with Dominic?" asked Sammi.

"Because they read it in the *National Daily*, that's how!" roared Cicero.

There was silence as the meaning of his words sank in. During training camp in Colorado, there had been a tell-all story in the *Na-*

tional Daily, but everyone assumed that the source was a disgruntled climber who had been cut from the team. This latest leak could only have come from someone at Mount Everest.

Tilt held his breath and did his best not to panic. *There's no way Cap could know it's me,* he kept repeating to himself. *There's no way Cap could know it's me. . . .*

Sammi spoke up. "What about Ethan Zaph? He knows Dominic had HAPE."

"But Ethan wasn't in boot camp," Perry pointed out.

Tilt came alive. "Maybe not in person," he argued, "but he had a lot of friends in that group. We were the top young climbers in the country. If he wanted info, he just had to pick up the phone."

"He could have said, 'Hi, it's Z-man. What's new at boot camp?'" Sammi agreed. "No one would suspect he was fishing."

Cicero was skeptical. "Why should Zaph care if Dominic gets a shot at Everest?"

"It's *his* record we're out to break," Tilt explained, thrilled to have a theory that deflected suspicion from himself. "Any trouble he can make for SummitQuest could affect our chances of getting to the top."

Cicero thought it over. "Maybe," he said finally. "But whoever it is, the walls have ears, so keep your mouths shut, especially around Zaph. Got it?"

Tilt cleared his throat. "Have you heard anything from Dominic? Is he getting better? You know, better enough to climb with us?"

"I decide whether Dominic climbs or not!" Cicero snapped testily. "Not the *National Daily* and whatever bigmouth is feeding them their information. And if I find out that it's one of you, I don't care if you're three steps from the summit — so help me, I'll yank you down to Base Camp myself and put you on the next yak to Kathmandu. Is that clear?"

Tilt nodded along with the others, his stomach tight.

Sammi wasn't the only one who lived on the edge.

By the time Dr. Oberman and Dominic made it to Base Camp, the SummitQuest team had returned from Camp One, rested, and set out again.

"How do you feel, kid?" asked Cicero over the walkie-talkie from Camp Two, nearly a mile above.

"Fantastic," Dominic told him. Tackling the

THE CLIMB

trek at a snail's pace had been frustrating, but his strength had returned in full force. "We can come up and meet you guys if you want."

"Cool your jets," laughed Cicero. "Get used to the altitude at Base Camp. We'll be back in a few days."

But even Base Camp — a place Dominic had been dreaming about for half his life — couldn't hold his interest for very long.

"Andrea," he suggested the next morning, "why don't we suit up and go into the Icefall?"

"You heard Cap," she told him. "We wait here for the rest of the group."

"We don't even have to make it to Camp One," he wheedled. "Come on, let's get our feet wet. I haven't strapped on crampons in six weeks."

"Dominic, you know better than anybody the dangers of going too high too fast. Do you have any idea how lucky you are? Not only are you alive, but you're probably going to get your chance at the mountain. Be grateful."

Dominic was nervous. The others were on their third acclimatization trip, and he hadn't even started yet. There were still weeks to go before they could try for the peak, but a lot could go wrong on Mount Everest. A few days of bad weather could put him so far behind schedule that he'd never be ready for a summit bid.

Stuck in a tent at Base Camp while the rest of them push for the top. Nothing, he thought, not even HAPE, could be worse than that!

The next morning, there was an accident on the Lhotse Face. One of the Japanese climbers was struck in the head by a falling rock.

A group of Sherpas were attempting a rescue. They had the man strapped to a ladder and were slowly carrying him down through the Icefall. This was nothing short of heroism — the Icefall was difficult and dangerous enough without having to maneuver a 180-pound climber attached to an eight-foot length of aluminum. As the only doctor presently in Base Camp, Andrea Oberman rushed the quarter mile to the mouth of the Icefall to await the patient. Dominic went with her.

Half an hour later, the party appeared. The rescuers were led by none other than Babu, supporting the front of the ladder/stretcher on his shoulders.

"What can I do to help?" Dominic asked Dr. Oberman.

The doctor had no time for him. "Stand clear, Dominic. This man may have a fractured skull."

THE CLIMB

She turned to Babu. "Get on the radio and set up a helicopter evacuation!" The barked orders continued to the group in general. "Let's move him back to camp! Bring extra blankets! Where's the best place to land a chopper around here?"

The Japanese mountaineer was carried off. Dominic made a move to follow, but hesitated. There were plenty of volunteers for this rescue. He'd only get in the way.

He peered up into the shattered glacier.

So dangerous. Why was he drawn to it?

The answer came immediately: *I'm a climber.*

"You're all crazy," his mother had said years before, when Mr. Alexis had decided to spend Thanksgiving scaling Half Dome in Yosemite. Chris had been only twelve for that trip — one of the youngest ever to take on the famous wall. Nine-and-a-half-year-old Dominic had burned with jealousy. It had always been that way — Chris was older; Chris was bigger; Chris was better. Even at training camp for SummitQuest, Chris had been considered a sure thing; Dominic had been expected to disappear in the first cut.

Yet Dominic, not Chris, was the Alexis brother standing at the entrance to the Khumbu Icefall. Dominic was at the base of mighty Everest.

And what was he doing?

Waiting.

That was when his eyes fell on the assortment of equipment lying on the moraine ten yards away. Since it was so difficult to walk in crampons over the Base Camp rocks, most Everesters left their footgear by the entrance to the Icefall. Camp, after all, was still a quarter mile away. For an exhausted, dehydrated climber returning from the upper mountain, it was a way to save precious energy.

Dominic's crampons were easy to find — they were the smallest ones there by at least three sizes. His ice ax, also smaller, lay beside them. He hefted it experimentally.

You promised Cap you'd stay put, he reminded himself.

But every time he turned the thought over in his head, it lost a little more shine, fading next to a new notion, growing in intensity.

I'll only go in for an hour or so. Just to get the feel of it.

THE CLIMB

CHAPTER TEN

To Dominic, the Khumbu Icefall was the most beautiful place on Earth.

Of course he knew his surroundings could be lethal. Climbers in the Icefall were like ants on a bowling ball — the slightest movement could crush you with a force millions of times your own weight. Even the greatest alpinists in history — Cap Cicero included — had a healthy fear of the Icefall. Dominic climbed cautiously, with a humble respect for the hazards all around. But he could not bring himself to be afraid. Instead, he was filled with wonderment at this vertical labyrinth of deep blue crystal. Every ray of sunlight that managed to squeeze down between Everest and Nuptse was multiplied to infinity by a wonderland of irregular prisms.

When he came to the first ladder, disappointment washed over him. That was the deal he'd made with himself. He would ascend only as far as the Icefall's first crevasse. Then it would be time to turn around. He was not dressed properly — sweats and a jacket instead of the standard one-piece wind suit. He had found light gloves in

EVEREST

the pockets, but not the Gore-Tex mitts for high-altitude mountaineering.

He frowned. On the other hand, the Icefall was rarely windy, and the day was just beginning to warm. He'd only been climbing for forty minutes. It didn't make sense to come this far without crossing one of the Khumbu's notorious ladders.

Over and back — that's all. Just so I'll know what to expect.

His crampons scraped at the rungs of the ladder. Awkward steps. His eyes began to fill with tears. Not tears of terror, but the emotion of feeling eighty years of mountaineering history under his feet. This wasn't a drill, or a practice climb designed to *simulate* Everest. This was the real thing.

A sudden voice behind him interrupted his reverie.

"Just walk, sahib. No look down hole. Pretend not there."

Startled, Dominic craned his neck to glance over his shoulder. At the foot of the ladder stood three Sherpas carrying enormous loads.

The leader stared at him. "A child?"

"I'm with SummitQuest," Dominic called back a little defensively. "Cap Cicero's team." He hurried across the ladder.

THE CLIMB

One by one, the Sherpas followed, joining him on the other side of the crevasse. They were barely breathing hard despite the huge packs each man carried. Sherpas were employed to ferry gear and supplies to the high camps on the mountain. They received little credit for their efforts, but without them, no expedition would have a chance at the summit.

The Sirdar looked him up and down. "You very young." Unlike Babu, who had lived in the West, most Sherpas spoke broken English with thick accents.

Dominic nodded. "We're all kids on SummitQuest," he admitted, "but I'm the youngest."

"You stay with us," the Sirdar decided. "No climb alone. Icefall dangerous."

But I was just about to go back down —

Dominic opened his mouth to say it, but bit his lip instead. How could he pass up a chance to climb with Sherpas, the legendary unsung heroes of Everest? *Just a little farther,* he decided. *Then I'll turn around.* After all, the descent would be much quicker. Andrea had her hands full with the injured Japanese climber. Dominic would be back in Base Camp before she even missed him.

He climbed a while longer, marveling at the porters' ease despite their backbreaking burdens.

Then it happened. On a steep, tricky scramble, there was a sudden snap. A crampon tumbled down the rime, its broken strap trailing behind it. The climbers stood frozen as it skittered out of reach and disappeared into the space between two blocks of ice.

The tallest Sherpa dropped his pack and one-footed it down the slope in search of his gear. Negotiating the Icefall was difficult enough under the best of circumstances. Without crampons, it was practically suicidal.

The man peered into the gap, then looked up with a gesture of helplessness that was clear in any language. The crampon was gone for good.

For Dominic, it was a sobering reminder: Yes, Everest was climbable. But let the slightest thing go wrong — something as simple as a broken strap — and all bets were off.

The Sherpas held a worried conference. Pasang could not continue his carry to Camp One. He would be able to make it back to Base Camp on one crampon, but that meant his load would have to sit in the Icefall until one of the others could come back for it.

As they debated all of their options, Dominic shrugged into the heavy shoulder harness and lifted Pasang's pack. "I'll take it."

The Sirdar stared at him. "Too heavy for boy."

"I can manage," Dominic assured them.

THE CLIMB

But the Sherpas insisted on transferring some of Dominic's load to their own. By the time Pasang left them and the climb resumed, Dominic guessed that his pack held twenty-five or thirty pounds of equipment.

It occurred to him that this might be unwise — to carry a load to nearly twenty thousand feet so soon after his bout with HAPE. But the truth was he felt remarkably strong. Most climbers wound up gasping for breath on their first trip through the Icefall. And sure, he found the air thin, but it didn't seem to be slowing him down.

Maybe Dr. Oberman was right. His extra week along the trekking route had trained his blood to carry more oxygen to the brain. He was *acclimatized*!

The gear turned out to be headed for the This Way Up expedition. Awaiting it at Camp One was none other than Ethan Zaph.

The youngest summiteer in Everest history did a double take when he saw Dominic unloading his pack. "What are *you* doing here? You went home! You had HAPE!"

Dominic shrugged. "I got better."

And he turned to follow his Sherpa team back into the Icefall for the descent, leaving Ethan standing there with his jaw dropped.

They were down in a little over two hours.

Pasang met them on the moraine, carrying steaming cups of Sherpa tea. There was one for Dominic as well. In all his life, nothing had ever tasted sweeter.

There was other good news besides Pasang's safe return on only one crampon. The injured Japanese climber had been safely evacuated by helicopter and was expected to recover.

"Congratulations," Dominic told Dr. Oberman when he joined her at the SummitQuest camp. "I hear the guy's going to be okay."

"Thanks." She looked him up and down. "You're all sweaty. What have you been up to?"

Oh, about 19,500 feet, he thought with a grin. Aloud, he said, "I helped out some Sherpas."

He didn't mention that this had been the greatest day of his life. Or that his mind was now occupied with a single thought: *I've got to get back up there!*

CHAPTER ELEVEN

http://www.summathletic.com/everest/cwm

The Western Cwm, the highest canyon on the planet, is located between the Nuptse wall and the West Shoulder of Everest. It has been nicknamed the "Crevasse Highway." Here, the Khumbu glacier splits into hundreds of pieces, separated by crevasses measuring as much as eighty feet across.

Camp Two, at 21,300 feet, is also known as Advance Base Camp, or ABC. Unlike the tiny Camp One, it is a bustling community of more than one hundred tents and the main destination for acclimatization. Climbers can and do spend as long as a week at a time here, adjusting their bodies to the thin air they'll encounter higher on the mountain. At ABC, the biggest enemy is not the altitude, the extreme heat of day or cold of night, or even the yawning crevasses.

EVEREST

CLICK HERE to see members of SummitQuest grappling with the mind-numb-
ing boredom of Camp Two, where nothing
ever happens.

Perry was chipping ice to melt for drinking
water when he saw the creature. It was about
nine feet tall and walked upright, its light brown
fur standing out against the terraced ice of the
West Shoulder — seventy yards away and closing fast!

He was about to yell for Cicero when there
was a terrific commotion in the This Way Up
camp. The half-demented voice of Nestor Ali
rang out, "Get your camera! It's a yeti! A *real*
one!"

He burst out of his tent lens first, shooting pictures at the speed of light.

That was when Perry noticed that the "yeti"
was wearing crampons. The mythical abominable snowman beat its chest and came running
toward Nestor. The climber/journalist dropped
his camera in the snow and took off running, with
no crampons, wearing only his soft-soled boot liners. He was soon flat on his back on the hard-
packed snow.

The yeti advanced menacingly on him. Then,

THE CLIMB

only a few feet away from the kill, the giant creature split in half. The top hit the rime and rolled away, giggling. The bottom was Ethan Zaph.

By this time, a large crowd of climbers had gathered to watch as Nestor scrambled to his feet.

"Very funny, guys! Very funny!" he ranted, his boot liners slipping. "I bet you'd be laughing your heads off if I'd run straight into a crevasse!"

Ethan was in hysterics. "We got you, Nestor! We've been carrying this fur coat for weeks! *Weeks!* Ever since Namche!" He picked up the coat to reveal the top half of the Yeti, the Sherpa Pasang.

For a group of bored-stiff climbers at Camp Two, these events were the equivalent of Academy Award entertainment. Raucous laughter and wild cheering rocked the Cwm. Even seasoned veterans like Cicero guffawed their approval at this distraction from the serious business of climbing a behemoth.

At last, even Nestor good-naturedly joined the party. "Okay," he said, "but if my camera's broken — "

A low rumbling in the Cwm rose above the merriment.

Babu was the first to stop chuckling, followed

by Cicero, who called for silence. There was an explosion like a kiloton of dynamite, and the snow pack on the West Shoulder disintegrated and began to roar down at them.

"*Run!*" bellowed Cicero.

No instruction was ever less necessary. There was a mass stampede for the Nuptse side of the valley. Perry stumbled, but Sneezy hauled him up by a fistful of sweatshirt and dragged him out of harm's way.

The avalanche thundered down to the Cwm, kicking up a cloud of ice crystals that rose hundreds of feet in the air. The churning wall of snow pounced on Camp Two, shattering the outer ring of tents and leaving the others half buried.

Then, all at once, it was over. The silence of the Cwm belied the furious activity of the previous moments.

The head counts began. The various expeditions took inventory of their snow-covered personnel and reported no one missing. Except —

"Wait a minute!" Cicero's voice rang out. "Where's Moon?"

Desperately, Babu, Sneezy, Tilt, and Perry searched faces. Sammi was nowhere to be found.

"*Sammi!*" Cicero raced for the compound,

THE CLIMB

wading through thigh-high powder. Using his hands as a shovel, he dug out the tent flap and zipped it open.

There sat Sammi Moon, cross-legged on her air mattress, completely lost in the musical world of her Walkman. Through the pummeling beat and raging guitars of Green Day, she had simply not noticed the avalanche.

Weak with relief, Cicero reached out and snatched the headphones from her ears. "Hey," he said hoarsely, "ever consider turning down the volume on that thing?"

"Thanks, Dad," Sammi grinned. She looked up at him and stared. The team leader was frosted white from head to toe. "Man, that must have been some snowball fight. I miss all the good stuff."

CHAPTER TWELVE

Climbers and Sherpas alike set about the task of digging out the tents. In a few hours, Advance Base Camp was up and running again.

Although no one had been injured, four campsites had been destroyed. One of these belonged to This Way Up. So Ethan, Nestor, and their teammates and Sherpas headed back down toward the Icefall. With Ethan's departure came a release of tension in the SummitQuest group. Most of them suspected Ethan of leaking information about them to the *National Daily*. Only Tilt knew the truth.

Porters continued to plod up the Cwm, carrying loads destined for Camp Three on the Lhotse Face and Camp Four on the South Col. ABC was the obvious rest stop, and it was not uncommon to see as many as thirty Sherpas sitting on the snowpack, eating candy bars and drinking tea.

Cicero and Sneezy were huddled over the video camera, examining the day's footage. The images they chose would be E-mailed by satellite phone directly from Camp Two to Summit's Web

THE CLIMB

site designers in Colorado. Scenes from the expedition could be on-line in a matter of hours.

Babu tapped Cicero on the shoulder. "Got a minute?"

"What's up?"

"I've been hearing the Sherpas talking about someone they call the 'little sahib.' The word is there's this kid — just a boy — who's been helping them carry loads through the Icefall for the last couple of days."

Cicero's face flamed red. "I'll kill him!"

"That's impossible!" exclaimed Sneezy. "How could it be Dominic? The kid was in a Gamow bag a week ago."

"Then who is it?" snarled Cicero. "One of the dozens of other thirteen-year-olds hanging around Mount Everest?"

"For what it's worth," added Babu, "they say he climbs like one of us."

Cicero reached for the radio and hailed Base Camp. A moment later, Dr. Oberman answered his call.

"This is Andrea."

"Where's Dominic?" Cicero practically barked at her.

"He's around somewhere," came the reply. "You know Dominic; he marches to the beat of a different drummer. He's made friends with some of the Sherpas, and they honestly seem to love him."

"Of course they love him!" howled Cicero. "He's been doing their work for them!"

"What work?"

"He's carrying loads up the Icefall!"

There was a pause, then the doctor's voice said quietly but clearly, "I'll kill him."

"Get in line!" growled Cicero. "Listen, if you find him, sit on him. I'm coming down." He began to strap on his crampons.

Babu reached for his own gear.

"God, no!" Cicero exclaimed. "I need you here to keep an eye on these three so they don't start a summit push without us!" He shouldered a small pack. "What happened to us, Babu? We've been guiding this peak forever. How did we lose control?"

Babu shrugged. "We've got a good system that works on this mountain, but it's based on everybody being adults. If you tell a forty-year-old lawyer, 'Stay out of the Icefall,' and he doesn't, that's *his* problem. But if the same happens with a thirteen-year-old kid, you feel like it's your fault and you've let him down. We're climbers, Cap, not baby-sitters."

As Cicero began to descend the Cwm from Camp Two, his mind was in turmoil. Dominic. It

THE CLIMB

was always Dominic. Cicero had known in boot camp that the kid was too young and too small. But the boy's surprising skill and indomitable spirit had won him over.

And what's my reward for having faith in him?

Who got HAPE on the trek? Who turned into the *National Daily*'s poster boy for "Send This Baby Home"? Summit headquarters had even begun to receive inquiries from the Nepalese authorities about why such a young child was listed on their climbing permit.

And now the little brat wouldn't stay out of the Icefall.

So lost was he in his internal rant that he barely even looked at the line of porters passing him in the other direction. They were Sherpas, climbing under heavy packs and making it look easy. He was almost past them when, with his peripheral vision, he noticed that one of them — the smallest — was wearing a SummitQuest hat.

"Freeze!"

Dominic looked up, surprised. "Oh, hi, Cap."

Cicero went to top volume. "You were sick, mister! Do you have any idea how *stupid* this is? And carrying all that weight makes it twice as likely that you'll have a relapse of HAPE!"

Dominic shrugged, load and all. "I feel really good."

Cicero stared at the boy. He *looked* really good, too. Cicero had guided enough expeditions to recognize a climber in difficulty. Dominic was rosy-cheeked and breathing well. He moved with a spring in his step despite a pack that must have weighed forty pounds.

But that didn't excuse the disobedience. "When I say stay in Base Camp, what code word is in there that tells you to start climbing? And now you're in the Cwm, so I guess the Icefall isn't good enough for you anymore! Where were you planning to stop? The summit? Or were you going to continue on to the moon?"

Dominic looked stricken. "I'm sorry, Cap. It just sort of got away from me."

Cicero was not receptive to his argument. "Too much candy on Halloween Night — *that* gets away from you! Not the Icefall! Climbing through the most inhospitable landscape on the planet is something you do *on purpose*! Give me one good reason why I shouldn't pack you off to Kathmandu right now."

"I'll go down, Cap. I promise. I just have to deliver this load to the Japanese camp at ABC."

Cicero swallowed his exasperation. That was

classic Dominic. Even when he was in big trouble, he wouldn't duck out on his responsibilities to a bunch of Japanese climbers he had never met.

"Give me that." The team leader yanked the pack off Dominic's back and hefted it himself. "You can sleep at Camp Two tonight and descend with the whole group tomorrow." A grunt of effort escaped him. "You carried this?"

The Sherpas laughed.

"Little sahib strong like yak," their Sirdar assured him. "For him, air no thin. Thick like sea level."

Cicero turned his face away to hide a smile of pride.

Welcome back, kid.

CHAPTER THIRTEEN

Base Camp was at full capacity, a bustling town of five hundred inhabitants, not including the porters and yak trains that arrived several times each day. Expeditions were constantly heading in and out of the Icefall. Teams pushed to higher and higher camps to complete their final acclimatization trips. SummitQuest bounced back and forth between base and ABC, venturing as far as the bergschrund, the deep crevasse that separated the Western Cwm from the Lhotse Face. It was late April, and soon the weather windows would start opening. When that happened — when conditions on the upper mountain cleared for a brief period — everyone had to be ready. Most of the time, the Everest summit was battered by jet-stream winds so strong that they could be heard in Base Camp, more than two vertical miles below. The sound was like the roar of a freight train.

Dominic had been banned from carrying loads through the Icefall, but he still spent a lot of his spare time with his newfound Sherpa friends. Pasang was even introducing him to the language. In return, Dominic was trying to teach him the words to "I've Been Working on the Railroad," the only English recording in Pasang's tiny home village.

The young man found the vocabulary very difficult. "What it means — *fiddly-eye-oh?*"

Dominic's Sherpa connections also provided him with every single piece of gossip in Base Camp. The Sherpas had the lowdown on everybody. Dominic knew who had the best summit chances (This Way Up) and the worst (the Guamanian brothers). Adventure Consultants had the best food, the Israelis had the best computer games, and the Canadians were the most polite. The strongest climber on the mountain that year was Babu Pemba, who turned out to be a kind of local hero. They also had a lot of respect for Cap Cicero and Ethan Zaph.

Sammi Moon turned out to be quite famous among the Sherpas because she was involved in every softball game, every Frisbee catch, and every arm-wrestling match at Base Camp. By contrast, no one had noticed Perry at all. If the reluctant climber hadn't had such striking red hair, he might have been totally invisible.

Tilt, however, had a reputation all his own. He had discovered that the yak drivers were so poor that they would do practically anything to earn a few extra rupees — mere pennies in U.S. money. So he kept a staff of personal servants to perform such tasks as rewinding his videotapes, tying his bootlaces, and recharging his laptop computer. The climbing Sherpas hated him for it.

"Sherpas poor, yes," said Pasang angrily, "but no slaves."

For his own part, Dominic was disgusted and embarrassed to be part of the same team as Tilt Crowley.

"Why can't he rewind his own videotapes?" he muttered to Pasang. "He spends all day cooped up in that tent. What else does he have to do?"

E-mail Message
TO: bv@national-daily.com
SUBJECT: Dominic's return

Cap has brought that poor sick kid back to Base Camp. They don't care about Dominic. They just want the glory of putting a thirteen-year-old on the summit.

That lousy Dominic! Every time Tilt thought about it, he wanted to break something. Dominic couldn't stay sick like everybody else with HAPE.

He had to come roaring back, carrying loads up the Icefall with the baboons.

And Cicero thinks the sun shines out of his little shrimp butt!

The thought made Tilt smolder. *If I went into the Icefall without permission, I'd be on a plane home tomorrow.*

It wasn't fair. Dominic got HAPE, and it actually *helped* him acclimatize. He was dancing around the Cwm while the rest of them were hammered by the altitude.

Not that the little runt was going to summit. But his chances had to be improved because he could breathe the thin air.

There must be some way to turn this around!

The really crazy part is that the Sherpas are taking advantage of Dominic, forcing him to haul heavy loads up through the Icefall. And Cap is doing nothing to stop it. Back in the States, you could go to jail for something like that, couldn't you? But in this dump, nobody cares.

There, he thought with a grim smile. *That ought to keep the pot boiling.* By this time, Tilt had learned to anticipate the chain of events: The story comes out in the *National Daily*; outraged people complain to Summit; Summit chews out Cap Cicero.

And, he reflected with satisfaction, Cicero blames the whole thing on Ethan Zaph.

If Ethan was not too popular around the SummitQuest campsite, his teammate, Nestor Ali, was becoming a great favorite. Young, and even younger at heart, Nestor was easygoing, friendly, and always good for a laugh. The yeti incident at ABC had only cemented his reputation as Everest clown. He was welcome in every tent and could often be found sitting around the flat stone slab that served as SummitQuest's dinner table.

"I don't think Ethan could be doing what you think he's doing," Nestor was saying one day over an omelet lunch. "Sure, he has the media contacts — he's a famous guy. But he doesn't care about records and being a big shot. He's a tunnel-vision climber. When he's taking aim at the summit, he forgets the rest of us are even here."

"Don't you think we're all like that?" Dominic asked thoughtfully. "I know I'm totally focused on getting my brother's sand to the top."

Nestor looked bewildered. "You're going to put *sand* on the summit? Why? To make sure nobody slips off?"

Dominic laughed. "Chris has sand from the Dead Sea," he explained, flipping up the leather string so the vial showed above his collar. "You know — from the bottom of the world to the top. Like that. If I get to the summit, I'll leave it up there for Chris. He should really be here, not me."

"I promised Caleb I'd take him to the top," Sammi said sheepishly. "I've got a picture of the two of us skydiving last summer — free fall."

"My uncle gave me an old piton from his rock-climbing days," Perry ventured. "He says it saved his life when he was twenty."

"Pretty lame for a billionaire," put in Tilt. "You'd think he'd give you the Hope diamond or something."

"This cost almost as much," Perry chuckled wanly. "It had to be pulled out of a cliff in the Canadian Rockies. It took a five-man team to find it and get it down."

"What about you, Nestor?" prompted Sammi. "Got anything for the pinnacle of the world?"

"My Slinky," Nestor replied readily.

"Slinky?" Perry repeated. "Like the kids' toy? Why would you want to leave *that* on the summit?"

"The ads say those things can 'walk' down any sloped surface," Nestor explained. "Well, if that's true, I can start it going at the top and it should boing all the way down the Kangshung face eleven thousand feet into Tibet."

There were howls of laughter from everyone but Tilt.

"You guys are nuts," he snorted.

"Well, what are *you* taking to the summit?" Sammi challenged.

Tilt kicked back on the air mattress. "Myself," he boasted. "And a camera to prove I got there."

CHAPTER FOURTEEN

www.summathletic.com/everest/
lhotseface

Above the Western Cwm looms the mile-high wall of ice known as the Lhotse Face. It is the steepest part of the southeast ridge route and grows steeper as the climber ascends.

CLICK HERE to see the SummitQuest team front-pointing up the sixty-degree slope, watched over by the spectacular peak of Lhotse, the fourth highest mountain in the world.

Lhotse, my butt! Perry thought to himself. He couldn't see any peak, spectacular or otherwise, towering above them. His universe at that moment consisted of a single rope that angled nearly straight up until it disappeared into a snow squall. For all he could tell, the upper end was attached to the Goodyear blimp.

He knew Lhotse was there only because the

rocks that kept pelting down had to be coming from somewhere. It was like climbing in a shooting gallery. And if one of them ever hit him . . .

He was clipped to the nylon line by means of a jumar, a device that enabled him to ascend the rope, but would lock automatically if he happened to fall.

Slide jumar up six inches. Left foot. Right foot. Repeat fifty million times.

The slope was too steep for conventional walking, yet not quite vertical enough for frontpointing. He found himself trying to do both — flat steps and toe steps — an awkward, ankletwisting combination more common on a ballet stage than in the Himalayas.

But no ballet dancer could handle twentythree thousand feet!

"Doing fine, Noonan," called Cicero from below.

But Perry was not doing fine. The altitude was showing itself as a jackhammer against every single muscle he tried to move. The air was so thin that there was literally nothing to breathe. Every few feet he had to stop to rest, to take several more gasping sucks at the punishing atmosphere in the hope of inhaling a decent amount of oxygen so he could keep going.

The radiant heat of the Western Cwm may as

well have happened in another life. The Lhotse Face was capital-C Cold. His climber's watch registered it as twelve below zero. But that didn't account for the chill factor from a brutalizing wind.

Three hours of pure agony seemed to bring him closer to nowhere. On top of all its other miseries, the Lhotse Face was endless. Sneezy had put it best at Camp Two last night: "There's lotsa face up there!"

At 23,700 feet, they encountered two members of the Japanese team descending after a night at Camp Three. Perry had been dreading this. Since there was only a single fixed rope, climbers could not pass each other without one of them unhooking from the line. It would only be for a second or two, but at that moment, he or she would be connected to the mountain by nothing more than crampons.

And then the maneuver was upon him. The first man unhooked and stepped deftly around Perry. His partner seemed to be having a much harder time. He came down to Perry's level and just hung there, waiting. He was gasping as if he'd just run a marathon; his arms hung limp at his sides. There wasn't an ounce of extra energy in him.

Perry really had no choice. With a silent

prayer, he disconnected his jumar and moved to step around the other climber. Just as Perry was about to clip on again, the exhausted man somehow lost traction in his crampons and began to slide down the ice. His rope caught Perry just below the knees, dislodging both of the boy's front points from the Lhotse Face.

For an instant of exquisite terror, Perry Noonan was off that mountain. Then, all in the space of a split second, his jumar snapped into place, and the device's teeth bit into the rope, stopping a fall that had never really started.

He dangled there, motionless and palpitating, until his mind came back to him. Kicking both front points, he dropped to the face and hugged it as if he were trying to insert himself inside the ice.

"I'm alive," he mumbled. "I'm alive . . ."

He was still repeating those words an hour later when he finally arrived at Camp Three. The feeling of being untethered from the mountain, waiting for gravity to pitch him into the abyss, was with him for a very long time.

At twenty-four thousand feet, Camp Three was a place unfit for human habitation. For starters, there was no real camp — not in the sense of a

common area where people could sit and talk comfortably. Four two-person tents were perched precariously on ice that was pitched steeper than a log flume.

"Are you sure you made it small enough?" Tilt grumbled at Babu.

The Sirdar laughed. "Do you know how long it took four of us to hack out platforms flat enough for these tents? Nine hours. If you don't like it, try the Hilton."

They held a team powwow, nearly five miles above sea level across a slanted conference table of blue ice. The only way to do this was for the eight climbers to lie in the tents with their heads poking out the flaps, facing each other.

"I know exactly how you guys feel," said Cicero. "You can barely breathe; you've got pounding headaches; and energy-wise, if you had to scratch your noses, you wouldn't have the energy to raise your fingers that high. Now listen carefully, because I'm going to blow your minds: You're ready."

They looked at him dumbly.

"You are. We sleep here tonight, down to ABC tomorrow, and then back to Base Camp. Then we rest up and wait for good weather. And our next stop" — he rolled over and pointed straight up — "is *there*."

All eyes followed along. The overcast was beginning to break up and, a vertical mile above, the pinnacle of Everest peeked out from behind the bulk of the southwest face. The powerful jetstream winds blew a plume of ice crystals off the summit half a mile into the troposphere.

CHAPTER FIFTEEN

Tilt Crowley was watching *The Matrix* for the eighth time in the kitchen tent at Base Camp. Absently, he popped open his lunch, a single serving tin of tuna.

"Ugh!"

The tuna can was filled with sardines again! The merchants of Namche Bazaar were a bunch of crooks. They charged the expeditions top dollar and sold them mislabeled cat food. The word around Base Camp was that the French expedition had dropped a fortune on two cases of caviar and ended up with forty-eight single servings of refried beans.

Maybe I'll get rich enough to buy Mount Everest and kick all the Sherpas out!

"Cap! Cap!" It was Sammi's voice, obviously in a state of high excitement. A second later, she came bursting through the flap, Perry at her heels. "Where's Cap?"

"Don't know, don't care," yawned Tilt, pitching his tin of sardines through the opening out to the moraine.

EVEREST

"Some Nepal government guys just helicoptered into camp!" Perry panted. "They're nosing around, asking questions about Dominic!"

Tilt was instantly alert. "What did you tell them?"

"What do you think I told them?" Sammi snapped. "I said, 'Dominic who?' If these two were sent because of the *National Daily*, they could be here to kick Dominic off the mountain!"

Tilt leaped to his feet. "Where's the shrimp now?"

They found Dominic in the This Way Up mess tent, drinking tea with Nestor, Pasang, and Gombu, the team's Base Camp Sirdar.

Sammi filled him in on the developments. "You've got to hide!" she finished.

"Oh, come on," scoffed Tilt. "What can they do to him? He's on the climbing permit. He's legal."

"That's not the problem," argued Nestor. "The government here can drive you crazy, even if you're legit. They'll delay you for weeks, crawling all over you with a microscope. By the time you get the okay, the monsoon will roll in, and it'll be too late in the season to climb."

Dominic thought it over. "I'll disappear for a while."

THE CLIMB

"Whatever you do, do it fast," urged Perry, peering out the flap. "They just left our tent, and they're headed this way."

Gombu flipped open the expedition's pantry chest and began removing boxes of crackers, cookies, and cereal by the armload. "You safe in here!" he exclaimed, pushing Dominic inside. The others helped pile the light boxes on top of the fugitive.

"You don't have to bury him!" Tilt exploded. "Nobody's going to look in there anyway."

That was exactly the problem, Tilt thought to himself. The government guys weren't going to find Dominic unless Tilt ratted him out.

But how can I do that in front of Sammi and Perry?

"Shut the lid!" hissed Nestor. "They're almost here!"

And then the two officials were upon them. They wore olive green paramilitary uniforms and black berets. One of them held a murky faxed photograph of Dominic, an old school picture re-produced from one of the articles in the *National Daily.*

"We seek this boy," the leader said.

"He's not here," Nestor replied.

The two spoke to the Sherpas in Nepalese, and got very short answers and very long shrugs.

Tilt had the panicky feeling that they were about to leave. Both men were breathing hard — Base Camp was at high altitude, even for the people of Nepal. *Search the box.* He tried to send the message telepathically. *He's in the pantry chest.* But why would they ransack any one tent before looking in the over three hundred others first?

He decided that the Nepalese needed a little help. Perched on a camp stove were four aluminum nesting pots. He could "accidentally" hip-check the cookware, which would clatter onto the pantry chest. With any luck, Dominic would be startled and cry out, thereby giving himself away.

"I have to go to the bathroom," Tilt mumbled and started forward. He was just angling into position, was about to deliver the blow, when —

"Who's talking to my people without me?"

Cicero burst through the flap, angry and arrogant as only a legend can afford to be. Tilt had no choice but to retreat as his team leader confronted the officials.

The constable with the fax stepped forward. "Cap Cicero, this is your climber, no?"

As he reached for the picture, Cicero intercepted a beseeching look from Sammi and noted that Perry's freckles were standing out like polka dots, so white was his face.

THE CLIMB

"Right," said Cicero. "Dominic Alexis."

"Where is he, please?"

Cicero never even paused. "Down in the valley somewhere. He's not going to climb. Too young, too small."

"A wise choice," the other man approved. "This news will be welcome at headquarters."

Perhaps closer to the truth, the news was welcomed by the two constables. They looked pathetically grateful to be able to head for their helicopter, which would take them away from 17,600 feet.

Ethan Zaph ducked in through the tent flap, peering quizzically over his shoulder. "What were those two guys doing here?"

Sammi fairly exploded in his face. "Like you don't know, rat!"

Cicero put a hand on her shoulder. "Take it easy, Moon."

Sammi was in no mood to be soothed. "Those two were looking to grab Dominic and kick him off the mountain!" she seethed at Ethan. "Because *you've* been feeding the *National Daily* lies about SummitQuest!"

Ethan stared at her, thunderstruck. Then he turned to Cicero. "What's she talking about, Cap? I know you guys don't like me because I quit your team. But why would you think I'd stab another climber in the back?"

"We don't know what to think, kid," said Cicero. "We're grappling with a lot of things ourselves. Don't take it personally."

"No, take it personally," Sammi snarled. "That's how I meant it."

Ethan's temper flared. "I haven't done anything to you or your team! You can believe that or stuff it — I don't really care! I didn't tip off the Nepalese, but I'll tell you this, though: They're right. This mountain is mean, and it's no place for a little kid. It's not right for Dominic, who could be in danger, and it's not right for the climbers who might have to put *themselves* in danger to rescue him." The well-known smiling face that adorned so many ads for climbing equipment was bright red with anger. "I didn't come into my own mess tent to take this kind of heat! *All I wanted was a lousy cookie!*"

He flung open the pantry chest and yanked out a bag of Oreos to find Dominic's distorted face peering up at him through the clear plastic of a bottle of vinegar.

"*Whoa!!*"

CHAPTER SIXTEEN

The weather report sent Base Camp into a frenzy of activity. The forecasting services all seemed to agree. There were clear days ahead, and several of them. The moment for a summit bid was now.

Sneezy filmed Cicero's pep talk, which turned out to be short.

"No panic. Same climb. We're just going to the end this time, that's all."

They dug their crampons into the crisp blue ice of the Khumbu Icefall.

That night they slept at ABC and spent the following day resting on the Cwm.

Cicero had little sympathy for their impatience. "Think of it as a trip to Miami Beach. It's the last heat any of us will feel for a good long time."

The next morning they were up well before the sun in an attempt to be free of the Cwm before the day's eighty-degree temperature swing. Miami Beach was fine for shorts and T-shirts, but not wind suits and heavy gear. Soon they were

EVEREST

back on the Lhotse Face for another torturous slog up steep sheer ice.

It took every ounce of will for Perry to put himself back up there again. Surprisingly, it wasn't quite as terrible as he remembered. How could it be? The acclimatization actually seemed to be working. He could almost breathe, and the effects of altitude felt more like a bad flu than a pile driver to the head. He had promised himself, though, that he was not unhooking his jumar from a fixed line if the entire British royal family wanted to get around him.

In fact, he did get passed, not by royalty, but by the first of several This Way Up summit teams. Ethan, Nestor, and Pasang climbed by on their way to the peak of Lhotse, dead ahead, yet impossibly far away.

Noticing the pure misery on Perry's face, Nestor hefted his ice ax like a microphone and boomed, " 'We have nothing to fear but fear itself!' "

"In that case," Perry panted back. "I should be pretty darn scared."

The other SummitQuest climbers offered their encouragement to Nestor and Pasang as they labored past. No one said a word to Ethan Zaph.

That night at Camp Three, Cicero held classes

in Oxygen 101. For the rest of the climb, each SummitQuest team member would wear portable breathing equipment — an oxygen mask and regulator hooked up to a sleek, ultralight cylinder of compressed gas. Tomorrow they would be crossing the important threshold of twenty-five thousand feet. There was no camp there, or even any milestone. But twenty-five thousand feet marked the beginning of Everest's infamous Death Zone.

"Supplemental oxygen *helps* you survive in the Death Zone. Remember I said *helps*. Because nobody, on *any* amount of O's, can last up there for long. Make no mistake — when you go that high, you're dying. Brain cells are disappearing, your heart beats at triple speed, and your blood gets thick like molasses. We're all on borrowed time above twenty-five K. The O's just let you borrow a little more of it, that's all."

Sammi, who included deep-sea diving on her list of extreme hobbies, had no trouble getting used to her oxygen mask. But the boys found them vastly uncomfortable, and even scary. Perry could not get over the feeling that he was suffocating, even though he was getting more oxygen, not less. Dominic found it spooky to hear the sound of his own breathing reverberating in his ears.

Tilt felt the same way. "It's like Darth Vader breath," he complained, tossing his mask aside. "I'll get the hang of it tomorrow."

"You'll get the hang of it *now*," Cicero insisted. "Nobody sleeps till you're totally comfortable in that rig."

Nobody slept anyway. The stakes were getting too high.

www.summathletic.com/everest/ southcol

No, they're not astronauts; they're the youngest expedition in the history of Mount Everest in full high-altitude gear, including oxygen. At this point in the climb our heroes might as well be walking on the moon. The atmosphere is virtually unbreathable, and they are far beyond the rescue range of modern technology.

The route to Camp Four is the highest left turn on the planet, an ascending traverse across the Yellow Band — five hundred feet of steep, crumbling limestone. Next comes a rock climb in the sky over the Geneva Spur, a decaying black club overlooking the Cwm by nearly a vertical mile.

It is not far now — the South Col, at the edge of Earth's atmosphere at twenty-six thousand feet. This barren wasteland of ice and stone is the site of Camp Four, the last stop before the summit. With nighttime temperatures of eighty below zero in lethal alliance with wind gusts more than one hundred miles per hour, this is not a relaxing place. Yet relax they must. For at midnight, they will walk right into the teeth of the worst conditions the mountain has to offer. **CLICK HERE** to see the SummitQuest climbers at Camp Four trying to grab a scant few hours of sleep before their final test on top of the world.

"I can't sleep," Dominic mumbled into his oxygen mask.

"Who asked you to?" roared Tilt. "I just need you to shut up long enough for *me* to get some rest!"

Perry tried to keep the peace in the close quarters. Due to the difficulty of ferrying equipment this high, the eight SummitQuest climbers were crammed into two three-person tents. "Come on, Tilt. We're all nervous."

This was not strictly true. The others were nervous. Perry Noonan was scared out of his wits.

He was playing a chess game in his head in a vain attempt to divert his mind. But he could get no further than three or four moves before his discomfort and fear brought him back to the Death Zone.

"I'm so pumped," said Sammi, pulling the mask from her face so she could be heard. "I mean, think about it. There's nothing about this moment that isn't extreme. Breathing extreme air in extreme cold and extreme wind, getting ready to take on the ultimate extreme mountain!"

Perry fiddled with his mask. "Who can sleep in this getup?"

Tilt pushed him back down on his sleeping bag. "That's easy for you to say. You don't need rest. You're going to quit before we hit the ridge. I'm going the distance tonight so — everybody — shut up!"

Dominic crawled to the entrance. "I'm going to check the radio. See if any of the other teams made the summit today."

Outside, the arctic blast of wind nearly bent him double. Nylon flapped against aluminum poles at such high frequency that Camp Four gave off an electric buzz. The seven-foot walk to the guides' tent seemed like a struggle. He poked his head inside. Dr. Oberman and Sneezy were trying to get some sleep. Cicero and Babu were

at the radio. Babu was the only one not breathing bottled gas. He never climbed with it — not even at the summit.

The stout Sherpa was the first to notice him. "Who's there?"

I must look like a storm trooper from Star Wars *in this oxygen rig,* Dominic reminded himself, pulling the mask aside.

Cicero yanked him in and zipped the flap shut. "You should be sleeping, kid."

Dominic shrugged. Few ever slept on the Col prior to a midnight climb. The conditions, the altitude, and the nervousness seldom allowed it. After a summit push, when the body has had every molecule of strength, will, and, at last, awareness wrung from it — that was the time for sleep. "Did anybody get to the top today?"

Babu shook his head. "The Guamanians are back. They didn't get very far. Some of the Japanese are still out there. They made it to the South Summit before turning around." He added, "But they're doing fine."

No sooner had the words crossed his lips than a barrage of angry words exploded from the radio. It was a full-fledged screaming argument — and definitely not in Japanese.

Cicero ripped off his mask, grabbed the microphone, and boomed, "This is Cap Cicero! Identify yourselves!"

"Cap, it's me — Nestor!" The voice sounded as exhausted as it was enraged. "I'm with Ethan and Pasang! We're above twenty-seven on Lhotse and — somebody messed up! I don't know who — maybe the staff at Base Camp — "

"What's going on out there?" Cicero roared.

"We're out of rope!"

Out of rope! Dominic could hardly believe his ears. There were many reasons for an ascent to fail — a storm, an accident, or the human body just reaching its limit. But to have to turn back because there wasn't enough rope to stretch all the way to the top — that was agony. They were only a few hundred feet below the Lhotse summit!

"Don't do anything stupid!" Cicero ordered in a commanding tone. "You climb without ropes, and somebody's going to slip!"

"But we're *there*, man!" Nestor was moaning. "We're off the ice! No more crampons even! Just a rock gully all the way to the peak!"

"Is Zaph there! Let me talk to Zaph — "

Suddenly, a Sherpa voice — Pasang's — cried, *"Rockfall!"*

There was an audible thud, then Ethan yelled, "Nestor's hit! Grab him!"

"What's going on?" Cicero bellowed into the radio.

His only response was violent rustling and static.

"What's happening? Who's out there?"

Ethan's voice, now distant, screamed, "Nestor! Wake up! *Wake up!*" and then the signal went dead.

CHAPTER SEVENTEEN

Sneezy and Dr. Oberman weren't sleeping anymore. By this time, the four guides and Dominic were crowded around the small radio. Cicero called all the other expeditions. No one was anywhere near the climbers in trouble. The closest teams were at Camp Four. The Guamanians were exhausted from their failed summit bid, and the Japanese were still on the mountain. SummitQuest alone was in any shape to offer assistance.

"If Nestor's really unconscious," the doctor said grimly, "there's no way two men can get him down the face from that altitude."

"We've got to help him!" exclaimed Dominic.

Cicero glared at him. "You're going to stay here and sit tight with the others. We'll look for them."

Sneezy was surprised. "All of us? Shouldn't somebody stick with the kids?"

Cicero shook his head. "Zaph's climbing without O's. Maybe he can handle himself, but I doubt he's got the strength for a rescue. We don't

want to drag ourselves all the way out there just to be caught short."

Babu nodded. "We'll have to traverse to the face until we hit their fixed line. Then we can head up the ropes and catch them descending."

"If they're not doing it headfirst at sixty miles an hour," Sneezy said pointedly.

Dominic nodded. "I'll tell the others."

The team leader grabbed his arm. "You know what this means, right?"

And Dominic did. There would be no summit bid tonight. Even if Cicero and the guides could effect a quick rescue and be back at Camp Four by midnight, they would be far too fatigued to set out for the top of Everest. In all likelihood, the team would have to retreat to ABC, or even Base Camp, to wait for another weather window.

He swallowed hard. Everest was fickle. They might not get another chance.

Dominic didn't hesitate. It was the unwritten rule of mountaineering: A rescue takes precedence over everything. Even a shot at the pinnacle of the world.

"Go!"

"The radio!"

Pasang watched as Nestor's walkie-talkie skittered down the Lhotse Face and disappeared from view. By the time it reached the Western Cwm more than a mile below, it would be traveling at unimaginable speed.

He helped Ethan turn Nestor over on his back — not an easy task at over twenty-seven thousand feet. Ethan flipped up the journalist's oxygen mask and listened tensely.

"He's still breathing. Thank God."

The boulder that hit Nestor had come out of nowhere, a flying projectile the size of a microwave oven. It had struck him squarely in the backpack, momentarily dislodging him from the mountain and leaving him hanging from the fixed ropes.

"Breathing *now*," Pasang agreed. "But what next?"

It was a good question. Near the summit, the western ramparts of Lhotse straightened to near vertical, and the treacherous face sloped upward at eighty degrees in places. For two climbers to get an unconscious companion down even as far as Camp Three would be impossible.

Ethan thought it over. The walkie-talkie was gone. Nobody knew they were in trouble. Descent wasn't an option, so . . .

"We'll go up," he decided.

"Without rope?" the Sherpa exclaimed. "One slip and — "

"Down is *ice*," Ethan argued. "Up is rock.

THE CLIMB

Down is far; up is close. We can practically crawl to the summit from here, dragging Nestor behind us. From there, we can take the ridge down to the South Col. One of the teams is bound to have a doctor at Camp Four."

"No fixed ropes on ridge, either," Pasang pointed out. "Cornices. Very dangerous."

"But possible. It's Nestor's only chance." He slapped the unconscious journalist's cheeks. "Come on, buddy, wake up!"

Nestor did not stir.

"All right," Pasang assented finally. "We go to summit."

Tilt stood on the black rocks of the South Col and gazed bleakly at the sun going down on the Western Cwm. It was one of the truly spectacular sights on Planet Earth, but he saw none of it.

Stinkin' Nestor!

Every time he thought about it, white-hot rage boiled through his brain.

Why this? Why now?

When Tilt thought ahead to the future, *every single thing in it* depended on this summit bid! The summit *was* his future. And it was *happening!* From here at twenty-six thousand feet, the top seemed so close he could practically hit it with a spitball. . . .

And then that clown has to go and get himself nailed by a rock!

He had always known Cicero was a jerk, but he never would have believed the mountaineering legend could be such a sucker. Why would he jeopardize the whole expedition just to rescue Nestor?

Nothing against Nestor, but why can't somebody else save him? His own expedition — they should be doing this! Not Cap! Not SummitQuest!

But Nestor's This Way Up teammates were all at Camp Two or lower. A group had started up the Cwm to help him on the way down. But by then this weather window would be history. There might be another; there might not. It would be decided by pure luck.

Not something you want to stake your whole future on.

The attack came from behind. Arms reached around his sides, and someone wrestled him down. Shocked and afraid, Tilt hit the rocky ground and rolled free. His assailant was a Sherpa in full climbing gear, including oxygen mask and goggles. The man scrambled up and made another run at Tilt.

"What do you want?" bawled Tilt.

But the Sherpa kept coming, stumbling like a

punch-drunk boxer. Terrified, Tilt backed away, casting a nervous eye over his shoulder. He was very near the point where the flat South Col rounded into the steep Lhotse Face — a deadly fall.

"Get away from me!"

The Sherpa reached for him. Then, as if the effort of lifting his arms had sapped all his remaining strength, he collapsed to his knees. A moment later, he was on all fours, gasping into his mask.

Light dawned on Tilt. *This guy isn't fighting me! He's so exhausted he can't even stand!*

On Cicero's orders, the teen climbers had moved to the guides' tent in order to keep an eye on the radio. Tilt hustled the Sherpa inside and pulled off the mask and goggles.

"Pasang!" cried Dominic in dismay. The normally confident climber was shivering uncontrollably.

They wrapped Pasang in blankets. Perry made him a cup of hot chocolate to warm him up.

"How's Nestor?" probed Dominic.

"Nestor very bad," the Sherpa reported gravely. "I think maybe will die on mountain."

"What are you talking about?" cried Sammi. "Aren't they bringing him down?"

Pasang looked blank.

Dominic grabbed his arm. "Cap, Babu, Sneezy, and Andrea left a few hours ago to help you guys up on the face."

The Sherpa put his head in his hands and moaned aloud. "Very big mistake! Very bad!" His eyes were filled with horror. "Ethan say, 'No safe climb down face. Climb summit and down ridge.'"

There was a breathless pause as the terrible truth sank in. Cicero and the guides were searching for Ethan and Nestor on the Lhotse Face. And all this time, the two had summited and were somewhere along the northeast ridge. It was a colossal mixup — one with consequences that could prove to be deadly.

A roar of laughter broke the stunned silence. "This is just fantastic!" Tilt exploded. "We throw away our summit chance so Cap can stage a rescue, but there's no one there to rescue anymore! Tell you what — when we get back to the States, we can go to Hollywood and sell the movie rights to *Climbing with Morons!*"

"Come on, Tilt," Perry said feelingly. "Nestor could die up there."

"No just Nestor!" Pasang's horror story had one final wrinkle. After hauling Nestor's unconscious body to the summit, they had started down Lhotse's northeast ridge. Pasang took Ethan's

pack, and Ethan carried Nestor piggyback style. It was an unbelievable feat of strength — especially for someone climbing without oxygen. But after an hour of descent, Ethan had collapsed. It was not a misstep or a fall. The famous young alpinist had just run completely out of steam.

"I try give Ethan my O's," Pasang went on, tears trickling down his frost-nipped cheeks. "But he say no — go Camp Four. Find Cap Cicero."

"If he wanted to climb with Cap, he shouldn't have quit SummitQuest!" Tilt snapped irritably.

"Cap has no hard feelings about that," Sammi countered. "He was ready to go after Nestor and Ethan. He thinks he's doing it right now, but he's in the wrong place!"

And then Dominic said, quietly but firmly, "We'll do it."

CHAPTER EIGHTEEN

"Do what?" Perry looked at him in alarm. "You don't mean — "

"We'll climb up the ridge and get Nestor and Ethan."

"Oh, no, you don't," warned Tilt. "I signed on to climb one mountain — Everest. Nobody said anything about Lhotse!"

Sammi got in his face, pressing her oxygen mask right up against his. "I'm on to you, Crowley. You're a jerk — but not a big enough jerk to let people die."

Dominic hunched over the radio. "Cap. Cap, come in please."

Cicero's voice came out of the tinny speaker. The team leader sounded totally spent. "Doesn't look good, kid. We've been on the face for three hours, and there's no sign of them. I think maybe they fell."

Dominic took a deep breath. "Brace yourself, Cap — they're on the northeast ridge." He explained the latest developments from Pasang. "Nestor's out cold, and Ethan — I guess he just kind of hit the wall. We're going to climb up and see if we can bring them down."

"No!!" barked Cicero. "Stay put! We'll come after them!"

Dominic looked pointedly at Pasang. The Sherpa shook his head. Two hours minimum for the guides to return; perhaps another hour to recuperate before starting up the ridge. Nestor and Ethan didn't have that much time.

"We think that might take too long," Dominic said carefully. "Nestor's hurt bad, and Ethan's got no oxygen high in the Death Zone."

"That's an unknown ridge, and there's maybe half an hour of daylight left! I absolutely forbid — "

Sammi reached around the radio and pulled out the battery pack. The set went dead. "These things are so unreliable at altitude," she said calmly.

Their first stop was the equipment dump between the two tents. There, they loaded up — oxygen bottles, a spare breathing rig for Ethan, and helmet lamps. Perry was throwing heavy coils of rope over his shoulders and around his neck.

"Whoa, Perry," called Sammi. "We're not climbing to Tibet, you know."

"There's not a single fixed line on that ridge!" Perry shot back, stuffing his knapsack with ice screws. "If we don't do this right, somebody is going to end up dead!"

She squinted at his face, barely visible behind goggles and mask. *He's petrified,* she thought, *but maybe that's a good thing.* Perry's fear made him a mediocre mountaineer, but it had also turned him into a master of ropes, pegs, screws, and pitons. He had trained himself to belay an elephant — not a bad guy to have around when the chips were down.

Pasang had to be physically restrained from coming with them. "You won't make it. You're too tired," Dominic told him kindly but firmly. "We can rescue two, but not three." At last, the exhausted Sherpa agreed to wait for them in the tent.

For safety, they roped themselves together in pairs — Sammi and Perry, Tilt and Dominic. It was not yet dark, but the temperature gauge on Dominic's watch read forty-nine degrees below zero. They could only guess at the windchill.

The first obstacle of their ascent was a towering triangular wall of wind-scoured ice. It stretched from the Col fifty stories up to the northeast ridge, which began at its tip.

THE CLIMB

Perry tried without success to place a screw near its base. "The ice is barely an inch thick. I don't think it's safe."

Sammi front-pointed past him. "You know how to make it safe?" she called. "Don't fall!"

They were twenty feet up when Tilt's crampons lost their hold of the thin rime. He slid down the wall, and as he did, Perry's screws popped out of the ice one by one. Tilt was unhurt as he tumbled to the Col — but only because the accident hadn't taken place four hundred feet higher.

"You stupid idiot!!" he roared, not at his companions, but at Lhotse itself. "I wouldn't even be climbing here if it wasn't for lousy Ethan Zaph, whose record is going to stand forever! I can't break it because I'm too busy rescuing *him!*"

They climbed on, determined to reach the ridge before darkness fell. Perry inched along, stubbornly laying down a line. The others said nothing. They knew that the rope was practically useless. Anything heavier than a dictionary would rip the screws clear out of the mountain.

But it's a fixed route, he reassured himself. It took his mind off the truth — that he was hanging off the fourth highest mountain on the planet, supported by nothing more than the half-inch of front points he could plant in the wall. Somewhere much deeper inside him, he was repeating Sammi's words: *Don't fall . . . don't fall . . .*

A crampon shattered the thin layer of verglas, leaving him hanging on to his ax for dear life. Frantically, he kicked at the face searching for a purchase. But every stab of his foot broke the ice up even more, leaving nothing but inhospitable naked rock.

"You okay, Perry?" Sammi called down at him.

No, I'm not okay! he wanted to shriek back. *Three hundred feet off the Col, and I've got nowhere to stick a crampon! It's like trying to climb a moonbeam!*

But he knew that was the Death Zone talking. At extreme altitude, the brain wasn't receiving enough oxygen to work properly. That was why so many smart mountaineers made bad decisions in the Himalayas.

Come on, Perry, he exhorted himself. *Think!*

Carefully, he scraped his crampons along the exposed stone until he found a tiny ledge about the thickness of a pea. Pressing his side-points down on it, he heaved himself up to more stable ice. *Kick, kick, thunk,* and he was on the way up again.

Night fell, forcing them to ascend to the apex

of the triangle by the eerie glow of their helmet lamps. Once on the ridge, the going was easier, but no less hazardous. The feel of their crampons crunching into hard-packed snow filled them with confidence. But that same snow had been wind-blown to form massive cornices. It was impossible to tell where solid rock ended and unsupported cornice began. Break through, and your fate would be a mile-and-a-half plunge to the Kang-shung glacier far below.

Every step drew them farther into the Death Zone. The effort of putting one foot in front of the other became less an act of mountaineering and more an exercise in suffering. Even with bottled oxygen, breathing became gasping.

Ten steps, then a break, Sammi ordered herself. Soon she was resting every seven. Then every five.

For nearly a thousand vertical feet, they slogged over rock and corniced snow. Notches in the ridge created small cliffs, ranging in height from ten to fifteen feet. At home, they would have been routine scrambles. Here, more than five miles above sea level, they presented punishing obstacles that left the four sobbing with sheer fatigue.

Agonizingly slowly, Perry twisted screws into the bulletproof ice and roped the jagged steps.

"Hurry up, Noonan!" shouted Tilt from below. "We're freezing to death down here!"

Anywhere else, his words would be an exaggeration. But the altimeter on Dominic's watch read 27,479 feet, and the air temperature had dropped to −66°F. Despite their exhaustion, Tilt, Sammi, and Dominic danced on the spot as they waited for Perry. Frostbite rarely struck a mountaineer in motion; it was the standing around that caused the extremities to freeze.

"Where are Ethan and Nestor?" shivered Sammi, pounding her mitts together to maintain circulation. "We're only a few hundred feet below the summit."

"The famous Ethan Zaph," growled Tilt. "When we're finished rescuing him, I'm going to throw him off the mountain!"

Perry was near the top of the notch, looking to place one final screw. "I can't find any ice!" he called down to the others. Here the wind had blasted the ridge down to bare shale. He looked around for another route up. The gash in the mountain continued on both sides as far as the glow of his helmet lamp would allow him to see.

The frustration grew inside him, overshadowing even his fear. A human life depended on their success — two lives, probably. How could they turn back now?

"Use the piton!" Dominic called from below.

"I didn't bring any!" Perry cried, beginning to lose control. He'd assumed the entire route would be covered with ice. It was a mistake — *his* mistake. And because of it, two people were going to die. . . .

"Your *uncle's* piton!" Dominic insisted.

Oh. Perry hesitated. *That piton.* Uncle Joe had sent five guys to the wilds of Alberta to recover that dumb peg. It was meant for the summit of Everest, not some no-name notch on Lhotse!

He'll be furious if I waste it.

At that moment, it occurred to him how crazy that was. He was hanging off a rock a zillion feet up in a windchill of minus infinity — and he was worried about what Uncle Joe might say?

"No," he said aloud into the punishing wind. Then, louder: "No!" The thoughts came in an emotional flood, washing away the tension of the climb. *I love you, Uncle Joe, but if I'm so spooked by you that I'd let two people die — that's just plain wrong!*

He pulled off his small knapsack and reached inside, coming up with the twenty-five-year-old peg. Fifteen thousand dollars — more than its weight in gold, probably. That's what Uncle Joe said it had cost to get it back — a weathered, rusty piece of iron.

Well, easy come, easy go! Perry found a good crack and hammered the piton in with the flat end of his ice ax. Then he strung the rope through its ring and heaved himself up to the top of the step.

And screamed.

CHAPTER NINETEEN

Sammi, Dominic, and Tilt jumared up the rope as fast as the altitude would allow their weary arms to move. One by one, they scrambled over the prow of shale. There they found Perry, on his hands and knees, dry-heaving into his respirator. A few feet in front of him, sprawled on the rocks, lay the dead body of a climber.

Dominic felt his legs begin to wobble. The victim seemed to be male, although it was impossible to tell. The face was partially mummified by the blistering cold, flesh receding to reveal the contours of a human skull. A death mask in the sky.

For the SummitQuest climbers, already at the outer limit of their endurance, the shock of it stopped them in their tracks. They knew that there were many such grisly sights in the Himalayas — alpinists who lost their lives so high up that their bodies could never be safely recovered. But to crest a rise and find yourself staring directly into the face of death was something no mountaineer could ever be prepared for. Even Tilt was visibly

shaken, his eyes wide with horror, wheezing into his oxygen system.

"It's Nestor!" Perry was blubbering. "We're too late! He's dead!"

Sammi grabbed him by his shoulders. "It can't be! This guy's been here for years! Look at him!"

"No!" He shook her off angrily, but he knew she was right. So much deformity could not possibly have happened so quickly. Yet this news, which should have heartened him, only wrenched even more sobs from him.

"Shut up! Shut up!" Tilt was yelling more from fear than anger. *If this wimp doesn't stop crying, I'm going to lose it!* "It's just a dead guy with freezer burn!"

"There was a team up here in the mid-nineties," Dominic babbled, none too steady himself. "Italians, I think. This could be one of — "

"You shut up, too!" Tilt roared. "If you all don't shut up, I swear I'll — "

And then they heard it, faint but crystal clear — a distant voice calling, "Hey!"

Sammi's keen eyes spotted the dim amber ghost of a fading helmet lamp, a half-mile farther up the ridge. "Ethan," she breathed.

The body forgotten, they rushed along the jagged slope with the renewed vigor of climbers

THE CLIMB

on a mission. They stopped only to remove their crampons for better progress on the bare rock. Here, any snow that touched Lhotse was immediately flung out over the Kangshung glacier by wrenching wind gusts that threatened to dislodge the rescuers from the mountain.

The four bent into the gale and sped up. They had seen death; it had almost overwhelmed them. But now they reached down deep and found hidden reserves of strength because they didn't want that fate for their fellow climbers.

"Ethan!" shouted Sammi.

"Over here." Now the response was close. It was a sound they had not heard before — that famous voice, hollow with exhaustion and defeat.

And suddenly, the two lost climbers were right in front of them. Dominic hardly recognized the top young mountaineer in the world. Ethan sat cross-legged, meek and trembling over Nestor's unmoving form. The journalist's face was white as chalk under his oxygen mask.

Ethan regarded Dominic without recognition at first. Then, "You! Are you everywhere or something? How could you be — ?" He seemed to lose his train of thought partway through the question. He had been in the Death Zone without oxygen for more than eleven hours.

Sammi and Perry hooked up the spare breathing rig and placed the mask over Ethan's mouth and nose. He perked up immediately. "We couldn't wake him up," he said, pointing at Nestor. "We were at the summit — wait, no. On the face — no — " His oxygen-starved brain could not seem to organize his thoughts.

"I'd be getting ready for a summit bid if it wasn't for you," Tilt accused, which only confused Ethan further.

Sammi and Perry rolled Nestor onto his side, allowing Dominic to turn the flow on his gas regulator up to four liters per minute — the maximum.

The back of Nestor's wind suit and his knapsack were crusted with tiny red crystals. "What's that?" asked Perry.

"Blood," replied Sammi. "Frozen blood." She turned to Dominic, perplexed. "He was hit by rockfall. The injuries should be mostly internal, right?"

Dominic tried to remove the knapsack. It wouldn't budge. Frowning, Dominic zipped it open and fumbled around inside. His mitts fell on a coil of some kind of wire. He pulled it out to realize he was holding Nestor's summit Slinky. The unimaginable cold of the Death Zone had made the thin metal so brittle that it shattered in Dominic's hands.

THE CLIMB

There was something else in there. He adjusted his helmet lamp and shone it inside the small pack. The others gathered around. In an instant, the nature of Nestor's injury became completely clear.

"Oh, my God," gasped Perry.

The journalist had been climbing with his crampons in his knapsack in the rock gully near the top of Lhotse. The falling stone had struck the pack, driving the razor-sharp crampon points through the fabric of his wind suit, into his back.

"Ouch," commented Tilt.

"It's like being stabbed by ten knives," added Sammi with a wince.

Dominic tried again to yank the knapsack free. But the crampon points were in so deep that Nestor's entire body was stuck to the pack and would not separate from it. Finally, Sammi, Perry, and Dominic held on to him, while Tilt, the strongest, heaved with all his might.

"Aaaaaaaah!!" Nestor howled in pain as the crampons were torn from his flesh.

Tilt staggered in reverse and went down, the knapsack clutched in his arms. Nestor got up on all fours. "My back! My back!"

"Nestor, it's Dominic! Dominic Alexis!" Breathlessly, he tried to explain what had happened during the time the journalist had been unconscious. "You're two hundred feet below the summit of Lhotse and you've got ten stab wounds in your back. We've got to get you down to Dr. Oberman."

"Can you walk?" asked Sammi.

With great effort and much assistance, Nestor struggled to his feet. "I'll never make it," he moaned, panting from the effort. "It hurts so much!"

"He's lucky he's at this altitude," Sammi whispered to Perry. "Blood's thicker than mud up here. At sea level, he would have bled to death by now."

"At sea level, they would have sent an ambulance," Perry retorted.

The good news was that Ethan could now walk on his own. Nestor was another story. With Sammi supporting the right arm and Dominic under the left, he could barely put one foot in front of the other. They were facing a third of a mile of vertical descent down to Camp Four. On the tricky and perilous ridge, it might as well have been a light-year.

They checked their oxygen equipment, replacing empty bottles and clearing ice from masks and regulator tubes. It was decided that Sammi, Perry, and Dominic would all rope themselves to Nestor. With luck, the three of them might be

THE CLIMB

able to guide the injured journalist through the tough journey ahead. Tilt alone would handle Ethan.

"You're lucky I don't handle you right off a cliff, superstar," Tilt grumbled, tethering himself to Ethan's harness.

Progress was slow, and maneuvering Nestor down the many drop-offs proved to be time-consuming and difficult. Soon the ridge was snow-covered again, and they had to stop to reaffix their crampons. The menacing cornices called for extra-special care, which delayed them even more.

Tilt spent the entire descent griping at Ethan. "The great Ethan Zaph. Don't make me laugh. If you're so great, how come we had to rescue your sorry butt?"

Poor Ethan had no strength to defend himself. Baby steps down the ridge were all he could manage.

Me! he lamented. *The strongest young climber ever!*

He was depressed, but grateful. He knew that these kids had just saved his life. The little guy especially — *I was wrong about him.* Few could function at this altitude, let alone take charge. For a thirteen-year-old to show this kind of poise and

ability in the Death Zone was flat-out unbelievable.

Suddenly, the snow beneath his feet disintegrated. In an instant of exquisite terror, he realized that he was not on the ridge at all, but on a
cornice curling improbably far out over the Kangshung Face. And then gravity took him and flung
him downward.

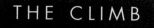

CHAPTER TWENTY

"Your ax!" bellowed Tilt, frozen with fear. In a few seconds, the rope would play out, and more than two hundred pounds of plummeting climber would pull him off the mountain.

Ethan reached for his ice tool — *one last chance!* But as he fumbled for the handle, it was already too late. He was sliding down the rock, picking up speed, his mind empty of all thoughts but one: *When you fall a mile and a half, are you still alive when you hit the bottom?*

Tilt Crowley threw himself to the snow, locked his arms around the biggest boulder he could find, and hung on for dear life.

"*Oof!!*"

The jolt slammed his face against hard granite. The force on his harness was so great that his entire body was lifted up in the air. Everything went momentarily black. But he held on to the rock, to the ridge, to Lhotse, to life.

His eyes fluttered open. He had done it! He could feel Ethan's weight dangling at the other end of the rope. The question remained: Was it *dead* weight? Had the boy survived the fall?

EVEREST

A faint cry from below. "Help!"

Sammi and Dominic grabbed for the rope, but Tilt pushed them aside. "I don't need *you!*" He planted his crampons and got to his feet, leaning away from the precipice, two hands on the taut line. "Hey, Zaph!" he roared triumphantly out over the abyss. "You call yourself strong? You don't know the meaning of the word! *This* is strong!" Single-handedly, he began hauling in the line. Sammi and Dominic joined in.

Minutes later, a trembling Ethan, pop-eyed and ashen-faced, crested the ridge. He collapsed into Tilt's arms, gasping and wheezing.

"Settle down," Tilt ordered in an irritated tone. "I don't even like you."

"You don't like anybody," grinned Sammi. She put an arm around Tilt's shoulders. "That was amazing — and I don't amaze easily."

"The greatest belay I've ever seen," added Perry.

"Big deal," snorted Tilt. "By the time the press gets through with it, it'll be Zaph the hero belaying the rest of us by his nose hairs."

It would be a solid hour before Ethan would release his death grip on Tilt's arm.

At exactly 10:30 P.M., the alarm on Dominic's watch began beeping. A rueful laugh escaped him. In another life, on another mountain, that was the signal to wake up and get ready for their assault on the peak of Everest. It was time to melt ice to make tea and hot chocolate. Time to force down oatmeal and Summit bars, energy for the climb ahead.

Everest. It seemed distant somehow. As if it had never been their original goal, and the plan had always been a perilous rescue on the upper reaches of Lhotse.

Attempted rescue, he corrected himself. By no means was this a done deal. They were well below twenty-seven thousand feet now, but Ethan was flagging and Nestor was deteriorating badly. Dominic was pretty sure that if it weren't for the physical support of his fellow climbers, the journalist would have lacked even the strength to stand up.

No one noticed when Nestor began to gasp, sucking hungrily for oxygen that was no longer there. He tried to sound the alert, but he didn't have the air. All that came out were two croaking syllables: "Help me." He collapsed to the snow.

Sammi checked for a blockage in his breathing tube, but it was clear. Perry checked the gauge on Nestor's oxygen bottle. "Empty!"

"We're such idiots!" Sammi exclaimed. "He's

drawing O's twice as fast as the rest of us! Of course he's going to run out first!"

Dominic fumbled desperately inside his pack, looking for a spare cylinder. *This is my fault!* he thought frantically, *I should have known better! I should have seen it coming.*

He slapped the new bottle into place, and Sammi hooked it into the regulator. They watched expectantly. Nestor's breathing stabilized, but he did not come to.

For twenty precious minutes, they tried to wake him, shaking him, slapping him, screaming in his ears, and even pressing snow against his cheeks. But in a windchill approaching one hundred degrees below zero, twenty minutes of inactivity was more than a delay; it was a foolhardy risk to life and limb. In the Death Zone, climbing was the body's natural heater, its last line of defense against frostbite and hypothermia. They had to keep going.

Tilt grabbed Nestor under the arms; Sammi took his legs. For a while, the ridge unfolded gently before them, and they made good time. Nestor's labored footsteps had been so slow that they were actually moving faster this way. Then they rounded a bend, and the lights of their helmet lamps seemed to disappear into blackness.

THE CLIMB

Dominic looked down. They were five hundred feet above the South Col, at the apex of the triangular ice wall.

Sammi shone her lamp over the steep slope. "Oh, boy."

Perry was the first to panic. "We'll never get him down this!"

"Wait!" Ethan pointed. "Fixed line!"

Tilt shook his head. "Worthless." He yanked the top screw out of the ice. The entire rope dislodged from the mountain, anchors popping down its full length.

The conference was short.

"We'll have to leave him," Sammi decided. "The guides must be back at Camp Four by now. Maybe Andrea can climb up here and give him a shot or something."

"Nestor doesn't have that kind of time," Dominic argued. "We've got to get him down *now*."

Tilt turned on him angrily. "How, shrimp? You know why they don't bring dead bodies back from the upper mountain? Because it's impossible! And unconscious guys are dead guys in training!"

"He's right," said Perry sadly. "To get off this rock, you've got to *walk* off."

Even Ethan agreed there was nothing they

could do for his teammate anymore. "We'll leave him and go for help."

Dominic was not swayed. Who knew for sure if Dr. Oberman was on the Col? And even if she was, it would still mean a long climb down, a longer one back up again, and then a difficult descent with Nestor.

His eyes fell on the dislodged rope, which lay before Tilt, a loose ice screw flopped on its side. "We'll lower him down."

"We don't have enough rope," Perry protested.

Dominic pulled the tether cord out of his harness. "Tie them all together. We can make it."

"We can't," Tilt insisted. "We're not even close. That's got to be five hundred feet!"

But Dominic was adamant. "We'll get him down. I swear."

CHAPTER TWENTY-ONE

They knotted the nylon lines together and tied one end to Nestor's harness. Then they eased the journalist over the top. Dominic followed on his front points and ice ax.

Sammi looked at him dubiously. "I hope you know what you're doing. You're still way short."

"Trust me," Dominic promised, and was gone.

Tilt and Perry let out the rope, and Nestor slid slowly down the wall of ice. Dominic kept pace. *Kick, Kick, thunk. Kick, kick, thunk . . .*

They had been descending for only about twenty minutes when Nestor's progress abruptly halted.

"That's the end!" Sammi shouted down from the ridge.

Dominic pushed his mask aside and bellowed, "Give me a minute!" He looked around and found his helmet lamp shining right at it, exactly where he'd expected it to be. There, maybe ten feet to his left, was another fixed line. It had taken Perry three pitches to reach the top of the triangular wall. This was the second length. Still another waited below.

EVEREST

Front-pointing efficiently, Dominic traversed to the rope and yanked it free of the mountain's thin rind, sending ice screws tumbling down to the Col. Now came the hard part — keeping Nestor secure while adding on the new length. He plastered his shoulder to the slope, wedging the journalist in place as he worked.

"What's going on?" came Sammi's call.

Dominic fastened the knot. "Reel it in!" he ordered.

High above, confusion turned to dismay as Tilt and Perry hauled the slackened rope effortlessly upward.

"What did he do with Nestor?" Tilt muttered in consternation. "What's going on?"

Sammi watched in bewilderment as the double fisherman's knot rose into the glow of her helmet lamp. Her eyes widened in sudden understanding. "He found the second rope!"

"And there's another one after that!" Perry exclaimed excitedly.

"Unbelievable!" breathed Ethan, energized by the genius of the thirteen-year-old's plan. He flipped up his mask. "Go, Dominic! Do it, kid!"

When they felt Nestor's weight on the line, Tilt and Perry resumed lowering the rope. Below, Dominic continued his descent alongside the journalist's inert form. The work was hard — front-

THE CLIMB

pointing with only one ice tool was more difficult than with two. His right arm and shoulder throbbed with pain, but inside he was celebrating. *It's going to work. We're going to get Nestor to the Col.* From there, he wasn't sure of the next step, but he was confident his friend would be in good hands. *If Andrea can revive him, Cap and Babu can get him down. He's got a chance. A helicopter can land as high as twenty-thousand feet. It isn't easy, but it's possible.*

So absorbed was he in figuring the angles of the rescue that he barely heard Sammi yelling. He was too far away to make out her exact words, but he realized that Nestor's descent had been halted once more.

His eyes scanned the ice for the final fixed rope. It wasn't there.

The realization was like a cannon shot to the pit of his stomach. There was no rope. It had fallen, or blown away in the permanent gale of the Death Zone. He checked the altimeter on his watch: 26,148. They were still well over a hundred feet above the Col. And Nestor was stranded, dangling like a yo-yo on a string.

Dominic's head filled with a blizzard of bad ideas. *I'll front-point down and look for help!* But what if there *was* no help? *I'll climb back up again!* What good would that do?

His eyes filled with tears. Maybe they were right — the people who said he didn't belong here. Oh, sure, he could handle himself physically on the mountain. But what about *mentally*? The pressure to do the right thing when someone's life hung in the balance. Was any thirteen-year-old ever ready for that emotional roller-coaster ride?

The last words hung meaningfully in his thoughts. Roller-coaster ride . . .

Roller-coaster ride!

With a deep sense of purpose, he sat Nestor upright on the slope, and maneuvered himself behind, wrapping his arms around the journalist's waist as if the two of them were seated in tandem on a toboggan. In fact, that image was exactly Dominic's plan. It was, in climbing lingo, a glissade — a controlled slide.

Well, this won't be very controlled, but it's Nestor's only chance.

Control was a pretty big concern here because the Col was only 150 yards wide. Veering too far to the left would mean a four-thousand-foot drop over the Lhotse Face. A mistake to the right would send them screaming down the Kangshung.

With trembling hands, Dominic drew his brother's vial of Dead Sea sand out of his wind-suit collar. "If you're really magic," he whispered, "now's the time." And with that, he drew back his ax and cut the rope.

He dug the tool into the ice, dragging it behind them in an attempt to control their speed. It worked for the first thirty feet or so, but then gravity took over, and the mountain ripped it violently from his hand. With monstrous acceleration, they rocketed down the steep slope. He felt the wind rip the helmet lamp from his head and toss it contemptuously over the Kangshung Face. Clamping his arms around Nestor, he hung on as the ripples of ice passed beneath them at horrifying velocity.

He fought down an impulse to dig in his crampons to slow the slide. At this pace, the move would only catapult him straight up and send him tumbling to his death. *Hang in there,* he urged himself. He couldn't begin to imagine their speed — eighty miles an hour? Ninety? The altimeter on his watch was flying like the tenths-of-a-second timer on an NBA clock.

The roaring in his ears drowned out the howling of the wind, and his vision began to darken at the corners. "Stay awake!" he screamed at himself, as if the act of yelling might somehow keep him from losing consciousness. But he was fading, his eyes actually closing, when the rocks of the South Col seized his momentum and used it to bounce him around like a Ping-Pong ball.

The instant Sammi saw the two helmet lamps speeding down the wall, she knew.

"Hey!" cried Perry in alarm. "The rope went slack!"

Ethan stared at the ghostly circles of light flying down the mountain. "They fell!"

"That's not it!" exclaimed Sammi as the lamps accelerated in perfect lockstep. "They're *sliding!*"

"That shrimp," said Tilt, shaking his head. "He's crazier than *you* are!"

They watched, transfixed, as one of the lamps suddenly somersaulted away from the other, careening wildly before it disappeared down the Kangshung Face.

"What was — ?" Perry let his voice trail off into the gut-tightening silence. Even the labored sounds of the oxygen gear shut down as the team held its collective breath, paralyzed with dread. At that moment, the answer to Perry's unfinished question seemed pretty clear. They had just seen one of their friends — Nestor or Dominic — plunge to a terrible end.

Tilt heaved himself over the precipice and be-

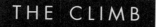

gan front-pointing furiously down the ice. "I'm going down there."

"Me first!" Sammi was hot on his heels.

"What about Ethan?" asked Perry.

But the revitalized Ethan was already on his way down. Perry had no choice but to follow.

CHAPTER TWENTY-TWO

Pain.

That was Dominic's next reality. His aching body throbbed all over. His mother's words came to mind, repeated often to her climbing men: "You'll break every bone in your body!"

Well, Mom, you were right. I finally did it.

No. That wasn't so. While he hurt just about everywhere, he didn't seem to be *badly* hurt *anywhere*. Just one big bruise from head to toe.

Nothing broken, everything still attached. He sprang up.

The powerful beam from a helmet lamp almost knocked him over again. He squinted below the light until he could make out the gawking face of Cap Cicero, plainly amazed to see him alive at all, let alone upright.

In the space of a split second, the team leader's face went from surprise to joy to blind rage. "You little maniac! You know how many climbers would have tried that slide? One! The *craziest* one! And I'm looking right at him — "

"Where's Nestor?" Dominic interrupted urgently.

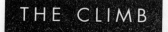
THE CLIMB

"Andrea's got him. This Way Up has a rescue team on its way to the Col."

Dominic watched as the doctor directed Babu and Sneezy to carry the unconscious journalist to the tent.

"He's got ten crampon punctures in his back," he advised her. "He's probably hypoxic, too. And you'd better check for frostbite."

She stared at him and then blinked. "Dominic — the old monk at Thyangboche — the vision — "

"Huh?" he asked. After the night's rescue, their visit to the monastery seemed as if it had happened in another life.

"You've got — " The doctor was practically stammering. "You've got shiny coils all around you!"

Dominic looked down to find the remains of Nestor's Slinky hanging off his wind-suit — silver metal spirals that glistened in the artificial light. The strange lama's prediction — they had called it a hallucination. And yet it had come true.

Cicero had no time for reminiscences. "What about the others?"

Dominic pointed south, where four dim circles of light inched down the invisible wall like night sprites descending from the sky. "Ethan Zaph is the fourth."

The team leader frowned. "How nervous should I be?"

"The ice is too thin, and they've got no ropes, and — " Dominic thought it over. Sure, it was a nasty climb. But compared to all they'd been through that endless night, it was a walk in the park. "They'll make it," he said confidently.

If only he felt the same way about Nestor.

Nestor's ordeal was far from over. At Camp Four, Dr. Oberman stitched up the wounds on his back and gave him a heavy dose of antibiotics to ward off infection. He did not regain consciousness.

The team of This Way Up Sherpas arrived at three A.M. They rested briefly and set out at first light, carrying Nestor in a Gamow bag folded inside a two-person tent. Pasang and Ethan descended with them to assist in the rescue.

Late in the day, the This Way Up climbers arrived at ABC to learn that a rare and risky helicopter evacuation had been set up for the lower Cwm, just beyond Camp One at the top of the Icefall. Cicero and the team were on the Lhotse Face when it happened. They held their breath as they watched, knowing well that the chopper was flying at the very upper edge of its range. At 19,500 feet, the air was too thin to provide the rotor blades with much lift.

The young alpinists watched in agony as the

helicopter had to abort its first two approaches. Then, on the third try, the pilot managed to hover three feet off the glacier — low enough for the injured journalist to be loaded aboard.

Sixty seconds later, the chopper was a tiny dot in the sky. Nestor was on his way to a hospital in Kathmandu.

Only then did SummitQuest start descending — and breathing — again.

The mood at Base Camp was somber for the next two days, and it wasn't just because of the tense vigil by the satellite phone waiting for news of Nestor.

The weather had deteriorated badly. On the summit ridge, a howling blizzard was dumping four feet of snow on already treacherous ground. The weather satellites predicted that it would go on for at least a week.

Babu and some of the other Sherpas thought this might be the onset of the summer monsoon. If they were right, climbing season was over.

"Stick a fork in us," Sammi predicted gloomily. "We're done."

The thought that their summit chances might be finished had sent Tilt's mood into a tailspin. Since returning from the Icefall, he had left his sleeping bag only to eat his meals in stony silence. He had not spoken except to scream at Perry for being "too happy."

"I'm happy I'm not dead!" Perry shot back through the flurries that fell over Base Camp. "And I'm happy I might not get another chance to be dead!"

"You'll be dead if you don't shut up," Tilt promised. "And it won't take any mountain to do it."

Could SummitQuest really be over? Dominic checked with Cicero several times each day.

"Fifty-fifty, kid," was the reply. Then later, as the forecast worsened. "Seventy-thirty."

Dominic stubbornly refused to accept that the expedition was in jeopardy. He picked out a new ice ax to replace the one he had lost during his glissade to the Col. He was walking in circles in the snow, getting used to the new weight in his hand, when Pasang ran up, howling like a madman. The excited Sherpa grabbed him by the arm and dragged him to the This Way Up mess tent, where a grinning Ethan Zaph handed him the satellite phone.

"The *National Daily* was right! Everest is no place for a thirteen-year-old! And now an innocent Slinky is dead!"

"Nestor!" Dominic cried delightedly. "You're okay!"

THE CLIMB

"Well, sort of," said the voice on the other end of the line. "You know, considering I'm flat on my face with tubes coming out of places I didn't even know I had."

"But you're alive," Dominic insisted.

"Thanks to you, Dominic. That's what I'm calling about. I just want you to know that I'll never forget how you risked your life to save me."

"That's what climbers *do*."

"That's what *you* do," Nestor corrected. "There isn't anyone like you. Not on this planet. If it wasn't for you, I'd still be on that ridge, and we Puerto-Rican Pakistanis don't freeze well. You take care, kid. You're going to be famous someday."

"Safe home, Nestor. We'll miss you." Dominic passed the phone to another ecstatic teammate, and Ethan pulled him aside. "It wasn't me who tipped off the Nepalese about you. You've got to believe me on that."

Dominic nodded slowly. "But you still think I don't belong."

The famous young alpinist shook his head vehemently. "You guys saved our lives! There's something special about you, kid. You more than belong! When the gods made Everest, they probably had you in mind." He put a hand on Dominic's shoulder. "I was wrong and I'm sorry. I'll climb with you any day."

Dominic was melancholy. "I don't think any of us are going to be climbing any time soon."

He stepped out of the tent. A light dusting of powder covered the moraine, belying the violent weather higher up.

We were at 27,700 feet on Lhotse! he thought to himself. *Just a quarter mile lower than the Everest summit! We can do this! The top of the world is within reach! All we need is a chance!*

The snow continued, settling on Base Camp and on Dominic's dreams.

BOOK THREE: THE SUMMIT

EVEREST

For Daisy Samantha Korman
My Summit

PROLOGUE

The wind pounced on them above twenty-five thousand feet.

As the youngest expedition in Everest history scrambled up the Geneva Spur, the onslaught began — overpowering, unpredictable gusts that threatened to pluck the climbers off the mountain and hurl them into space.

Amazingly, this was nothing new to them. This was the second time the team had stood atop the Spur, a mammoth club of decaying black rock in the infamous Death Zone high on Everest. Their last summit bid had been scuttled when they'd been called away to perform a daring high-altitude rescue. For two very long weeks, the SummitQuest climbers had waited at Base Camp, begging fate for the weather to offer a second chance at the peak.

Now they had it. And, as team leader Cap Cicero put it, "We're not going to let a little breeze get in our way."

Clad in full-body wind suits, oxygen masks, and goggles, the SummitQuest mountaineers looked like something out of a science fiction movie. This was fitting, since the pinnacle of the world was as inhospitable a place as any alien planet.

Bent double into the teeth of the gale, they slogged on, gasping bottled oxygen, moving slowly, but always moving. At extreme altitude, the mere effort of putting one foot in front of the other is the equivalent of pushing a boulder up a steep hill. It takes massive reserves of strength and will. And it takes the ability to fight through pain.

A sudden howling blast drove thirteen-year-old Dominic Alexis back a step. Cicero reached out a hand to steady his youngest and smallest alpinist. Then he guided the boy into line behind him in an effort to shelter him from the worst of the fierce wind.

Cicero's confident stance belied an inner concern: *If the blow's this bad here, it's bound to be murderous higher up.*

Normally, conditions like this would have sent a team back to Base Camp to wait for better weather. But it was the twenty-first of May, very late in the climbing season. Any day, Everest's summer monsoon could begin, effectively shutting down the mountain. They climbed now because they could not be sure they would get another chance.

The team leader had no way of knowing that summer would come late that year. Nor could he have foreseen that, before Everest slipped into the monsoon, it would claim the life of one of his young climbers.

CHAPTER ONE

Camp Four was a handful of tents on the South Col, the desolate, wind-scoured valley between the titanic peaks of Everest and Lhotse. At twenty-six thousand feet, it was more than a mile higher than Mount McKinley, the loftiest pinnacle in North America, and two miles higher than any point in the lower forty-eight states.

True to Cicero's expectations, conditions were appalling on the Col. The air temperature was $-17°$ F, made bone-cracking by a wind that, at sea level, would have been considered a Category 2 hurricane.

"We can't climb in this!" complained Perry Noonan, shouting to be heard over the howling gale. "It's going to be a million below zero at the summit!"

"It could die down in an hour," soothed Lenny "Sneezy" Tkakzuk, panning the bleak wasteland of rock and ice with his camera. It was Sneezy's job to document their adventures on videotape. The footage would be E-mailed via satellite phone to their sponsor, Summit Athletic Corporation, for release on the Internet.

EVEREST

"Or it could stay like this for two weeks!" Perry countered.

"It's not rocket science," put in Babu Pemba, the head Sherpa guide, or Sirdar. "If it eases up, we climb. If it doesn't, we turn around."

"I'm not going down," announced Tilt Crowley defiantly. "This is our last chance. I don't care about the rest of you guys. *I'm* going to the summit."

Cicero glared at him. "You'll go where I tell you to, Crowley. Now let's all try to get some rest. Standing here freezing isn't going to change the weather."

It was just before three P.M. The summit bid was to begin in nine hours — an all-night marathon climb, returning before dark the next day.

If everything goes as planned, Perry reminded himself. The problem was that in the Death Zone nothing ever went as planned.

In the teen climbers' tent, Tilt, Perry, Dominic, and their fourth teammate, Samantha Moon, the only girl, snacked on Summit Energy Bars and waited for the stove to melt ice. At this altitude, fire burned at such a low temperature that a simple cup of instant soup or hot chocolate could take more than an hour to prepare.

Perry had come to detest this whole ritual. Just

THE SUMMIT

being in the thin air and low atmospheric pressure felt like a debilitating flu. *Who wants to eat and drink when you're sick as a dog?* he thought to himself. *Especially when you have to slave to boil water.*

The simple truth was that Perry was not the most gung-ho climber in the group. He had only qualified for the team because his uncle, Joe Sullivan, was the founder and president of Summit Athletic.

Even now, at twenty-six thousand feet, probably dying a little with each bottled breath, Perry was amazed that he had never said those simple words to Uncle Joe: *I don't want to go.*

It wasn't that his uncle was a tyrant. But the same force of personality that had built a multi-billion-dollar empire had created a man who wouldn't dream of seeking anyone's opinion. He was accustomed to being in charge. He would never think of asking, "Perry, do you want to go to Everest?" What climber wouldn't?

Perry wouldn't. And didn't. And he was disgusted with himself that he wasn't safe at home right now, instead of trying to boil water in a place where water wouldn't boil.

Sleeping in an oxygen mask was an adventure. Usually it depended on how exhausted you were. Most climbers never slept at all at Camp

Four. But even for those who succeeded, it was more like a series of five-minute catnaps in the course of several hours of icy discomfort.

Tilt was the exception. Not only did he sleep in his breathing rig — he snored.

Sammi bounced a plastic cup off the sturdy shape inside the bedroll. At only fourteen years old, Tilt was the second youngest of the group, but he was built like an NFL linebacker.

"Come on, Crowley! Lose the buzz saw!"

"Don't wake him up," Perry pleaded.

The red-haired boy would have given much to avoid Tilt's in-your-face sarcasm, if only for a few extra minutes. Tilt would not have won any popularity contests with the climbers or the guides. Even the friendly Sherpas steered clear of him after they learned that he referred to them as "baboons," a takeoff on Babu's name.

Eventually, they all found sleep, even Perry. His uneasy dreams placed him on a toboggan on an endless hill. The other riders were cheering.

What are they, crazy? Don't they see there's no bottom?

And then something shoved him hard from behind.

Caught in hazy semiconsciousness, he was still plummeting down when the force struck again. This time he saw what it was. Buffeted by

THE SUMMIT

the howling gale outside, the wall of the tent was *moving!*

A new and even more terrifying sensation followed — the nylon floor, skidding beneath them. He could feel the rock and ice surface of the Col passing below.

That was enough for Perry. He started screaming.

"Shut up, wimp — " Tilt began.

Then the world turned upside down. Overpowered by the wind, the light aluminum tent frame folded like a beach chair. And they were rolling.

"Do something!" howled Sammi.

But nothing could be done. Perry was immobilized in his sleeping bag, his face pressed against the tent floor. The others somersaulted over him as the four rattled around inside the nylon tumbleweed.

Trussed up and helpless, Perry could only estimate how far the gale was blowing them. If they rolled over the side of the Col, his toboggan nightmare would become a horrifying reality. It would be a four-thousand-foot slide down the steep Lhotse Face.

"Oof!"

A heavy weight landed on top of them, and the tent stopped rolling. Scant seconds later, a knife blade cut through the windproof fabric, missing Perry's nose by an inch and a half. Cicero was there, hauling them out one at a time, while big Babu lay across the wreckage of the tent.

Perry stared, his thoughts a mixture of awe and relief. Another fifteen feet would have put them over the side of the Col and into oblivion.

The instant Babu released his grip, the wind launched the shredded tent high over the Lhotse Face. The SummitQuest team watched it soar like a kite until it was out of sight.

Hunched together for protection from the gale, they surveyed what used to be Camp Four. Not a single tent was still standing. Sneezy and Andrea Oberman, the expedition doctor, struggled to salvage equipment where the guides' shelter had once been. Not far away, the tents of This Way Up, another expedition, were in tatters.

Tilt was like a wild man. "Let's go *right now*! Once we bag the summit, the whole lousy mountain can cave in for all I care!"

"Tilt — *think*," Dr. Oberman ordered. "Even if we could climb in this wind, we've got nowhere to come back to. Camp Four is *gone*!"

"So we won't stop at the Col!" Tilt raved. "We'll go all the way down to Camp Three! We've got an early start! We can make it!"

Cicero grabbed him by the front of his wind suit. "Get a hold of yourself, Crowley. You may be going to the summit someday, but not today."

Dominic spoke up. He was so small and so quiet that people often forgot he was there. Yet despite his youth and size, his climbing instincts were too good to ignore. "We should leave right away," he suggested. "As it is, we'll be descending the Lhotse Face in the dark."

The fear and shock in the group receded, leaving disappointed resignation. Their second failed summit bid. They knew the drill: a night at Camp Three, another at Camp Two on the Western Cwm, and then down to base through the treacherous Khumbu Icefall.

Sammi groaned into her mask. "I can't face Base Camp again."

"We're not going to Base Camp," Cicero informed her. "We'll head down into the valley."

Tilt's eyes bulged. "We're *leaving?*"

"We'll lose some altitude, breathe some decent air, get some real sleep." Cicero flipped up his goggles and regarded them intently. "Then we'll call up Summit and see if it's time for us to go home."

CHAPTER TWO

www.summathletic.com/everest/valley

Foiled by the mountain a second time, the youngest Everesters in history descend into the Khumbu Valley to the village of Gorak Shep, a day's trek from Base Camp. Here they await word from Summit Athletic headquarters. Is their adventure over?

The answer comes back a resounding "Climb on!" But Everest itself will have the final card to play. Is there one more window of good climbing weather left this season? The team can only wait and hope.

In the meantime, they force all tension aside and use this delay as a chance to catch up on the news back home. **CLICK HERE** to see the climbers chatting with families and friends on the satellite telephone — an example of how modern

technology can transform a primitive setting.

"It's a pack of lies!" Cicero bellowed into the
handset.

On the screen of his laptop computer was
a newspaper article from the *National Daily*,
E-mailed from Summit Athletic headquarters in
Colorado.

MIDDLE SCHOOL HIJINX AT 27,000 FEET

The so-called mountaineers of SummitQuest
continue to prove that filling a climbing team
with children for the sake of grabbing head-
lines is more than just cynical; it is downright
dangerous — not just to the teens themselves,
but to other expeditions as well.

By far the most shocking example of this took
place recently when thirteen-year-old, ninety-
pound Dominic Alexis took injured climber
Nestor Ali on a reckless 150-foot slide high
on Lhotse, the fourth-highest mountain in the
world. By the time the incident was over,
dozens of climbers had risked their lives in
rescue attempts, and Ali had to be airlifted to
a hospital in a costly helicopter evacuation. . . .

"I saw that slide!" Cicero raged. "It was the only way to get the guy down from there. I don't know if I would have had the guts to do it myself!"

"Unbelievable," muttered Sammi to Dominic as Cicero raved into the phone. "I mean, you were the hero of that rescue. And they blame you for putting Nestor in the hospital."

"It's your fault, all right," added Perry. "Your fault he's still alive."

Dominic shrugged helplessly. "They're not lying, exactly. Everything in the article happened. It goes to show how the media can distort the truth just by the way they report the facts."

"I'll tell you what it shows, shrimp," sneered Tilt. "It shows that somebody hates us. And we all know who's got the most to lose if we summit."

Sammi made a face. "Ethan Zaph."

The famous Ethan Zaph was a member of the This Way Up team and the current record holder as the youngest alpinist ever to conquer Everest. If any of the SummitQuest climbers made it to the top, that record would be broken. Someone was feeding the *National Daily* embarrassing and misleading information about SummitQuest. Sammi was pretty sure she'd found the culprit.

Dominic did not agree. "How could it be Ethan? He was one of the guys we rescued."

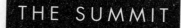

"Yeah," agreed Tilt. "And isn't it convenient that rescuing those two kept us off the summit so his precious record could stand forever?"

Even Sammi didn't buy that theory. "I don't think he faked it; I just think he's a rat!"

Tilt made no reply. He was the only one of them who knew for certain where the *National Daily* was getting its information. At first, he had done it strictly for the money. Not everyone had a billionaire uncle like Perry. And climbing gear and clothing was expensive stuff — more than a lousy paper route would pay for.

But lately a second motive had taken over his secret E-mailed reports to the *National Daily*. Tilt's plan was to become the new Ethan Zaph — a younger summiteer who would win even more fame and fortune. There was only one problem: Dominic was even younger than Tilt. If he summited, too, *he'd* be the new record holder, and Tilt would be downgraded to also-ran. Who cared about the *second* youngest guy to bag Everest?

Dominic could make it, too. The shrimp led a charmed life, as if he'd been sprinkled with fairy dust or something! Every move he made turned out to be the right one; everybody loved him; the Sherpas treated him like a cherished younger brother. The only thing he *didn't* have going for him was the fact that he was young and small. And Tilt made sure that the *National Daily* hammered that piece of information into the public's head. Now a lot of people felt that Summit Athletic had put a baby on a mean mountain.

The fact that everyone blamed the *National Daily* on Ethan Zaph — well, that was just gravy. If Cicero ever found out Tilt was the leak, he'd be off the team faster than you could say Kathmandu.

Outside the window of this ramshackle excuse for a hotel, it was snowing. Every flake that fell here usually meant ten tons on the upper mountain. Tilt's brow clouded. None of this would matter if they couldn't get another chance to push for the summit.

Cicero slammed down the phone, fuming.

Sammi read his mind. "I say we head back to Base Camp and squeeze the truth out of Ethan Zaph."

"Forget it," said the team leader with a sigh. "In the next few days, we're either going up or going home. What possible difference could it make?"

CHAPTER THREE

Sneezy was E-mailing video footage from in and around Gorak Shep to Summit's Web designers in Colorado when he heard the helicopter. He was instantly alert. The villages of the Khumbu region were barely out of the Stone Age. High tech around here referred to the yak trains that ferried climbing equipment to and from Base Camp. A chopper meant business, and the only big business was Everest.

"Cap — "

Cicero was already at the window, watching the landing. "Here comes trouble," he said tersely.

The two men who strode across the hard dirt compound to the lodge wore paramilitary uniforms and black berets. They represented the government of Nepal, and had visited SummitQuest once before, at Base Camp. At that time, the articles in the *National Daily* had just come to the attention of the Nepalese climbing officials.

"Where's Dominic?" the cameraman whispered.

"Rock scrambling with Babu and Sammi in the hills," Cicero replied.

And then the men were ducking through the tiny door, their faces grim.

"Cap Cicero." The junior officer held out a murky faxed copy of the latest *National Daily* article. "The boy is here?"

"The boy is not here," said Cicero, tight-lipped.

"Where is he, please?"

"The boy is not here," Cicero repeated. "You've got something to say, say it to me."

"Three weeks ago, we came looking for the boy Dominic Alexis, and you told us he had departed. This was a lie, yes?"

Cicero shrugged. "The kid was sick. Then he got better."

"You assured us he would not climb," the man persisted. "And look what he did."

Sneezy spoke up. "He saved two lives."

"Which one cannot do unless one is on the mountain!" The young officer's irritation was growing.

"Enough of this hairsplitting!" snapped the ranking official. "Cap Cicero, we are here to inform you of a decision by our government. The boy, Dominic Alexis, is no longer on your climbing permit. He will not climb."

"You can't change the rules in the middle of the game!" exclaimed Cicero. "Nepal took big money from Summit Athletic for that permit. Dominic's on my team. If I climb, he climbs."

"Should that happen," replied the younger man, "you yourself, Cap Cicero, will be banned from climbing in Nepal. This would be a *lifetime* ban."

Cicero pointed out the window, where a long procession of heavily laden yaks could be seen coming down the trail from Base Camp. "In case you haven't noticed, the season is pretty much over."

"You cloud the subject well," said the senior officer. "But I hope you will listen well, too. This is not an idle threat, and we will not be fooled again."

The two uniformed men stalked back to their waiting helicopter, their military bearing slightly wilted by the altitude at seventeen thousand feet. Soon the chopper was airborne and gone.

Sneezy let out the long breath he'd been holding. "What are you going to do, Cap?"

The famous alpinist snorted. "You think I'm going to let a pair of tin-plated bureaucrats break up my team? What can they do — climb to the Col and arrest me? Did you see them? They were practically suffocating, and we aren't even at Base Camp."

"It's no joke," Sneezy insisted. "They're not

just two guys. They're a whole government. If you get banned, you're off Everest for good."

Cicero shrugged. "There are other mountains."

"But there's only one top of the world."

"You let me worry about that," said Cicero. "And don't say a word about this to anyone, especially Dominic. The kid's already stressed that the weather won't break. The last thing I want to do is mess with his head."

In the dingy dormitory room directly next door, Tilt Crowley took his ear away from the wall. He was smiling.

Dominic sprang fluidly up the lower slopes of the small peak Kala Pattar, planting his hands and feet with swiftness and authority. The freedom of this climb exhilarated him. Everest was the ultimate challenge, but there an alpinist was burdened by heavy equipment, footgear, and clothing. To do this — find some rocks and just go — was an undeniable pleasure.

He clamped both hands on a granite knob, chinned himself to the ledge above it —

And cried out in shock.

Strong hands grabbed him under the arms and hoisted him bodily up to the flat rock surface.

"Nice moves, shrimp."

THE SUMMIT

Dominic stared at Tilt. "What are you doing here? What happened to 'I only climb when it counts?' "

Tilt shrugged. "Gotta stay in shape." He took in his surroundings with an expression of distaste. "Pretty kindergarten stuff. You know — compared to where we've been."

Dominic nodded. "It's not exactly the Icefall. But think about it. We're over seventeen thousand feet. To get this at home, you've got to go to Alaska."

"Listen, shrimp, there's something you should know, because Cap's sure not going to tell you. Those two Nepal government guys were back this morning. You're off the climbing permit now. And they said if Cap takes you on the mountain, they're going to ban him from Nepal for life."

Dominic grew still. He had always considered that the *National Daily* articles could cause trouble for him. But never had it occurred to him that his problems might harm the career of a legend like Cicero.

Cap Cicero. That name had always been spoken with reverence around the Alexis home. Perhaps America's greatest living alpinist. Even now, after months together, it blew Dominic's mind that he was actually climbing with the man.

"You know," Tilt went on, "Everest is a big adventure for you and me. But for Cap, it's his living. If he gets kicked out of Nepal, it's not just good-bye, Everest. Three quarters of the world's highest mountains are right here. It would ruin him."

"It's not fair," Dominic said quietly. "If their problem is with me, why take it out on Cap?"

Tilt laughed mirthlessly. "Not fair! It's their country and their mountain, so they get to jerk everybody around all they please."

Dominic sat down on the hard granite of Kala Pattar. From here, Everest's triangular west side loomed over the valley, its cold indifference taunting him. The upper third of the mountain was shrouded in gray mist — a mammoth snowstorm, no doubt. The summit was still unreachable.

But even if that blizzard passed, opening up a window of clear weather, and even if SummitQuest took one final stab at the top, Dominic Alexis would not be with them.

The thought pained him grievously, bringing tears to his eyes. He could not remember ever wanting anything as much as he wanted to stand on that summit.

But it would never happen. He could not — would not — be the factor that ended the career of the great Cap Cicero.

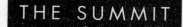
THE SUMMIT

CHAPTER FOUR

SummitQuest subscribed to five international weather forecasting services. They all called within the space of half an hour. The British were first with the good news: The impossible had happened. There was no monsoon, at least not yet. The jet stream was pulling north of the mountain, creating a pocket of clear weather that would be over Everest in two days. It would be brief, but a team with the right timing would have just enough of a window to push to the summit and get back down again.

"We've got our shot!" Cicero crowed ecstatically.

The news touched off a flurry of activity in Gorak Shep. They were still a day's walk from Base Camp. They had to leave immediately in order to be in position to take advantage of this gift from the climbing gods.

As they trekked up the path along the lower Khumbu glacier toward Base Camp, Perry's feet dragged on the moraine. Of all the lousy luck in the world, this had to win the Kewpie doll! He had rooted so long and so hard for the monsoon

EVEREST

to come and end his hideous adventure. Even now, as they could physically see the blizzard moving off the peak of Everest, he still couldn't bring himself to accept the fact that they had a go. Again!

When they arrived at Base Camp late in the day, the place looked so different that it was almost a shock. So many tents were gone, so many camps deserted. Three weeks before, this settlement on the lateral moraine had been a bustling city of more than five hundred climbers and staff. Less than a quarter now remained — the diehards who had waited against all odds for this one last shot at the top.

So far, this had been the worst Everest season in recent memory. Not one single climber had reached the summit. If that pathetic statistic held, it would be the first time since 1977.

In the cavernous SummitQuest kitchen tent, Cicero briefed the Sherpa staff on what was to come. The climbing Sherpas were to leave before first light to repair the ladders and fixed ropes, and to rebuild Camp Four, which had been destroyed in the windstorm. The summit push would begin the morning after. There would be no margin for error. This late in the season, the good weather simply could not hold. Any delay would spell an end to their chances.

A group of Sherpas from other expeditions came over to welcome Dominic back to Base Camp. Pasang, who worked for This Way Up, confirmed that his team would also be launching a last-ditch summit attack.

"Is Ethan going up?" asked Dominic.

Pasang nodded. "But this time climb with oxygen. Safer." Most Sherpas spoke with heavy accents. Babu was the exception.

"Gee, what was his first clue?" Sammi asked sarcastically. "When we had to drag him down Lhotse like a sack of potatoes?"

Pasang looked wounded. He had been climbing with Nestor and Ethan that day, and blamed himself for their mishap.

"She doesn't mean anything by it," Dominic told him apologetically. "She still thinks Ethan's behind all the trouble with that newspaper."

"And what about you, little sahib?" Pasang asked, using the nickname the Sherpas had bestowed on Dominic. "No monsoon, you get last chance. But no seem happy."

Dominic swallowed hard and said the words that he had not yet worked up the courage to speak aloud: "I'm not going."

Pasang's reaction was surprise; Sammi's was something more.

"What are you — crazy? This is what we prayed for! Of course you're going!"

"I'm not," said Dominic. "I decided yesterday."

"Why?" she demanded. "Because of the *National Daily*? Give me thirty seconds, and I'll go over there and feed Zaph his sat phone!"

"Keep your voice down," Dominic hissed. "Cap doesn't know yet."

"He does now!" exclaimed Sammi through clenched teeth. She marched off in search of the team leader.

Dominic watched her determined stride and knew she was going to rat him out. Sammi Moon never bluffed.

Pasang looked completely bewildered. "Why no climb?"

Dominic caught a quizzical look from Perry and an approving nod from Tilt. And then Cicero was bearing down on him.

The team leader didn't waste words. He grabbed Dominic by the wrist, hauled him out of the tent, and confronted him on the Base Camp rocks.

"This better be good!"

Dominic was close to tears. "I can't go. I'll cheer you guys on from Base Camp."

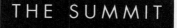

THE SUMMIT

"Why?" Cicero bellowed. "Is it that stupid newspaper? Who cares what they print?"

"I had two shots at the summit and I can't face it again," Dominic lied. "I'm scared."

Cicero snorted in disgust. "I've seen you jump off a mountain in Alaska. I've seen you use a Himalayan peak like it was a kiddie slide. You're not scared of anything. Now I want the truth."

Dominic took a deep breath. "I can't let you get kicked out of Nepal."

Cicero was taken aback. "How do you know about that?"

"I hear things," said Dominic defiantly.

"Ask Babu about Nepalese climbing officials!" Cicero raged. "The Sherpas have a saying — I don't remember the exact words, but it translates to: 'Those guys couldn't find yak droppings in the middle of a herd of yaks!' "

Dominic was stubborn. "This could cost you your career."

"Good choice of words," the team leader agreed. "My career. Which means it's *my* problem, not yours. Listen, kid, I didn't want you on this team. I tried everything to cut you. But I couldn't because you're special. A lot of guys can tackle mountains and get to the top. But when you climb, the whole thing becomes larger than life, like it's a work of art! And every swing of your ice ax and kick of your crampons is a brush stroke. One of these days, they could talk about the great Everest heroes, Mallory, Hillary, Messner, and *Alexis*! It all starts right here, right now — if you'll let it."

But Dominic was adamant. He couldn't picture himself as a future climbing legend. The thought that Cicero, his own hero, saw him that way confused and flustered him.

But the fact remained: If he was responsible for the destruction of Cap Cicero, he would never forgive himself.

E-mail Message
TO: CalebS@zipnet.usa
Subject: All Systems Go!!

Dear Caleb,

Guess what? The jet stream moved off the summit. Or maybe the summit moved off the jet stream. I don't really understand which. Who cares? The point is WE'RE GETTING ANOTHER CHANCE!

It's four o'clock in the morning, but I'm way too amped to sleep. Caleb, it's so extreme up there that it makes

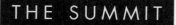

THE SUMMIT

everything else we've done seem like patty-cakes. I wish you could go with me. We'd ROCK that hill — ha, ha. Get it? There's a lot of rock up there — you know, under all the ice. When I plant our picture on the top, I'm going to say, "You haven't seen the last of *this* couple!"

Keep your fingers crossed for me, Caleb. The second I hit the Icefall, I'm climbing in overdrive. The only way to beat an extreme mountain is to go totally ballistic.

Love,
Sammi

P.S.: I haven't heard from you in a while, so please E-mail back. How are exams coming along? I'll be in summer school to make up what I missed. Maybe you should flunk so we can go together (just kidding).

CHAPTER FIVE

The next morning, Dominic found Ethan Zaph in the This Way Up mess tent, sharpening his crampon points with a graphite file. The face that had adorned the cover of so many mountaineering magazines glanced up only briefly before returning to work. "Hey, Dominic. All set for tomorrow?"

Dominic swallowed hard. "I'm sitting this one out."

Ethan stopped filing. "Why?"

Even now, after two full days to get used to the idea, the words were difficult to say. "Nepal took me off Cap's permit."

"Because of the *National Daily*?"

Dominic nodded.

Ethan was distraught. "Dominic — I swear — it wasn't me!"

"I believe you," said Dominic. "Sammi and Tilt don't, but I do."

"You can still climb," Ethan told him. "By the time the Nepalese find out, you'll be off the mountain and gone. What can they do to you?"

Dominic shook his head sadly. "If I go, Cap gets banned from Nepal for life. And let's face it,

Nepal *is* his life." He reached under his collar and drew a thin leather strap over his head. On it dangled a small glass vial filled with sand. The necklace belonged to Christian Alexis, Dominic's older brother.

"It's Chris's," he explained. "Sand from the Dead Sea — the lowest point on Earth. He wanted to leave it on the summit. When he got cut from the team, he passed it on to me. And now that I'm not going — "

Ethan accepted the trinket, peering through the glass at the loose grains inside. " 'From the bottom of the world to the top,' " he said, quoting Chris's motto. He and Chris had climbed together. The American Junior Alpine Association ranked them numbers one and two, with Ethan in the lead after his conquest of Everest. He slipped the strap around his own neck and regarded the younger boy intently. "Why me? Why not give it to one of your teammates?"

Dominic shrugged. "You made the summit before. You've got the best chance of getting there again. I can live with not climbing" — a lie — "but I really don't want to let Chris down."

"I'll get it to where it needs to go," Ethan said confidently.

"Thanks." The look that passed between them plainly said that both recognized the truth — in the Death Zone, nothing could ever be certain.

The famous face wore a thoughtful expression as Dominic walked away.

E-mail Message
TO: Jsullivan001@summathletic.com
SUBJECT: Tomorrow's climb

Dear Uncle Joe,

You're probably going to kill me for this, but . . .

Perry leaned on the backspace bar, erasing the line.

I know it's crazy that I waited so long before telling you . . .

Another line disappeared from the screen of his laptop.

Are you sitting down? This may come as a shock . . .

Delete.

I DON'T WANT TO GO!!

He slammed the computer shut. *Tilt's right,* he thought sadly. *I am a wimp.*

Not because he was afraid of Everest. Any sane person would be. No, Perry was a coward for not having the guts to tell Uncle Joe the truth. Not even via E-mail from nine thousand miles away.

The SummitQuest camp was a beehive of activity as climbers and guides prepared for action. Wind suits were checked for wear, goggles and Gore-Tex mitts painstakingly counted. The word had just come over the radio from the advance team of Sherpas. They had arrived at Camp Two. The route was in good shape so far, although the days of heavy snow made for treacherous avalanche conditions.

The report had touched off wild celebration. Backslaps and high fives flew in all directions.

Perry stared at the scene of jubilation. *Wait a minute! Am I the only one who heard that?*

"Uh — excuse me," he said, tapping Cicero on the shoulder. "What was that last part? You know, about the avalanche conditions?"

"Oh, that." The team leader shrugged. "There's a lot of fresh snow up there. Sometimes it falls down."

That was what he had to say about the very real possibility of all of them being swept to their deaths by a tidal wave of roaring snow. Not that

Perry needed further proof that he didn't belong with these lunatics.

Of Perry's teammates, Dominic alone was untouched by the outbreak of summit fever. Perry didn't even try to conceal his envy. Once again, Dominic had a perfect excuse not to climb. And instead of being grateful, he was shattered.

Not shattered enough to change his mind, though. Perry watched as Cicero, Sneezy, Dr. Oberman, even Sammi begged him to reconsider his decision. Cicero was practically screaming: "Don't you dare do this for *me*! I don't care if I never see this stupid hill again as long as I live! I want you up there with me, kid!"

Dominic didn't budge. He had arrived at a course of action that he judged to be right, and he was about as movable as the mountain he now refused to climb. At five the next morning, when the rest of the team suited up and headed into the predawn chill, the boy didn't utter a word. He just waved, as if they were going next door, and not to the top of the world.

Cicero was flushed with emotion. "I'll get you back here some day, Dominic. As long as I've got something to say about what happens on this mountain, I'll find a way."

They started across the moraine. Dominic did not watch them go.

THE SUMMIT

A quarter mile along, they stopped to strap on crampons — boot attachments featuring twelve sharp metal points for biting into ice and hard-packed snow. They were surprised to see a helicopter parked on the thinning rocks near the entrance to the Khumbu Icefall. Two shadowy figures approached.

Sammi squinted into the gloom. "It's them," she confirmed. "It's those Nepal government creeps."

"He's in Base Camp," snapped Cicero as the younger official began peering into faces. "Are you happy?"

"Our concern is for young Dominic's safety first and foremost," the senior officer informed him.

"I'm all choked up," Cicero snorted, and led his team onto the ice.

The two government men waited until the SummitQuest climbers had disappeared into the blue crystalline wilderness above. Then, dizzy and gasping from the thin air, they piled back into the chopper and begged the pilot to get them out of there.

It was a thousand times harder than Dominic had thought it would be.

He lay in his sleeping bag, the heavy down

fabric tucked up to his chin despite the warming morning. Icy droplets rained down on him as the sun thawed out the frozen condensation in the tent. Khumbu water torture, the climbers called it.

No torture could compare with the agony of staying behind.

All at once the flap was flung aside, and light flooded the small shelter. "Suit up, Alexis," announced Ethan Zaph. "We've got a mountain to get on top of."

"No offense, but go away," Dominic grumbled. "You should be halfway to Camp One by now."

"I'm serious," Ethan persisted. "The Icefall gets unstable as the day heats up."

Dominic cast him a resentful look. "Don't pour salt in my wounds, okay? You know I can't climb."

"You can't climb with Cap," Ethan amended. "Nobody said anything about climbing with me."

"And I'm sure those Nepalese officials are going to see the difference," Dominic said sarcastically.

"Those Nepalese officials went home," Ethan pointed out. "But, yeah, they'll see the difference. How can they blame Cap when he doesn't even know you're up there? You'll climb with This Way Up, with our equipment, eating our food, sleeping in our camps. Nestor isn't here, remember? I can't think of anybody who deserves to take his place more than you."

Dominic stared at him, thunderstruck. It was true. Nestor Ali was home after a week in a Kathmandu hospital. There was a spot open on This Way Up. "But — " he managed, "you could get in big trouble."

"I was in big trouble," Ethan reminded him. "Three weeks ago, I was at 27,700 feet, flat out of steam, with an unconscious partner. And a thirteen-year-old kid convinced his team to come up and get us. Dominic, do you honestly think there's anything the Nepalese can do to make me worse off than I would have been if it wasn't for you? You saved my life; I'm saving your climb. Small payback, but you've got to let me."

Dominic rose on unsteady legs. He felt dazed, as if he had just woken up from a deep sleep. Convincing himself that his Everest dreams were over had taken so much willpower that he now considered it an unchangeable law of the universe: Two plus two equals four; Dominic doesn't climb.

Yet here was Ethan with an idea. . . .

"You were right," Ethan finished. "Nepal is Cap's whole life. But it isn't mine."

Dominic felt his brain and body coming alive

again as he examined the plan from every angle. It could work! If Cicero didn't even know he was on the mountain, how could the team leader possibly be held responsible? Dominic would just have to avoid the SummitQuest people at the camps along the route. They might bump into one another on the narrow ridges leading to the pinnacle. But that high up, they would be hidden behind wind suits, goggles, and oxygen masks — passing astronauts on a landscape so forbidding it would make the surface of the moon seem like a resort hotel. And anyway, in the throes of exhaustion, Cicero probably wouldn't even notice him. The team leader had said it himself: "Past twenty-eight thousand, you wouldn't recognize your own mother if she came at you with a Thermos of chicken soup."

Dominic regarded the bigger boy with tears in his eyes. "Give me ten minutes to get suited up."

"You've got five," said Ethan.

He was ready in three.

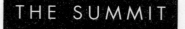

CHAPTER SIX

Mount Everest has claimed many lives in its history, but the Khumbu Icefall is its bloodiest battleground. Here the Khumbu glacier — really a frozen river — drops over a steep cliff. This sends millions of tons of slowly advancing ice careening down a half-mile escarpment. The glacier shatters into thousands of huge seracs, some of them the size of twenty-story buildings. It makes for spectacular scenery — a towering forest of jagged prisms the size of condominiums. But breathtaking as it is, the Icefall is not a place for sightseeing. The whole arrangement is moving, *falling*. The massive blue-white megaliths that lend the place its beauty might topple over without warning. Any unfortunate caught beneath an avalanching serac would be crushed like a bug.

A series of loud cracks punctuated the silence as hard glacial ice split and splintered beneath their feet. "Dangerous," Pasang said ominously. "No good climb so late in Icefall."

Ethan shot him a cockeyed grin. "You could have gone earlier. You wanted to wait for Dominic."

Pasang looked sheepish. There had been genuine dismay among the Sherpas when their "little sahib" had been grounded by the authorities. Pasang was privately determined to be at the boy's side all the way to the top. Dominic had many strikes against him, but the Sherpas of Everest were behind him one hundred percent. The SummitQuest Base Camp staff had even agreed to pretend he was with them whenever Cicero radioed in from the mountain.

"I'm just happy to be climbing," said Dominic. "All the way from Base, I was holding my breath. I half expected the entire Nepalese army to descend from the sky and arrest me."

"Well, they're sure not going to come looking for you up here," said Ethan. "So you're safe."

Crack!

A thin bridge of ice disintegrated beneath Dominic, and he was falling, dropping like a stone, straight into a crevasse. Desperately, he flailed with his ice ax, but he could not make firm contact with the dark wall.

He felt no fear, but only disbelief. Not that the mountain could kill, but that it could strike so fast — and without warning.

All at once, he came to a sudden jarring stop and dangled there, turning lazily.

The rope! he thought. *I'm still clipped onto*

the rope! Without it, he would surely be dead.

You're not safe yet! he reminded himself. *This line isn't made to handle that kind of jolt.*

"Dominic!"

He could barely hear Ethan's voice, although it was pretty clear that the older boy was screaming. "Dominic!"

He tried to yell, "I'm okay!" but it came out a high-pitched wheeze. He hacked madly at the glassy wall with his ice ax, but could not penetrate its smooth finish. He fared no better kicking with his crampons. Suspended in midair, he had no power behind his thrusts.

How can I get some of my weight off this rope?

His new teammates gave him the answer. Strong pulls on the line enabled him to get himself swinging. A stabbing kick with his right foot planted one front point; that purchase gave him the stability to stick the other.

With Ethan and Pasang steadying the rope from the surface, Dominic literally walked out. Pasang grabbed him by his wind suit and pulled him over the lip, where he collapsed on the ice.

Nobody spoke. There was nothing to say. There were certain near misses in mountaineering, mishaps that took climbers within a millimeter of disaster. Yet the only real damage they inflicted was to confidence. Physically, he was unharmed. This was exactly the same Dominic. Or was it?

"Okay," Ethan said huskily. "Your call. Was that a deal breaker?"

Dominic shook his head vehemently and panted. "Just give me a minute."

Ethan put an unsteady arm around his shoulders. Pasang squeezed Dominic's climbing mitt and would not let go. All three knew it had been that close.

www.summathletic.com/everest/abc

The final summit push begins with a day-long ascent, bypassing Camp One to Camp Two, or Advance Base Camp (ABC). Here in the radiant solar heat of the world's highest canyon, a team normally pauses for a day before taking on the upper mountain. But for the youngest expedition in Everest history, there will be no rest. Their weather window is razor thin, leaving no margin for error. They will climb tomorrow and the day after, followed by a summit marathon that will test them as they have never before been tested. **CLICK HERE** to see them preparing for one last shot at the peak. None of them will ever

THE SUMMIT

know such tunnel vision again. Every effort, every action, every breath is bent to the task of reaching the world's pinnacle. Not so much as a single thought is wasted on any other purpose.

Perry sat in the small tent, crouched over his laptop computer.

Dear Uncle Joe,

Before I set out for the highest point on the planet, there's something you should know: I'm no climber. What's more, I never was one.

It's not your fault, but in a way, it is. Because you never really asked how I felt when the crags got tougher and the cliffs got steeper. I just wanted to spend time with the uncle I idolized, and climbing was the way to do it. But somewhere in there, the cost of a mistake went from a few scrapes and bruises to my bones and maybe even my life.

Why couldn't we just stay home and play chess or something like that? Do

you even know I'm good at chess? I told you about fifty times. But you were determined for your nephew to have the alpine career you never got to have. This was always about you, not me. *Fortune* magazine voted you the sharpest CEO in American business. Yet you never even noticed that the higher we climbed, the less I looked down.

Well, Uncle Joe, where I'm going to-morrow, there's nowhere to look but down. There's a certain point where you get so scared that you just don't care anymore. I may not have the guts to stand up to you and save myself from the Death Zone. But I'm sure not going to march to that fate without making sure you know exactly how I feel about it.

He maneuvered the trackball over the SEND icon and hovered there, trying to work up the courage to put his message through. How many others had he written and deleted unsent?

All at once, the tent flap was flung aside and a laughing Tilt dove in, nearly flattening Perry. "I just nailed one of the baboons with a snowball — direct hit, right between the eyes!" He spied the E-mail on the computer. "Hey, what are you writing?"

Red-faced, Perry slammed the screen shut. But the bully in Tilt was aroused. Whatever this was, Noonan didn't want it made public. And that meant that seeing it was a must. He made a grab for the laptop, but Perry pulled it away at the last second, taking the brunt of the big boy's lunge with his own body. The two went sprawling into the collapsible aluminum pole, and the tent came billowing down on them.

"*What's going on in there?*" Cicero's voice, not far away.

A second later, the orange nylon was snatched away, and the team leader stood over them, glaring down. "Anybody with sense," he seethed, "would have better things to do with his breath up here!"

"We were just fooling around," Tilt mumbled.

"Yeah, Crowley, you're a real fun guy," Cicero growled. "The next time I see you using the Sherpas for target practice, you'll be throwing your next snowball from Base Camp." From the remains of the shelter, he selected two large pots and shoved them into the hands of the combatants. "Go chop ice to melt for water. And not around camp, either. A hundred climbers have been using this place as an outhouse. I don't like surprises."

The team leader watched them storm off in opposite directions. Then he set about restoring the flattened tent. The first thing that caught his eye was the discarded laptop, which was jacked into the satellite phone.

The power light was on.

Perry got back first and placed the pot of ice chips on the camp stove. Then he turned anxiously to his computer. He frowned. It was off.

He booted the machine up again, but the message had disappeared.

I'll write it again, he thought urgently.

But he could already hear Tilt's crampons crunching on the glacier outside.

"Forget it," he mumbled aloud. His courage had vanished as completely as the E-mail he would never have been brave enough to send.

It was dusk when Dominic, Ethan, and Pasang marched into ABC. Dominic made sure to steer clear of the SummitQuest camp. He did catch a glimpse of Sneezy filming the sunset, but the sight depressed him. For months he had been part of this family, and now he was expelled, banished practically. He felt lonely and disconnected.

Except for Ethan, the This Way Up climbers ignored him as if he had leprosy. He was an illegal member of this team, and nobody wanted to risk trouble with the Nepalese authorities. Dominic understood, but he didn't like being an outcast.

When he thanked Angus Harris, the This Way Up expedition leader, for giving him this last chance at the summit, the burly Scotsman replied, "Sure thing, Nestor. Good luck up there."

Dominic just stared at him, bewildered.

"You see, when I look at my climbing permit, the name says Nestor Ali," Angus explained. "So that has to be you, if you catch my meaning."

"Got it." Dominic turned to walk away.

"Hey." Angus put a beefy hand on his shoulder. "If you happen to see the lad Dominic Alexis, tell him we'll never forget what he did for our people on Lhotse. He shouldn't take it personally if we're not sticking our necks out to be his best friend. He's aces with us."

"I'll give him the message," said Dominic.

CHAPTER SEVEN

The stone was the size of a cantaloupe. It fell from near the summit of Lhotse, and by the time it appeared out of the low overcast, it was traveling at close to two hundred miles per hour.

Babu saw it first and sounded the warning. "Rockfall!"

The climbers flattened themselves to the slope of the Lhotse Face. The lethal projectile rocketed into their midst, whizzing by a bare six inches from Sammi's ear.

"Missed me!" she sang out defiantly.

The Face was the most grueling part of the climb — a mile-long skating rink tilted sixty degrees. Its icy steepness could be safely attempted only by jumar, a device that allowed a mountaineer to ascend a fixed line, but locked up automatically in case of a fall. Each agonizing step gained six or seven inches of altitude along a single rope.

When Camp Three appeared, it always seemed close enough to touch. Yet the slant of the Face had a foreshortening effect. For two solid hours the image of the tents teased them, elusive

THE SUMMIT

as a desert mirage. Sneezy got there first and pointed his camera unsteadily down the incline as the others struggled up to the tiny platform chopped into the ice.

Meetings at Camp Three were held lying down with the climbers' heads sticking out of the tents, facing one another.

Dr. Oberman shone a penlight into the teens' eyes and began to ask a series of simple questions: "What is your address?" "How many seconds are in three minutes?" "Spell 'spaghetti.' " "What is your mother's maiden name?"

"Tilt doesn't have a mother," put in Sammi. "He was hatched."

"I've got a mother," growled Tilt. "And she could beat you to a pulp even easier than I could."

"If they'd let her out of solitary," Sammi returned.

"What are you laughing at?" Tilt boomed at Perry, who was snickering into his bedroll.

"They're fine," Dr. Oberman assured the team leader with a tolerant smile. "They're the same pinheads they were before we dragged them down to Gorak Shep."

"All right, we're still acclimatized," decided Cicero. "But no one can acclimatize to the summit ridge, so I want everybody on bottled O's starting now. We hit the Death Zone tomorrow, and we only get a few hours' rest before we push for the top. It's our last chance; let's make it count."

Later, Sammi hunched in her oxygen rig, the Scuba-like echoes of her breath resounding in her ears. She was bent over her laptop, pounding out a last-minute E-mail to her parents while waiting for the satellite phone to connect her to the Internet. The device became temperamental at altitude. Camp Four was even worse. Last time, Sneezy had waited over an hour to send his footage to Summit's Web designers in Colorado.

As if on cue, the link was established. Sammi blinked. There was a message from Caleb waiting for her. She clicked on it.

Hi, Sammi,

Sorry I haven't gotten back to you sooner. Things have been crazy around here. Not Everest crazy, I guess. But a lot has happened since you left for Kathmandu.

Remember Myrna Applebaum? It's weird — you know how we always used to laugh at her? Well, I met her

skateboarding a couple of weeks ago, and it turns out she's pretty cool. Her cousin runs the pro shop at that half-pipe in Lawton, so she gets a lot of practice and she's *awesome*! She's never been climbing, but I told her where you were, and we checked you out on the SummitQuest Web site. . . .

Sammi's brow furrowed as she continued to scan the message. For two weeks she'd heard *nothing* from Caleb. Now he finally E-mailed her, and *this* was what he had to say?

I'm at twenty-four thousand feet on Mount Everest. Why would Caleb think I care about Myrna Applebaum?

When the truth hit, she reacted not with shock or even hurt. It was pure amazement. *He's dumping me!*

Then, even more astounded: *He's dumping me for Myrna Applebaum!*

She was oddly sympathetic at first. She'd been gone for nine weeks now. A month of boot camp before that.

Her second thought was more to the point: That *jerk!*

If it comes down to being Caleb's girlfriend

or *being extreme, it's a pretty easy choice to make.*

She reached into her knapsack and came out with an eight-by-ten glossy photograph protected by a Zip-loc plastic bag. It was Sammi and Caleb skydiving. Their chutes hadn't opened yet, so the two were captured in free fall, hands tightly clasped.

Sammi didn't even look at him. It was her own blissful smile that saddened her. Her anticipation not just of this jump, but of a whole future that would never come to be.

Hey, loser — think you're going to the summit of E? In a single motion, she ripped the picture in half, cleanly separating herself from her ex-boyfriend. Then she folded his image into a paper airplane, and sailed it down the steep pitch of the Lhotse Face.

Not in this life.

When Sammi Moon hit the summit, it would be as a free woman.

Unlike the other campsites, there was no set location for Camp Three. The expeditions bedded down wherever their Sherpas chose to hack out platforms in the Face.

This Way Up's tents were carved into the

slope about sixty feet below SummitQuest's. Dominic, Ethan, and Pasang arrived around four o'clock and immediately began chopping ice to melt for soup and hot chocolate.

Dominic never saw the object that struck him full in the face. It was a terrifying moment because he was working unroped, and even a small falling rock could have swept him off the Lhotse Face. But the impact was light — a sudden slap.

"Hey!"

Then he noticed it, sitting in a rut in the ice — a small paper airplane.

Ethan was disgusted. "Real smart. You could put a guy off the mountain with a stunt like that."

Dominic stared at the image on the folded paper. "If I didn't know better," he said with a frown, "I'd swear that's Sammi's boyfriend."

He reached over to pick it up. But a gust of wind dislodged the airplane from the Face and sent it spiraling down toward the Western Cwm.

CHAPTER EIGHT

www.summathletic.com/everest/
yellowband

Trouble at 25,000 feet: SummitQuest cameraman Lenny Tkakzuk loses his goggles
while filming in the inhospitable Yellow
Band, a thick layer of crumbly limestone in
the mountain's midsection. Here, in a windchill approaching –100° F, a climber's eyeball
can actually freeze solid without protection.

Help comes from an unlikely source. A
Sherpa from an expedition called This
Way Up offers his own eyegear for the
remainder of today's ascent to Camp
Four. "Sherpas born in wind and cold," the
happy-go-lucky hero explains. "No need
goggles." **CLICK HERE** to see Pasang, the
savior of the Yellow Band. It's nice to have
friends in high places!

Dominic lay on his stomach, shivering against
the mustard-colored rock. Staying active was the

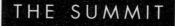

climber's first line of defense against the blistering cold of this altitude. What was going on up there? He couldn't make out the problem that had stopped SummitQuest in its tracks.

Ethan returned to report that the coast was clear. "Pasang had to lend Sneezy his goggles. Let's give Cap a head start and then get moving again."

Dominic nodded, his teeth chattering into his oxygen mask. The brutal chill penetrated deep into his gut, and his fingers felt useless, like fragile porcelain attachments. Ten minutes later the team resumed its climb, and he warmed a little, but his core was still ice.

"You wanted to see me, Cap?"

Perry ducked out of the merciless cold into the guides' tent at Camp Four. He frowned when he saw his open laptop on the communications table. "What are you doing with my computer?"

"Sorry for minding your business, Noonan." The team leader waved the red-haired boy in front of the small machine.

Perry looked around in bewilderment. Dr. Oberman, Sneezy, and Babu were regarding him intently. "What's going on?"

"You'll want to see this, Perry," the doctor said gently.

Perry turned his attention to the glowing screen — an E-mail from Uncle Joe:

Perry, why didn't you tell me? You mean more to me than all the summits in the world! I had no idea you felt this way.

Turn around and get off that mountain. Call from Base Camp, and I'll send a chopper to pick you up. My plane will be waiting at the Kathmandu airport. I'll make this up to you if it takes fifty years. . . .

"I sent your message from Camp Two," Cicero explained softly. "Part of my job — never climb with a client who doesn't want to be there."

Perry sat stunned, reading and rereading the E-mail. It was hard to believe that this whole nightmare was over. Nine weeks of discomfort, deprivation, backbreaking effort, and insane risk-taking. Plus a month of boot camp. And now — a few paragraphs over the Internet, and he was done.

I'm going home.

The relief that washed over him wasn't as

sweet as he'd expected it to be. What a waste! The time. The effort. The *fear*.

"You can start down with one of the Sherpas in the morning," Cicero went on. "Let me say one thing first: I didn't pick you. But you've turned into a heck of a mountaineer these past two months. You're as tough as anybody here. Maybe even tougher, because you had to suck it up for every step. I'd climb with you any day."

The guides nodded their agreement.

Perry was silent for a long time. Then he said, "I guess I should go pack my stuff."

His computer under his arm, he crossed the seven feet of gale-force wind that separated the two tents. Ferocious conditions.

Not my problem anymore.

"What's up?" asked Sammi.

"I'm going home." The words sounded strange — somehow unreal. "They're sending a helicopter to Base Camp for me."

She nodded distractedly and said nothing. Perry recognized her game face under the oxygen mask. Sammi's focus was made of the same titanium as her ice ax.

Not so Tilt. As Perry gathered his personal items together, the big boy kept up a gloating, I-told-you-so monologue.

"Oh, poor Perry, he can't hack it on Mount

Everest. The other kids are mean to him — he has to go crying home to Mommy. Uncle Joey, send a helicopter, send your Learjet — "

Perry was smoldering as he jammed a sweater into the pack. The words formed in his mind: *Shut up! Shut up!* But he didn't have the guts to say them aloud.

"What took you so long?" sneered Tilt. "I could have told you on day one of training camp: This wimp couldn't climb an anthill, let alone the highest mountain in the world!"

Cheeks flaming hot as his bright red hair, Perry wheeled on the bigger boy. And this time, the words did come: "Shut up, Crowley!"

Tilt was taken aback at first. Then his features relaxed into an unpleasant smile. "Who's gonna make me, Noonan? You?"

Perry set his jaw. There was only one way to quiet Tilt. And only one way to undo the waste of these past months. To make this miserable experience mean something.

The E-mail would be short and to the point. And this one he *would* have the guts to send: **Dear Uncle Joe —** *not yet***!!**

Perry Noonan was going to climb.

CHAPTER NINE

The plan was for a ten-thirty P.M. wake-up. Tilt was up by nine forty-five, melting ice for oatmeal.

He could not remember ever being this nervous. Tonight was the first night of his future. The blueprint for his life began right here, right now. Or not, if he messed up.

He wouldn't. He had been a monster on the climb up to the Col. Cicero had forced him to put on the brakes to keep from leaving the others far behind. He was in top shape, top acclimatization. He was even getting good at the eerie Darth Vader breathing of bottled oxygen.

Besides — and this was the best omen of them all — the shrimp was down at Base Camp. Dominic's amazing luck had run out. Surely that meant Tilt was bound for greatness.

Sammi and Perry awoke, and Tilt made them breakfast. Why not? He had to do something to keep busy or the butterflies in his stomach would devour him from the inside.

Cicero came in for some last-minute nagging. "I want to see three layers on your hands — ny-

EVEREST

lon gloves, wool mitts, Gore-Tex mitts. You're not getting out that flap till you show me."

Normally, Cicero's control-freak personality drove Tilt crazy. But this time, he stood quietly and let the team leader check every piece of gear and clothing.

"Just keep doing what you've been doing, Crowley. You'll make it."

"Thanks, Cap." It was the friendliest exchange that had ever passed between the two of them.

Since Tilt was ready early, it was decided that he would set out ahead of the others. Sneezy would accompany him. That way, SummitQuest would take its best shot at the peak early, with its cameraman on hand to film the triumphant Tilt standing on top of the world. Then, on the way down, Sneezy could hand the camera to one of the other guides as the second team passed them en route to the summit.

As Tilt waited for Sneezy on the rocks of the Col, he was surprised to see another alpinist braving the battering wind. He knew that two other teams were launching bids tonight — This Way Up and the Germans. But both of those expeditions were known for late starts. Who was this?

The slight figure wore a Gore-Tex mask, full

THE SUMMIT

oxygen rig, and goggles. It had to be a woman, and a little one at that. He was doing a mental inventory of female climbers when it hit him. The bright red wind suit. The small boots and crampons. The oversized ice ax.

Tilt moved closer, peering into the goggles. "Shrimp?"

The figure began backing away.

"Shrimp, it's me! Tilt!"

"*Shhh!*" Dominic pushed the oxygen mask aside so his warning could be heard. "Cap doesn't know I'm here!"

"*Why* are you here?" hissed Tilt. "How did you get here?"

"I'm climbing with Ethan Zaph," Dominic explained urgently. "Cap can't know so he won't be held responsible."

The frustration threatened to detonate Tilt like a grenade. Dominic Alexis! Somehow, the kid had managed to pull yet another rabbit out of his little runt hat! And here he was on the Col, poised to ruin Tilt's plans.

"Promise you won't tell," Dominic insisted. "Give me your word."

Telling Cicero — that was exactly what Tilt should do. But would it work? The team leader would never let Dominic quit so close to the top. Not even if he had to strap the shrimp onto his back and carry him kicking and screaming up the southeast ridge.

There was no way to keep Dominic from climbing at this point. What Tilt had to do was to find a way to prevent him from summiting. But how?

All at once, he had the answer. "The secret is safe with me," Tilt promised. "Listen, shrimp, I know we've had our problems. But I'm really glad you're getting your shot. Good luck tonight." He wrapped his arms around the smaller boy in a show of support.

"You, too," said Dominic.

As the young climbers embraced, Tilt reached around Dominic's back, found his oxygen regulator, and twisted the dial to maximum.

He broke away. "Hey, here comes Sneezy. You'd better not let him see you."

Tilt watched Dominic melt into the shadows. Gobbling bottled gas at a rate of four liters per minute, the shrimp would run out of oxygen by twenty-eight thousand feet, still more than a thousand below the summit. Cold, exhausted, and starved for air, he'd have no choice but to give up and return to Camp Four.

CHAPTER TEN

Dominic watched furtively as Sneezy and Tilt ascended the steep slope above the South Col. He squinted, trying to tell if they were front-pointing or climbing flat-footed. In the gloom, all he could make out were the hovering globes made by their helmet lamps glowing on black rock and white snow.

Where were Ethan and Pasang? It was dangerous to spend so much time standing around in brutal conditions, although Dominic felt surprisingly warm and strong. He had no way of knowing this was largely because he was breathing double the usual amount of supplemental oxygen.

Ethan wasn't at the tent, so Dominic headed for the This Way Up Sherpas' camp in search of Pasang. Inside, he found his Sherpa friend flat on his back with Ethan kneeling over him. When the beam of Dominic's helmet lamp penetrated the small shelter, Pasang cried out in agony.

"Douse that light!" ordered Ethan.

The tent went dark. "What's wrong?" Dominic asked anxiously.

The Sherpa's eyes were squeezed so tightly

shut that beads of sweat stood out on his forehead.

"Snow blindness," Ethan explained gravely.

Dominic was shocked. "How?" But he already knew. Pasang had climbed without goggles from the Yellow Band to the South Col. His eyes had survived the cold; the bright sun was another matter. This high up in the atmosphere, there was virtually no protection from ultraviolet radiation. The glare of a cloudless morning, reflecting off ice and pristine snow, had blinded Pasang. Although the condition was only temporary, the Sherpa's ascent was over.

Ethan was furious. "You know better! Why'd you do it?"

The guide shrugged miserably. "Sherpas' life very hard. Many climb, but only few jobs. But if Pasang on Summit Web site, maybe sahibs want hire this Sherpa."

Dominic put a hand on his shoulder. "It's okay. We understand." He had become so close to the Sherpas that he saw them merely as new friends. It was so easy to forget their poverty. Pasang was not a fellow adventurer. He was eking out a living the only way he knew how.

"I let you down, little sahib," he moaned to Dominic. "And my team. And myself."

Ethan tried to put a good face on it. "You've

THE SUMMIT

been up there three times already. You're hogging the summit! Give somebody else a chance, will you?"

"Go," urged Pasang. "Climb summit. I make tea when you return Camp Four."

"You sure you're okay?" asked Dominic.

"Go now!"

Dominic ducked out the flap and immediately ducked back in again. "It's Cap!" he hissed. "The whole team!"

Pasang had an idea. "There is" — he racked his brains for the words — "shortcut. Far west where Col curves down Lhotse Face. Much steep first, then simple walk to Balcony."

At 27,600 feet, the Balcony marked the start of the southeast ridge, the highway to the peak.

"If we can beat them to the ridge, we won't meet them again till we're on the way down," Dominic said excitedly.

The traverse to Pasang's shortcut was an easy ten-minute hike. There, at the northwest corner of the Col, Ethan and Dominic got their first glimpse of the Sherpa's definition of *much steep*. The "route" took them straight up a sheer cliff. It was so punctuated with both solid ice and naked rock that crampons would be a necessity one minute and a hazard the next.

"Pasang's going to owe us one first-class cup of tea," Ethan muttered.

There were no fixed lines. The two boys roped themselves together in the traditional style.

Their progress was exhausting and agonizingly slow. They inched up the wall, painstakingly placing CAM units and ice screws as they took turns belaying each other. An hour later, they had ascended a grand total of sixty feet.

Perry should be here, Dominic reflected, releasing a spring-loaded CAM in a small crack in Everest's hide. *This is his kind of climbing.* Dominic now respected the red-haired boy's rope work one hundred percent.

Ethan's fatigue and frustration were beginning to boil over. "Shortcut? *Nightmare* would be more like it! By the time we hit the ridge, everybody and his grandmother will be in front of us!"

Dominic could only shrug miserably as he struggled up the wall. A summit bid was a race against time. With every tick of the clock, the top of the world, in a sense, moved farther and farther away.

Only a quarter mile to the east, Sammi, Perry, Cicero, Dr. Oberman, and Babu were making much better time. They attacked the massive rock buttress of Everest's summit pyramid through a shallow gully. The terrain was not overly difficult, but the route was unroped, and the ice was like shatterproof glass. All was well as long as their crampons bit. If not — Perry didn't want to think about that.

Not thinking turned out to be a fairly easy thing to do. This high up, brain function was so impaired that thoughts were awkward and sluggish — if Perry managed to think at all beyond his movements. There was a brutal, yet strangely comforting simplicity to a summit push. This was no place for philosophers. The meaning of life lay in placing one foot in front of the other.

Fatigue came quickly. The South Col was barely out of the range of his helmet lamp, yet every few steps brought him to a standstill, leaning on his ax as he sucked breathlessly at his oxygen mask.

Cicero's reminders were gentle but firm. "You've got to climb faster, Perry. This expedition could put the youngest climber ever on that summit. But we could also summit the oldest if you don't hurry up."

Ten yards ahead, Sammi and Dr. Oberman were also flagging under the crushing effects of altitude. Her face contorted in a determined grimace, Sammi refused to rest, attacking the mountain with every cramponed step.

Only Babu seemed immune to the impossibly thin air of the upper mountain. Doubly amazing was the fact that he climbed without oxygen.

The guy's not human, Perry thought to himself. He kept an eye on the altimeter on his watch: 26,800 . . . 27,000 . . . 27,200 . . . Every vertical foot put more of a spring in Babu's step. They were almost at the Balcony. If this kept up, he'd be doing cartwheels on the summit!

Perry was never sure exactly how it happened. It wasn't a trip; not even a slip, really. But somehow, his crampons lost their purchase on the sheer ice.

When he first went down, he wasn't that scared yet. It felt like a routine skid, one of many on an icy climb. It was only when he became aware of the wind rushing past him, saw the blur of his surroundings flashing by in the gyrating glow of his helmet lamp, that panic set in.

He thought he heard Cicero's voice: *"Perry!"* But it might have been wishful thinking, his mind conjuring up the one person who could save him.

In a desperate attempt to slow his acceleration, Perry dug his crampons into the rime. His downward momentum stopped abruptly, and his slide became a head-over-heels tumble. Jolted and dizzy, never knowing which way was up, he closed his eyes and waited for his life to end. Would it be the rocks of the Col that snuffed him out? Or worse, would he be pitched down the seven-thousand-foot Kangshung Face? Or the four-thousand-foot Lhotse Face?

For God's sake, what difference does it make?

The jolts and bumps seemed to fade into a full-body numbness. All he knew was speed as gravity hurled him off this mountain he hated, and would now never escape.

Suddenly, he was airborne, flung by a ramp of ice. Those few seconds aloft brought with them a soul-crushing horror. For there was no way of telling if he was a few feet off the frozen slopes, or a mile and a half above the Kangshung glacier.

At the last second, he saw in the light of his helmet lamp the icy rock outcropping that swung up to meet him. The torch shattered. The universe went dark.

CHAPTER ELEVEN

www.summathletic.com/everest/
southeastridge

From the Balcony at 27,600 feet, the route to the summit follows the treacherous southeast ridge, a knife-edge of sloped rock more than five miles in the sky. It is one of the most lethal places on Earth. Huge snow cornices follow the line of the ridge, making each step a life-or-death gamble. Is there solid mountain underneath the drift, or are you stepping off into thin air? **CLICK HERE** to see fourteen-year-old Tilt Crowley breaking trail for his teammates to follow. A quarter mile above him, the summit waits. . . .

Sneezy slung the camera back over his shoulder and stumbled forward to catch up to Tilt. The guide had climbed Himalayan peaks before, but never had he experienced the hammer-blow effects of altitude like here on Everest. At twenty-

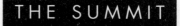

THE SUMMIT

eight thousand feet, they were higher than all but three of the world's mountains. Even with bottled oxygen, it was almost impossible to breathe. Panting, wheezing gasps were the best he could manage. His legs weighed forty tons each.

In spite of this, Tilt was moving onward and upward at an astounding pace. The teenager's strength was unbelievable. *He must smell it,* the guide thought to himself. *He knows he's going to the top.* Sneezy couldn't see anything standing in Tilt's way — certainly not Mount Everest.

"Hey!" he yelled. "*Hey!*"

Tilt held up, and a burst of tortured steps brought Sneezy alongside his charge.

"Slow down," he rasped. "If you summit without me, who's going to prove you got there?"

Behind the goggles, Tilt's eyes burned as if with fever. "Sorry. I'm just pumped! We're making great time, right? It isn't even sunrise yet."

Sneezy nodded. "If all goes well, it'll happen. What's going on in your mind, kid?"

Tilt grinned. "You have no idea."

The truth was that Tilt's thoughts were not with himself, but with Dominic. By the time the shrimp reached this altitude, he would be out of oxygen and forced to turn back.

The record would belong to Tilt.

*   *   *

Dominic lost track of time on the wall. It seemed endless, a vertical marathon that could only be tackled a single agonizing handhold at a time. Once he caught a glimpse of his watch and realized in dismay that four and a half hours had gone by.

Where's the ridge? he thought desperately. Could they be squandering their summit chances on this miserable cliff?

Fifteen feet above and to his left, he heard Ethan screaming with frustration — an almost unforgivable waste of energy and oxygen. Such was the anguished anxiety of feeling their bid slipping through their fingers.

The top of the wall never came. Instead, it rounded infuriatingly slowly into a mammoth buttress up against the upper mountain.

Weak and disoriented, Ethan and Dominic crawled atop the rock shoulder and took stock of their position. The ridge was nowhere to be found. Had they wasted this gargantuan effort?

Then Dominic saw it in the beam of his helmet lamp — a narrow arête carved into the mountain itself, a gently rising ramp perhaps eight inches wide.

Their eyes locked. It was a big risk. What would happen if they followed this path for hours only to have it disappear into the mountain? But

THE SUMMIT

the alternative was even less appetizing. The only other direction was down.

Ethan took the lead, walking the tightrope of the arête by gingerly placing one foot in front of the other. Half an hour later, they were unable to see anything that looked like the southeast ridge.

Up until that point, Dominic had thought only of how this detour might affect their chances of getting to the top. Now his mind began to fill with a deeper dread. Were they getting themselves lost high on mighty Everest?

All at once, their path cut sharply to the left, rounding a notch in the mountain's bulk. The arête widened into a ledge, and they stepped onto —

"The Balcony!" they chorused, weak with relief.

Above them stretched the ridge. Dominic squinted at the trail plowed through the shin-deep snow. Were these tracks left by Tilt and Sneezy? Probably. But what about Cicero and the rest of the team? Surely, they were ahead by now. And yet the new powder didn't seem to be trampled enough to indicate the passage of so many climbers.

Where was everybody? Had something gone wrong?

In the Death Zone, there was no time to keep

tabs on anyone else. Just staying alive was a full-time job up here.

They placed their spare oxygen bottles on the side of the path for pickup on the way down. Then they set out along the southeast ridge.

Had Dominic bothered to check the gauge on the cylinder that was hooked into his breathing system, he would have seen that his supply of gas was less than a quarter full.

Perry regained consciousness to find himself staring up into a ring of bright lights. Two thoughts occurred to him: 1) *I'm not dead* and 2) *I've stopped falling.*

He heard strange voices around him. They were speaking another language . . . German?

The German expedition!

"Where am I?"

Stupid question! If you're alive, what difference does it make?

The Germans seemed amazed to see his eyes open. "You *live?*" said a heavily accented voice. "After such a fall?"

Perry looked at his watch. The altimeter read 26,718. He had slid and rolled the height of a fifty-story building! Now he lay on a narrow ledge of dark ice. Four inches to his left, the lower ramparts of the summit pyramid fell away

into the Kangshung Face. Those few inches represented the difference between being here alive versus being eight thousand feet straight down in Tibet.

Another helmet lamp joined the group around him.

"Perry!" The voice was hoarse and breathless.

He focused on the man beneath the light. Even through the mask and goggles, he could see that Cicero's face was gray.

The sight of someone who cared — really cared — disintegrated the last of his control. The emotion burst from him like the opening of floodgates. The tears poured out — for the years spent climbing when he'd hated and feared it; for the things he'd never had the courage to say to his uncle; for the months spent on Everest, and in boot camp before that, culminating in this latest mishap, which had almost cost him his life.

Cicero gathered him up in powerful arms and moved him back from the edge of the abyss. Still sobbing, Perry latched on to his team leader as if he would never let go.

"It's over, kid," Cicero soothed. "You're going home."

CHAPTER TWELVE

Breaking dawn flooded the summit pyramid with radiant sun. The effect was almost unreal. The top of the world was coming into day. Beneath them, the rest of the Himalayan range was still draped in the dark of night.

Tilt barely noticed the mountain's light show. He stood with Sneezy just below the South Summit, where the fixed ropes ended. Their attention was focused on Everest's lesser pinnacle, fifty feet above them.

"This is as high as anyone's gotten this year," Sneezy shouted over the howl of the wind. "We'll have to fix line the rest of the way."

Tilt shook his head vehemently. "It'll take too much time."

Sneezy was surprised. "We're on point," he argued. "What about the team coming up behind us?"

"We don't even know they'll get this far," Tilt shot back. "I'm not risking my chance to lay rope for people who aren't coming!"

The cameraman was disgusted. "Eighty years of tradition on this mountain, but that's not as im-

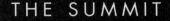

portant as you getting your name in the paper!
We made it this far because other people fixed
routes for us. Now it's our turn."

"What do I look like — a Sherpa?" Tilt
sneered. And he set himself to the steep snow
slope.

"Come back!" Sneezy's dilemma was clear.
Yes, the boy was acting selfishly and with disregard for every unwritten rule of mountaineering.
But it was Sneezy's responsibility as a guide to
stay with the kid. He was only fourteen! "You
can't go alone!"

"Watch me!" Tilt tossed over his shoulder.

"Let me belay you at least!" Sneezy hurried
up to join him. "That powder looks unstable."

The two roped themselves together and began
their attack on the rise. Tilt took the "sharp" end,
leading the way up. He burrowed his crampons
and ice ax deep into the snow to make solid contact with the husk of Everest. From Sneezy's view-
point below him, it looked more like swimming
than climbing. But their progress was steady despite the dizzying altitude.

Twenty minutes later, the two heaved themselves through a natural half arch of rock and
came to stand on the South Summit. The altitude
was 28,700 feet: 450 feet higher than K2, the
second-tallest mountain on Earth.

They were the first climbers this season to gaze up Everest's summit ridge.

The ridge was notorious in climbing circles. It was razor sharp and totally unforgiving. Your first wrong step would be your last. It was also unimaginably exposed — a daredevil's tiptoe between the Kangshung Face to the right and the Southwest Face to the left. Across this blew triple-digit wind gusts. But this year there was yet an added wrinkle. Two weeks of blizzards had coated this airless catwalk with a thick blanket of unpredictable shifting snow.

The homestretch began — slow, careful steps along the heavily corniced ridge. They remained roped together, but on this terrain, a belay was virtually impossible. A fall by one meant they were both gone. They used their ice axes as walking sticks to support them against fatigue and the onslaught of the wind. They knew that only one major obstacle lay in their path — a deep notch in the summit ridge that created a forty-foot cliff in the sky. This was the infamous Hillary Step, named for Sir Edmund Hillary, Everest's first conqueror.

Gradually, the snow-covered Step came into view. Hundreds of alpinists had faced it before. But to Tilt it was a message directed at him and no other: *One last battle and the war is won.*

THE SUMMIT

The two climbers looked up. Dozens of ropes stretched up the rocky gash, some of them half buried in the snow.

Tilt looked questioningly at his guide, but Sneezy shook his head. They had to resist the temptation to use these old lines. Years earlier, a solo climber at the end of the season had become entangled in the spaghetti of ropes. The following spring, his body had been discovered dangling from the Hillary Step, frozen solid.

Their climb had gone extraordinarily smoothly so far. But here, only two hundred vertical feet below the summit, Everest chose not to yield so easily.

Tilt started out, still in the lead, but he was impatient, and exhausted himself quickly. Sneezy tried next, a more measured, experienced approach. But he, too, was spent and gasping in a matter of minutes.

Tilt sat on the soft snow, glaring up at the Step with genuine malice. His dream would not end here, foiled by a glorified divot in the summit ridge. *You can't beat me! I won't be stopped!* And he was back at the rise, climbing it, almost wrestling with it.

Far on the right side of the notch, he found, beneath the powder, snow packed hard enough to support the front points of his crampons. Soon the points hit bare rock. But Tilt would not be denied. Jamming his ice ax into a crack, he grabbed on and literally chinned himself to the next handhold.

Watching from below, Sneezy was bug-eyed. At this altitude, the tiniest movement was considered a triumph. Tilt's display of arm strength was nothing short of miraculous. Fighting his own exhaustion, he brought out the camera. The world had to see this — the most storied obstacle in high-altitude mountaineering being conquered by raw power and sheer cussedness.

Roaring his defiance, Tilt scrambled atop the Step. Sneezy almost expected him to beat his chest and emit a Tarzan yell. But instead, he twisted an ice screw into the thick rime at the lip of the notch and dropped a length of nine-millimeter nylon line to Sneezy at the bottom. The guide tethered it to a second screw at the bottom. The Hillary Step was roped.

Slowly, but with growing excitement, Sneezy jumared up the rope. For him, too, this was a first ascent of Everest. The thrill was greater here than on any other mountain.

From here, the summit ridge looked like a gargantuan arrowhead of brilliant white rising above them. All detail disappeared in the gleam of the snow. Where was the top? Tilt couldn't see,

THE SUMMIT

but the route was obvious: Follow the ridge higher and higher — until there was no such thing as higher anymore.

The sky was mostly clear, but Tilt could feel tiny bee stings of ice on his face, the crystallized moisture that made up Everest's summit plume. The world was a different place up here near the edge of Earth's troposphere. Energy and exhaustion seemed to melt into each other. Here, there was only purpose. Tilt kept moving, one foot in front of the other, as if the summit were a magnet, pulling him ever upward.

Sneezy cleared the frost off the dial of his climber's watch. "Twenty-nine thousand feet!" he practically screamed. The number looked impossible, illogical, unreal.

They were almost there! They had to be! Tilt squinted into the glare. *Where's the peak? It should be right here! Is something wrong? Are we lost?*

And then the next step . . . was *down!*

CHAPTER THIRTEEN

It didn't register at first. *What's happening? The ridge goes up, not down!*

At that moment, Sneezy threw his arms around the youngest climber ever to summit the world's tallest mountain.

Tilt grabbed the guide's wrist and checked the number on the altimeter: 29,028. It didn't get any higher than that. Not on this planet.

The surge of joy that rose up in him reminded him of the depiction of a supernova that he'd once seen in a planetarium show — an explosion of white light growing in intensity as it radiated outward in waves.

He had done it! At this altitude, he had trouble wrapping his oxygen-deprived mind around the fact that he wasn't the same person who had awoken at the Col eleven hours ago. He was now living the very first minute of the rest of his life — he scanned the panorama — with the whole world literally at his feet.

The old Tilt Crowley, that ninth-grade nobody from Cincinnati, the one who earned money by delivering papers — he didn't exist anymore. Tilt

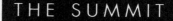

THE SUMMIT

was famous, a celebrity, a star. He was going to be rich.

Sneezy was shouting into the walkie-talkie. "We're here, Cap! We're on the summit! Right now!"

"How's Tilt?" came Cicero's voice.

"Strong — really strong! He led the Step like a pro! Where are you guys?"

"I'm at Camp Four," Cicero reported. "Perry took a dive."

"Is he okay?"

"Couple of broken ribs, Andrea says. Nothing serious. Sammi and Babu are on the southeast ridge. Let me talk to the kid."

The fourteen-year-old was still wild with excitement. "Cap, it's *amazing*! You've got to see it!"

"I've been," came the amused reply. "Now listen up. Andrea's already on the sat phone to Colorado. You're going to be in all the papers tonight. You ate this mountain for breakfast."

"Thanks, Cap."

"I know you feel like you're done for the day," the team leader went on, "but here's some advice you'd better take: A lot of climbers can get up that rock; the trick is to get yourself down again. So take your pictures, enjoy the view. Then get your butt back on the ridge, because you're only halfway there."

"Gotcha," replied Tilt. Nothing, not even Cicero's nagging, was going to spoil this moment for him.

He watched as Sneezy attempted to unfurl a Summit Athletic Corporation flag in the battering gale. From his apparently bottomless knapsack, the guide produced a telescoping aluminum flagpole. The two of them planted it in the snowpack next to the half-buried survey rod that marked the peak.

SummitQuest — Tilt had almost forgotten that he was part of an expedition. One that was an official success now that it had placed a member on the summit. A lot of credit would be claimed over this — by Perry's uncle, whose brainchild it was; Tony Devlin, who handled the business end; Cap Cicero, who led the team.

Take your bows, guys. I'm at the top, and I don't see any of you here.

This victory belonged to Tilt Crowley.

Babu put the walkie-talkie back in his wind-suit pocket and turned to Sammi, behind him on the ridge. "That was Cap. Lenny and Tilt are on the summit."

Sammi was astonished. "Already?" The two had been delayed by Perry's accident. They were barely beyond the Balcony. "Go, guys! They flew!"

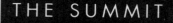

THE SUMMIT

"They made good time," Babu agreed. "But mostly, we're way behind schedule."

"Then what are we waiting for?" She increased her pace and pushed past him, gasping into her mask.

"Sammi!" He had to scramble to keep up with her. "You know, Cap put a two o'clock turnaround on us." The turnaround meant simply this: If you weren't on the top by two P.M., it was too late to keep climbing. At that time, all team members had to head back down to Camp Four, regardless of their position on the mountain. If they did not, they would end up descending in the dark at a time when their headlamp batteries would be most likely to fail.

"It's not two o'clock yet," said Sammi, tight-lipped.

"If you climb too fast, you'll burn yourself out," he warned.

She tried to grin, but through the pain of her effort, it came out a grimace. "Come on, Babu. You know me. I've only got one speed."

And Babu did know her. Over the past two months, he had come to admire the girl's tenacity and fearlessness. But he also knew Everest. Perry's accident had cost them a lot of time. To make up that time, they would need determination, skill, and luck.

Babu Pemba had been in this game long enough to realize that very few climbers could count on having all three at the same time.

Ethan and Dominic were approaching twenty-eight thousand feet when they first saw the two specks descending the southeast ridge above them.

Ethan looked at his watch. It was only ten-thirty A.M. If those dots in the snow were coming from the peak, then they were climbing at near-record pace.

He frowned. "Did the Germans send an early summit party?"

Dominic shook his head. "That has to be Tilt and Sneezy. I'll bet they made it."

"Probably," Ethan agreed. "Tilt never did take no for an answer." He grinned. "I guess that means I'm not important anymore."

As the ascending and descending pairs closed the gap, Dominic could see that the lead climber above — probably Tilt — was moving strongly. His partner was having a much tougher time. Every two or three steps, Sneezy would slump on his ice ax to snatch a few seconds of rest. He wasn't in danger, exactly. But he wasn't doing well.

Half an hour later, the two teams passed.

THE SUMMIT

Dominic pretended to lean forward into his climb, keeping his face averted. He didn't want Sneezy to recognize him and alert Cicero. He needn't have worried. The cameraman was so exhausted that he never moved his gaze from the narrow path in front of him.

Tilt, too, seemed content to let Dominic keep his secret. He confirmed their summit success with a single thumbs-up, and exchanged a high five with Ethan — the new record holder accepting the torch from the old.

Ethan put an arm around Sneezy and hugged the older man briefly. "One foot in front of the other, Lenny. That's all you have to do."

The guide could only grunt his acknowledgment and plod on.

Powering past, Tilt felt a pang of guilt. Zaph and the shrimp seemed genuinely happy for him. He almost turned around to warn Dominic that he was about to run out of oxygen, but fought the impulse down. Tilt was only in this generous mood because he now held the record. If the shrimp somehow managed to get his hands on a spare bottle of gas, and made it to the top, Tilt's time in the spotlight was going to be very short.

He reached out an arm to steady Sneezy, who was wobbling.

"Thanks," the cameraman panted. "Hey, was that Zaph?"

"That was him," Tilt confirmed. "The *second* youngest kid ever to summit Everest."

"Climbing with Pasang, right?" Sneezy persisted, trying to create order out of his jumbled thoughts.

"Yeah, Pasang. Right."

CHAPTER FOURTEEN

The ridge grew steeper as the sun rose in the sky. Ethan and Dominic slogged on, feeling the weariness as never before. Most Everesters agreed that this was the make-or-break section of the summit assault, the crucial second act of a three-part drama. The euphoria of reaching the Balcony has worn off, yet the next milestone, the South Summit, is a dangerous, oxygen-starved marathon away — more than one thousand vertical feet of unbreathable air, unbearable cold, and overpowering wind.

It was easy to despair at 28,300 feet. Here, higher up than all of the world's lesser peaks, the summit still seemed distant.

Don't think, Dominic commanded himself. He immersed his mind in the lore of history's great alpinists. All had doubted themselves on this jagged, inclined proving ground. Yet all had prevailed by following a credo that was so simplistic that it bordered on the childish: *Just keep moving.*

Suddenly, he was on his knees in the snow, struggling for his next breath. Desperately, he yanked off his mask and searched the plastic breathing tube for any sign of blockage. It was clear.

Ethan was at his side instantly. The older boy's eyes went straight to the tiny gauge on the oxygen cylinder. "You're out of O's!"

"That's impossible!" Dominic gasped. "I took a full bottle at the Col!"

"This thing's open to maximum!" Ethan exclaimed. "Of course it didn't last!"

"But — " The reply was fully formed in Dominic's head. He had personally set his oxygen to two liters per minute. Yet his brain could not communicate the words to his mouth. Confusion — that was another sign of hypoxia — oxygen starvation. The symptom that came next was even more alarming — a deep, whole-body chill that began in his fingers and toes and spread inward.

Ethan detached his own cylinder of gas and hooked it into Dominic's regulator.

Dominic took two deep breaths and then pushed the mask away. "You need this! I won't take it from you!"

Ethan shook his head. "I summited Lhotse without gas."

"We're *higher* than Lhotse!" Dominic argued. "And we're not done yet! We've got to descend to the Balcony and get our spare bottles!"

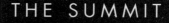

THE SUMMIT

"No!" Ethan wheezed. He hyperventilated for a moment as he adjusted to the thinner air. "If we go down, our summit bid is finished!"

Despairingly, Dominic knew it to be the truth. They were more than seven hundred feet above the Balcony. If they descended, every inch of that ground would have to be climbed again en route to the pinnacle. They would not have the strength. But mostly, they would not have the time.

"Let *me* go down," Dominic insisted. "This is my problem, and it shouldn't cost you your chance."

"This *is* my chance," Ethan countered. "The minute I hit the top last year, I knew one day I had to try this mountain without O's. I chickened out after what happened on Lhotse, but this is my wake-up call. If I don't give it my best shot, I'll be asking 'what if' for the rest of my life." And he hunched into the wind and continued up the corniced ridge.

Dominic watched for an uncertain moment and fell into line behind him.

He may not be the record holder anymore, Dominic thought to himself, *but he's already one of the all-time greats. I'm proud that he wants to climb with me.*

The wind shifted. Now it seemed to be blowing straight down from the top of the ridge, directly in their faces. Dominic found himself drifting ahead of Ethan. It was not so noticeable at first, but as they fought onward and upward, it became obvious that Ethan was losing ground. Without oxygen, the older boy was experiencing cold and fatigue much more acutely than Dominic. And every step drew them into even lower temperatures and even thinner air.

Dominic tried to slow his own pace to match Ethan's. It was easier said than done. In these conditions, movement and exertion were warmth and life; slowing down seemed as unnatural as the stately choreographed march of a wedding procession. Their progress dwindled to a snail's pace. It took them over two hours to get to the bottom of the steep slope of unstable snow that led up to the South Summit.

"Where are the ropes?" asked Dominic.

Ethan barely had the strength to shrug. "I'll lead."

It was like watching slow motion — Ethan, half buried in powder, wriggling up the fifty-foot pitch. He was about halfway to the top when it appeared to Dominic as if he had come to an abrupt halt. A moment later he was sliding down, his mitts still reaching for handholds. Had it not

THE SUMMIT

been for the sheer danger of their surroundings, it would have been comical — a scene from a Roadrunner cartoon.

Dominic made the decision quickly. He shrugged out of his oxygen system and placed the mask over Ethan's mouth and nose.

Ethan recovered quickly. "Give me a minute!" he croaked.

Dominic shook his head. He fought off the feeling of strangulation and struggled to settle his own breathing. *You can do this,* he told himself. *You're acclimatized.*

He set himself to the slope. The first burst of effort brought on a head rush that very nearly flattened him. But it passed. He began to inch his way up, and as he ascended without oxygen, he gained confidence that it really was possible.

Breathe. Breathe.

Partway up, he paused and lowered a rope to Ethan, who secured it at the bottom with an ice screw. The coil of line seemed abnormally heavy, and threw off his balance. But he caught himself and did not slip.

Breathe. Breathe.

The half tunnel that led to the South Summit seemed close now. He moved toward it, climbing, wading, crawling. The nylon line paid out as he ascended, roping the slope. But he didn't allow himself to think about that. The key to climbing without gas, he was finding, was pure focus. The South Summit above wasn't just the most important thing in the world; it *was* the world.

And soon he was on it, dizzy and gasping, but there. He fixed the rope to another screw. Fifty feet below, Ethan clipped on his jumar and moved up to join him.

It was one-forty P.M.

Poised on the wooden rail of the Terrace Bridge, Sammi Moon peered down between the toes of her sneakers at the rushing river of the gorge below. She didn't hesitate. She was off the bridge headfirst, dropping like a stone. The acceleration was even better than she'd expected, and she hurtled toward the water with spectacular speed.

When she felt the bungee cord begin to stretch, she knew a moment of disappointment. No! Faster! Don't let it stop!

The water was only a few feet away. But the full elastic resistance was pulling her back now, and would soon yank her up again. She longed to dunk her head in that ice-cold river, but the line wasn't long enough. Just a few inches short . . .

"Sammi!"

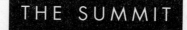

THE SUMMIT

She turned around to complain to the manager about not getting her head wet, and found herself staring into the concerned features of Babu Pemba. An arctic blast reminded her of where she was — hanging by the teeth of her jumar off a rope fixed to a notch in the southeast ridge above twenty-eight thousand feet. Mount Everest, Nepal, Asia.

"It's two o'clock," said Babu gently. "We go down."

"No!" She hauled herself up the line, sliding the jumar along. It was an explosion of energy, a Herculean effort, the best she could muster. It gained her a grand total of eight inches against the mountain. The summit was still a thousand vertical feet away.

"We're at least five hours from the top," Babu explained patiently. "That's if the weather holds out." He gazed to the south. To the left of the pinnacle of Lhotse, now actually below them, the peak Ama Dablam was wreathed in overcast that hadn't been there that morning. "I don't like the look of those clouds."

"Five hours is nothing up here!" Sammi complained. "You can spend five hours melting a liter of water! We can make it!"

"We can make it *up*," Babu agreed. "Not down. Not in the dark. We turn around."

Sammi was outraged. "You don't come nine thousand miles and climb twenty-eight thousand feet just to turn around!"

"That's *exactly* what you do," Babu countered. "I've been on seventeen expeditions; I've summited nine times. What do you think happened on the others? I turned back."

"Tilt made it," she offered defiantly.

"Tilt was lucky. Nothing happened to slow him down. What about Cap? His attempt ended before the Balcony. Does that make him a lousy climber? Sammi, you're good enough to bag this mountain. But things happen."

"Not to *me!*" she exclaimed bitterly. "When I do stuff, I do it till it's done! I live life to the extreme!"

"Not here, you don't," Babu said firmly. "There's only one kind of extreme on Everest — extremely dead. I don't know — maybe it's possible to stand on that summit at nightfall and climb all the way down in the dark. I'm never going to find out, because I'd have to bet my life on it. And I don't bet that high. What we need to settle now is — do you?"

Tears stung Sammi's eyes behind her goggles. It was not her failed bid that upset her. It had taken this man from an alien world to teach her something that she should have known all along

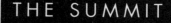

THE SUMMIT

— that these pursuits she considered extreme were not really extreme after all. Skydiving, snowboarding, bungee jumping — they were games, hobbies. But when presented with something truly life-and-death, Sammi Moon said no thanks.

She didn't doubt that this was the correct choice. But right now, the idea made her very sad.

She looked off to the south. "Yeah, you're probably right about those clouds."

And they started down.

Sammi carried her disappointment like an extra burden as they slogged along the ridge. Not summiting certainly didn't make the descent any easier, only shorter. It still called for exhausting effort. Supposedly, the air was thickening with every step. *Ha!* she thought. *That's a laugh.*

Babu was in the lead. He clipped onto a fixed rope and rappelled down a twenty-foot drop, expertly steering clear of the soft cornice below.

Sammi swung a leg over the lip and paused. To the left of the route, a pristine, forty-five-degree snowfield stretched downhill for almost two hundred feet. There, the ridge curled around, cutting it off and containing it. There must have been dozens of similar places in the Himalayas. But this one had come at exactly the right time.

She descended about halfway down the

drop. Then, "Hey, Babu!" She cut the rope with her ice ax, pushed off from the step, and swung out over the expanse of white. Letting go of the rope, she dropped to the snowfield, landing on the seat of her wind suit. The slide began on impact. She sailed down the slope in a blizzard of powder, shrieking in sheer delight all the way. As she had known it would, the ridge stopped her glissade, wiping her out at the bottom.

Awestruck, Babu watched her emerge from the billowing cloud, scramble up through the cornice, and rejoin the ridge far below. As his heart slowly began to beat again, he realized that the mountain the Sherpas called Jongmalungma had not defeated Sammi Moon.

THE SUMMIT

CHAPTER FIFTEEN

Cap Cicero climbed from Camp Four and met up with Tilt and Sneezy a short way above the Col.

The cameraman was uninjured, but so physically weary that an extra arm to lean on was welcome indeed. "I'm fine," he kept repeating, over and over. "Just a little out of steam."

"And look at you." The team leader turned his attention to Tilt. He had never been a Tilt Crowley fan, and still wasn't. But he had to be impressed by the boy's achievement today. "You look like you're ready to tackle K2."

"I'm dead," Tilt admitted happily. "I'm just so psyched — I don't think I can sleep!"

"You'll sleep," Cicero assured him. "But I want two liters of liquid in both of you first."

The descent to the Col was steep and nerve-racking. Tilt found himself taking timid steps, as if he were made of delicate crystal.

What am I? he thought in disgust. *A wimp like Perry Noonan?*

The truth was that Tilt was uneasy because he now had so much to lose. His future was in the bag. He couldn't afford to be reckless.

At Camp Four, he and Sneezy downed steaming mugs of Sherpa tea while Cicero E-mailed the video footage of their summit bid to Colorado.

Then the new Tilt Crowley jammed himself into a warm sleeping bag and plunged into a dreamworld where every climbing magazine had his face on its cover.

He awoke three hours later, still exhausted, but too excited to stay in his bedroll. He had waited fourteen long years to be somebody. He wasn't going to miss a minute of this.

As he ducked from his tent to the guides', the blast of wind seemed almost bearable to him, compared with the howling gale of the summit ridge.

Inside, he found Perry and Sneezy, both fast asleep. Otherwise, the shelter was deserted. He picked up the sat phone from Cicero's gear and hustled it back to his own tent. There was a very important message to be sent.

Part of his secret agreement with the *National Daily* stated that, if he made it to the top, all fees would be doubled. It was time for the youngest summiteer in Everest history to start seeing some cash.

He booted up his computer and began to type.

E-mail Message
TO: bv@national-daily.com
Subject: Did it!

Hit the summit today with guide Lenny Tkakzuk at 9:07 A.M. Perry fell and slid halfway to the Col on his butt. He's fine if you don't count broken ribs and gutlessness. Sammi and Dominic both quit before the top. Yeah, Dominic climbed after all with another team, but equipment problems stopped him around 28,000. . . .

The tent flap opened briefly, and Sammi dragged herself in, utterly spent from her climb. "Hey, Tilt, way to go!"

Startled, he slammed the computer closed to hide the incriminating E-mail. "Get out of here!"

She snorted. "I'm happy to see stardom hasn't done anything to change your sunny personality."

Tilt was chagrined. "Sorry," he mumbled. "You just kind of snuck up on me. How far did you get?"

"Not far enough," she groaned. "You know, you and Sneezy will probably end up the only ones to summit this season. Everybody else is turning around, too. The Germans never really got their act together. And the This Way Up teams are all heading down."

"How about that," chuckled Tilt. "The great Zaph turns out to be human after all."

Sammi frowned. "I didn't see Ethan. Are you sure he's climbing today?"

"He was going up the ridge when I was coming down! Him and — this other guy! But they had oxygen trouble. They should be at the Col by now."

She shrugged. "All I said was I didn't see him. He could be here." She yawned hugely. "I just wanted to say congrats. I've got to go get yelled at some more. I had a little fun on the descent, and Babu got all bent out of shape about it." And she wandered out.

It was a good thing that Sammi had been too bone weary to notice that Tilt had gone white to the ears. Ethan and Dominic *not back yet?* How could that be? The shrimp would have run out of oxygen eight hours ago! They could have *crawled* back by now!

A numbing dread growing in the pit of his stomach, he burst out of the flap and rushed over to the This Way Up camp, trying his best not to run. He found the returning climbers limp and disheveled, chugalugging vast amounts of tea and

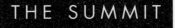

soup in an effort to hydrate themselves so they could lie down and pass out.

A few recognized him and called out their congratulations.

Tilt tried to sound casual. "When did Ethan get back?"

He got blank looks. No one could recall having seen This Way Up's most celebrated climber, either at camp or on the mountain.

Heart pounding, Tilt went from tent to tent. No Ethan, no Dominic.

"Ethan sleep red tent there," one of the Sherpas told him.

"Thanks." The two-person shelter was empty and had obviously been so all day. The stove was cold, and a tin cup sat on the nylon floor. It was half full of soup, now frozen solid.

Possibilities popped into his head, all of them worst-case. When the shrimp ran out of O's, he collapsed, and Zaph wouldn't leave him. Or he got lost, and Ethan was looking for him. Or he was so impaired that Ethan had to drag him, inch by inch, all the way back to Camp Four.

It didn't matter which scenario was the right one. None of this would be happening if Tilt hadn't tampered with Dominic's oxygen cylinder.

I only meant to turn the kid around, not kill him!

And now Ethan was missing, too, thanks to Tilt.

The irony of it nearly tore him in two. Here he was, at the greatest moment of his life, poised to drink in the sweet nectar of fame and fortune he had always craved. But how could he face himself, knowing that his success had been paid for with the lives of two innocent people?

If they die, I killed them!

A rush of adrenaline sent him pounding across the black rocks to his tent. He shook the layer of frozen perspiration out of his wind suit and dressed at lightning speed. Outside, he strapped on crampons and stuffed his pack with a walkie-talkie, spare helmet-lamp batteries, and two oxygen cylinders.

It occurred to him only briefly that it might be foolhardy to be climbing again so soon after a fourteen-hour round-trip sprint to the summit. The caution seemed far less important than the two alpinists he had deliberately put in danger.

Hang in there, shrimp! I'm coming to get you!

No one saw him hit the snowy slope. He was moving so fast that he was soon out of sight among the lengthening shadows.

CHAPTER SIXTEEN

The call came over the radio at six o'clock. Dorje, SummitQuest's Base Camp Sirdar and cook, sounded worried. A howling blizzard was dumping heavy snow on the Khumbu glacier. How were conditions at Camp Four?

Cicero peered through the flap. Light flurries had begun, but this was common on the Col. There was no sign of severe weather.

"We're fine up here," Cicero reported. "And you should be, too. If that squall was anything to worry about, the forecasting services would have given us a heads-up."

Perry looked around the cramped space. "Where's the sat phone?"

The team leader finally found it in the other tent, beside Sammi's slumbering form. It was still hooked into Tilt's computer. The second he pulled out the jack, the phone began to ring.

Cicero picked up the handset. "This is Cap."

It was the American forecasting service. They had been calling for hours. A major storm had formed unexpectedly, rising from the Khumbu valley right up to Mount Everest.

"So batten down the hatches," the meteorologist advised. "It'll be over by morning, but it's going to be a real interesting night. Your people are all off the mountain, right?"

"Of course," Cicero replied. Then it hit him. Where was Tilt?

Sammi stirred. Sleep was elusive, even for the weary, at twenty-six thousand feet. "What's going on, Cap?"

"Have you seen Crowley?"

"He's probably learning German so he can brag in every camp on the Col." She sat up. "He can't be far. His computer's still on."

"Don't you kids ever shut anything off?" Cicero asked irritably. Electricity was precious on the mountain, where the extreme cold drained batteries four times faster than normal. He opened the screen and reached for the power switch.

The E-mail recipient's address jumped out at him: **bv@national-daily.com.**

The *National Daily!*

Rage filled him. It was *Tilt* leaking information about SummitQuest to the *National Daily!* Tilt always screamed the loudest whenever Sammi tried to blame it on Ethan Zaph. And it was Crowley all along!

I should have known! Cicero ranted inwardly. Who else would do something this lousy? And keep on doing it when he saw how much trouble he was causing. Thanks to Tilt and the *National Daily*, poor Dominic was sitting at Base Camp, heartbroken!

The part that really burned Cicero was that Crowley was now the star of SummitQuest. They were all going to be expected to smile and pat him on the back while telling reporters what a great kid he was.

Instead of throttling the no-good . . .

Then he read the E-mail.

"Dominic?"

"Yeah, he really missed out," Sammi said wanly. "I wish I'd made it to the top, but I'd feel worse stuck on the sidelines."

Cicero bounded out of the tent, pulled aside his oxygen mask, and began to bellow, "Crowley! Crowley!"

Sammi was mystified. Of all people, Cap Cicero knew that no voice would carry very far through the screaming winds of Camp Four.

That was when she realized something she had not noticed before. She poked her head out the flap. "Cap!" she called up at him. "Tilt's wind suit! It's gone!"

Impossible, thought Cicero. There was no way the kid could have the strength to climb. Besides, where would he go? He had already made the summit.

He grabbed a walkie-talkie, feeling foolish. "Crowley," he mumbled. Then, louder, "Can you hear me, Crowley? Are you there?"

He was just about to put the handset away when Tilt's tired voice replied, "Hi, Cap."

"Where are you?" barked Cicero. "Why aren't you in camp?"

"The shrimp is out here somewhere," Tilt explained breathlessly. "He shadowed us up the mountain with This Way Up. With Zaph."

Cicero struggled for calm. "If they're climbing, they'll be coming back soon — "

"They should have been down hours ago!" Tilt interrupted. "They had oxygen trouble at twenty-eight thousand!"

"Oxygen trouble?" Suspicion edged into the team leader's voice. "And you know this because . . ."

Muffled sobs carried from the other end of the connection. "I didn't mean to hurt anybody! I was just trying to keep him off the summit! I wanted to be the youngest — I *need* to be the youngest — "

"*What did you do?*"

"I cranked his gas up to full." Tilt was weeping openly now. "Just to turn him around before the top! But something must have gone wrong!"

Of course something went wrong! Cicero wanted to howl. *Climbing Everest is hard enough when everything goes right!*

Money — that was the cause of all this. Oh, how Cicero yearned for the old days! Before the endorsements and the magazine covers and big companies like Summit that were willing to pour millions into no-holds-barred assaults on the great peaks. Back then, alpinists were dirt-poor fanatics who lived on macaroni and cheese until they could sign on with an expedition. Booby-trapping a teammate's oxygen was unheard of, because it didn't matter who was youngest or fastest or first. Records were for bragging rights, period. Yes, Tilt had done something terrible. But the real culprit was the cash and glitz that could turn athletes into terrorists.

With much effort, he swallowed his rage. Wherever Dominic was right now, it wasn't going to help the kid if Tilt got himself killed. "Listen, Crowley," he said through clenched teeth. "No one is blaming you. The stakes are as high as the altitude, and people do crazy things. But you've got to come back to camp. There's a storm brewing — a bad one. If you get caught out there, I can't help you."

Tilt was aghast. "The shrimp!" he cried, and the connection was broken.

"Crowley!" Cicero exclaimed, but there was no one on the other end.

Cap Cicero was renowned for coolness under fire, but right now he was anything but cool. Part of him was aware that he wasn't making much sense as he babbled a short explanation through the flap of the guides' shelter. "Talk that idiot down! Lie to him! Whatever he wants to hear! Just get him back!"

The snow was growing in intensity as he bounded across the Col to Angus Harris's tent in the This Way Up camp.

Harris was in his bedroll, just drifting off to sleep after eighteen hours on the mountain, when Cicero barged in.

"You let my kid climb without telling me?" Before the semiconscious Harris could manufacture a single word of reply, Cicero grabbed the other team leader's walkie-talkie. "Zaph, this is Cap Cicero! Can you hear me?"

"Let me explain — " Harris began groggily.

But right then Ethan's excited voice crackled from the handset.

"Cap, we're on the summit!"

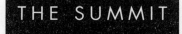

THE SUMMIT

CHAPTER SEVENTEEN

It had taken Ethan and Dominic more than four hours to ascend the summit ridge — double the usual time. One of them was always climbing in oxygenless slow motion. They passed the breathing apparatus back and forth, eating up valuable minutes.

At the Hillary Step, Ethan had tried to lower the rig to his companion. The cylinder slipped out of the loop, dropped forty feet, and disappeared into deep powder. In his fevered state, Dominic could not seem to locate it. Far above, Ethan pointed and screamed while the younger boy dug through the snow. By the time he had retrieved the bottle and jumared up the Step, another precious hour had passed.

But the summit! Dominic had seen well over a thousand photographs of the famous pinnacle. All of them, blown up to life size and arranged in a 360-degree panorama, could not begin to compare with the experience of being there.

He would not even permit himself to blink, for fear of missing a nanosecond of this ultimate experience. He and Ethan hugged and laughed like

EVEREST

madmen, trading breaths from their single mask. The full wrath of the jet stream battered them, packing the punch of a spectacular windchill. Dominic barely noticed. The many stumbling blocks that had littered his path on this unlikely ascent fell away like the vast expanse laid out before him in every direction. Too young and too small — maybe so. But Dominic Alexis was on top of the world.

Ethan reached inside his wind-suit collar and pulled the vial of Dead Sea sand over his head. "I think this belongs to you."

Dominic stared at the necklace. In his exhausted elation, he had completely forgotten Chris's memento from the lowest point on the globe. It was hard to believe that its long journey was finally over. It had traveled up so many crags, so many cliffs, so many mountains. And here, seven miles above its starting point, the keepsake had risen the full range of altitude the planet had to offer.

We did it, Chris. If only you could be here to see this with me.

Dominic's voice was hoarse as he spoke his brother's often-repeated words to the small vial: "Far from home, baby. You're far from home."

That was when the call had come over Ethan's walkie-talkie.

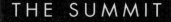

THE SUMMIT

"Shhh!" Dominic hissed. "Don't tell Cap I'm with you!"

"Do you think I'm deaf?" the tinny voice from the small speaker raged. "Let me talk to my climber!"

Dominic leaned over to the handset and bellowed, "No, Cap! You don't know I'm here!"

"Forget about that!" came the impatient reply. "Don't you see you're in trouble? *Nobody* summits this late! Neither of you is going to be anywhere if you don't get down from there!"

"We read you," agreed Ethan, much deflated. "We've had some delays — oxygen problems. We're descending."

"Not so fast," snapped Cicero. "There's a blizzard coming on the south side — a monster. It's already snowing at the Col. You can't beat it."

Dominic turned around. Angry dark clouds smothered the Khumbu glacier all the way into the valley, engulfing everything but the peak of Lhotse. On Everest, the storm was creeping up to the Balcony and the southeast ridge. They were trapped! "But — " he stammered, "but we can't just stay on the summit — "

"There's a British team on the North Face," Cicero told them. "They left a camp at twenty-seven thousand. That's a thousand feet closer, plus the mountain will block the storm for a while."

The North Face! Most Everest ascents followed the southern approach, but there were other, even more difficult, routes to the top.

"I don't know, Cap," Ethan said nervously. "It'll be dark soon, and neither of us has ever been on the north side."

"I'll talk you through it," Cicero promised. "You'll have to rappel down two big cliffs, but at least you'll be going down, not up."

Dominic hesitated. "Are you sure there isn't another way?" He had faith that his body would not let him down. It was his mind he didn't trust. In his oxygen-depleted state, did he have the powers of reason to learn a notoriously difficult new route in the dark, with a killer storm bearing down?

"Listen, kid," Cicero said patiently. "Things happen in mountaineering. A few dumb decisions, a little bad luck; before you know it, you're in a jam. You can survive this — but not on the southeast ridge."

Dominic's eyes met Ethan's. Cicero had climbed the North Face before. If anyone could guide them, he could.

Dominic knelt down and set Chris's necklace

in the firm snow beside the Summit Athletic flag Tilt and Sneezy had planted many hours earlier. He regarded it oddly. "No," he said suddenly, vehemently. This thing had meant good luck for him every step of the way. It had even led him to the winning entry in the contest that had qualified him for SummitQuest's boot camp.

Sorry, Chris, but I need it more than any mountain does!

Carefully, he picked up the glass bottle, unscrewed it, and let a few grains of Dead Sea sand fall to the pinnacle of the world. Then he closed the vial and strung the leather strap over his head. "Let's move."

At six fifty-five P.M., Ethan Zaph and Dominic Alexis stepped into the unknown on the North Face of Everest. As they left the summit, they entered another country. The ridge marked the border between Nepal and Tibet.

They had only been descending for twenty minutes when Cicero's voice on the walkie-talkie began to grow more faint amid the crackling static.

Ethan was alarmed. "Cap! We're losing you! The mountain's blocking the signal!"

"It doesn't work that way, kid," Cicero soothed.

But as they continued to negotiate the rocks,

the team leader faded into the howl of the jet stream.

"You're gone! You're totally gone!" Ethan shouted into the handset. "Cap! Can you read me?" He shook the unit violently. "This isn't supposed to happen! I can't even hear the static anymore!"

Dominic's mind wrestled with the altitude. "Dead batteries?"

"We've got no spares!" Ethan held the handset close enough to swallow it. "Cap! We need you! You can't leave us!"

But the walkie-talkie was silent. They were on their own on the treacherous North Face. Dominic felt the absence of Cicero's voice as sharply as if the team leader had been climbing right beside them.

He passed Ethan the oxygen mask, and the older boy gratefully took a gasping suck.

To their left, the peak of Cho Oyu, the sixth highest mountain on Earth, fell into darkness as the sun dipped farther beneath the horizon. Soon it would be Everest's turn.

Several hundred feet below them, the sullen gray clouds of the storm began to wrap around the base of the summit pyramid.

THE SUMMIT

CHAPTER EIGHTEEN

"Kid? Zaph?" In a rage, Cicero bounced the walkie-talkie off the wall of Angus Harris's small shelter.

"What?" the This Way Up team leader asked anxiously.

"Keep trying to reach them!" Cicero tossed over his shoulder as he scrambled through the flap. "I've got another missing kid to check on!"

Outside, the blizzard was revving up to its full fury. The rocks of the Col were already covered with three inches of fresh snow.

He could barely squeeze himself into the jam-packed SummitQuest guides' tent. Sammi had joined the vigil around the radio. Dr. Oberman hunched over the set, pleading with Tilt.

"Climbing is *suicide* in this weather!" she shrilled. "You summited; you're a star! Don't throw your life away just when you've got everything you always wanted!"

"I want the shrimp," Tilt panted in reply. "And Zaph. I'm not coming down without them."

Sammi grabbed the microphone from the doctor's hand. "Tilt, it's Sammi. Listen, Dominic and Ethan are safe on the Col."

"You're lying."

"They're at the Germans' camp," Sammi insisted. "Hanging with some of their Sherpas. You know Dominic and the Sherpas."

It brought a rueful laugh over the speaker. "Nice try."

Cicero considered giving Tilt the news that Ethan and Dominic had already summited and were currently descending the North Face, far out of anyone's reach.

No, he thought. *The kid's consumed with guilt. He might try to climb the mountain again and chase them down the other side.*

He hefted the microphone. "Crowley, if you don't get your butt down to Camp Four, I'm coming up after you."

"It's about time," Tilt shot back. "But don't worry about me. Find the shrimp."

And he broke the connection.

Nearly flattening Sneezy with a knee, Cicero began to pull on his wind suit. Babu reached for his own gear.

"This isn't smart," Dr. Oberman said seriously. "You guys are as good as it gets, but in these conditions, the mountain always has the upper hand."

Cicero could only shrug helplessly as he continued to dress. That had been the problem with SummitQuest from the beginning. The rules and procedures on Everest had been established for decades. But it was always assumed that the alpinists were *adults*. Certainly, if Tilt were twenty-four and not fourteen, no rescue party would be sent until after the storm. A ninth grader was a whole new ballgame.

Outside, they strapped on crampons and plucked helmet lamps from the equipment dump between the two tents. Babu switched his on. The sudden light only underscored the horrible weather. Driving snow blew horizontally across the Col. Visibility was practically zero.

Babu hesitated a moment. Then he selected an oxygen rig from the pile and shrugged into it, fitting the unfamiliar mask over his mouth and nose.

Cicero watched him soberly. In all the decades the two men had climbed together, Babu Pemba had never once breathed bottled gas, not even at the summit. That he felt the need to do so now was as urgent a warning as any forecasting service could ever give.

It was going to be a long night.

It turned out to be Ethan who drew the last lungful of bottled O's from their single cylinder. Dominic recognized the little choking gurgle that came from his companion.

"Empty?" he asked.

"Done." Panting, Ethan shrugged out of the apparatus and let it drop to the rocks.

It was not their first piece of bad news. As night finally enveloped the top of the world, they had switched on their helmet lamps to discover that only Dominic's was still working. One less asset. One less lifeline.

And the storm. It had begun slowly, but soon made up for lost time. The gale drove snow into their faces, standing them erect as they struggled to hunch forward. Powder covered the rocks almost immediately, making the route slippery and even more dangerous.

"What happened to Cap's cliffs?" Ethan shouted over the wind.

Dominic cleared the snow from his watch. They were just above twenty-eight thousand feet. He had read about the famous Steps of the north side. He wrestled with his hazy memory, trying to think back — trying to think *period*! The uppermost of the two cliffs — surely they should have reached it by now. . . .

"But how could we have missed it?" he asked.

"We veered east!"

"Yeah?" In the blinding blizzard, Dominic had

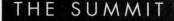

THE SUMMIT

no trouble believing it. But with a flutter of panic, he realized that it would have made just as much sense to him if Ethan had said they'd wandered to the west. "Are you sure?"

"I think so!" The older boy seemed less certain, confused.

They spun around desperately. The storm surrounded them like the curtain ringing an old-fashioned bathtub. Even with his helmet lamp, Dominic couldn't see much farther than a few feet through the squall. The more he looked, the more disoriented he became, until all directions seemed equally promising.

He was relieved when Ethan started off again. Dominic hurried ahead, leading the way with his torch.

The ground grew more jagged and unpredictable. For over an hour, they slowly descended. Dominic trained his helmet lamp downward, focusing on one footfall at a time. Ethan followed right behind, step-by-step in Dominic's tracks in the accumulating snow. It was the only safe course.

All at once, a blast of wind was followed by an instant of calm, creating a small gap in the blizzard's cloak. Dominic saw . . . *nothing*!

No rock. No ice. No slope, gentle or steep, unfolding ahead.

He got down on his hands and knees and crawled forward. *Stupid,* he scolded himself. *It was probably a hallucination.*

And then the beam of his helmet lamp shone on snow-covered ground — *sixty feet straight down.*

THE SUMMIT

CHAPTER NINETEEN

The cliff! They weren't lost after all!

The celebration was short-lived. Ethan and Dominic peered over the lip and examined the obstacle below. The step was formed by the crumbly mustard-colored rock of the Yellow Band. Ethan reached out and grabbed a handhold experimentally. It disintegrated in his hand.

"Doesn't matter," he said in answer to Dominic's apprehensive look. "We can't stay here."

Using the blunt end of his ice ax, Ethan pounded a piton into the top of the cliff. The rotten rock shattered around it. He tried several other places with similar results.

"Let me try." Dominic threaded a line through the peg's ring, and tightly wound it around a bulbous outcropping of limestone. Then he hammered the piton into a small crack beneath the boulder.

Ethan tested the cord, pulling with his full weight. Amazingly, it held. "I'll lead."

While Dominic shone his light on the route, Ethan attached his harness to the top rope and began to rappel carefully down. Whenever his crampons made contact with the brittle limestone of the cliff, he would dislodge a cascade of pebbles. Other than that, the descent was routine, and he was at the bottom in a matter of minutes.

"It's okay!" came the call from below.

Dominic clipped onto the line and heaved himself over the side.

The feeling of the rappel buoyed Dominic's spirit, dissipating the dread that gripped him. *This* was something he was good at, something he had control of. He stopped on a narrow, snow-covered ledge halfway down to catch his breath. But when he pushed off again, he was instantly aware that something was not right.

High above, a weak spot in the anchoring rock gave way under his weight. The outcropping broke in two, sending a large chunk of limestone tumbling over the lip of the cliff. He saw the boulder hurtling down at him for just a second before the piton popped out, and he was falling, too.

The warning formed in his mind: *Ethan, run!* In the blinding blizzard, his companion would not see him until it was too late. But the drop took away what little breath he had left.

Ethan cried out in shock as the younger boy landed on top of him. Dominic felt his ankle twist — a sharp, searing pain shot up his leg. The visible world lurched violently as his helmet lamp

THE SUMMIT

was jarred off his head. There was a sickening pop as the plummeting rock shattered the torch as if it had been aimed by an evil spirit.

The North Face went dark.

"Shrimp!!"

Tilt blundered around in the blizzard, his crampons plowing through nearly a foot of new powder to bite into the ice below. Last night, he had been charged with such high excitement that he had barely noticed a mountain beneath his feet. But now, Everest was making its presence felt. The steepness. The altitude. The weather. *Ugh!*

"Shrimp! Zaph!"

He knew that the chance that the two boys might hear his cries was outrageously slim. But what else could he do? It was his fault they were in trouble in the first place.

Keep moving. One foot in front of the other. No pain.

The howl of the gale abated for a moment, and Tilt could make out Cicero raving at him through the walkie-talkie. *". . . this-is-no-joke-Crowley-the-mountain-doesn't-care-that-you're-only-fourteen-you've-got-to-descend . . ."* Briefly, a smile replaced the grimace of fatigue on Tilt's face. The team leader was begging again. Just a few minutes ago, it had been gruesome tales of frostbite. Before that, threats. The climbers at Camp Four were trying to talk him down, too. He found their pleas kind of entertaining.

It's about time I got some attention on this expedition!

"Whoa!"

The beam of his helmet lamp illuminated his boot, frozen in midstride, about to step off the edge of the Kangshung Face.

In a panic, he overbalanced backward, and tumbled to the snow. He slid a little, then jammed his ax into the ice. At last, he stopped, his heartbeat a drumroll.

Man, that was close!

He got up again, dusting the snow from his wind suit. Where was he? The ascent to the Balcony was a straight shot from the South Col. It came nowhere near the Kangshung Face.

I must have wandered off. Understandable in the blinding snow.

Carefully, he climbed a few yards and began to retrace his steps. His tracks were already half buried under a coating of new powder.

As he headed back to the main route, a feeling of powerlessness took hold in the pit of his stomach. Getting lost in the blizzard was that easy — a single wrong turn had brought him

THE SUMMIT

within inches of disaster. Zaph and the shrimp could be anywhere, scattered over hundreds of millions of square feet of snow-obscured mountain.

Was there really any chance of ever finding them?

CHAPTER TWENTY

In the smothering dark at the base of the cliff, Ethan and Dominic took stock of themselves.

Dominic's ankle was sprained, but he could still walk in the tight supporting boot. Ethan's situation was more serious. A crampon point from Dominic's flailing foot had made a deep gash in Ethan's thigh. The cut itself was not an immediate danger. At this altitude, blood was the consistency of molasses, so bleeding was extremely slow. The problem was the slit in Ethan's wind suit, and in his sweatpants and thermal underwear underneath it. An Everester climbs in a cocoon. Once that shell is breached, there is no protection from the arctic cold of the Death Zone.

The contents of Ethan's knapsack were transferred to Dominic's. The younger boy wrapped the empty pack around Ethan's wound and lashed it on tight. They set out again, both hobbling — baby steps down the world's highest mountain. In the pitch-black, progress was almost nonexistent. Three painful, limping hours brought them only to 27,600 feet — the height of the Balcony on the south side. To keep from wandering in the zero visibility, they committed themselves to a narrow rock trench. It was a screaming wind tunnel in the gale, but at least it led down. They prayed it was in the right direction. The gully was so thin that they bumped and scraped their sides and shoulders on jagged formations of rock.

Another hour passed. The luminescent dial of Dominic's watch hovered before him like a floating spirit in the inky night. The blowing snow glowed an eerie green before it.

They held a nervous conference.

"Where's the second cliff?" panted Ethan, sucking air. "We should be there already."

"We must be off course," Dominic gasped. "Which means we'll never find that camp. We're going to have to bivouac."

Bivouac! To hole up and spend a night outside on the mountain. It was the last resort of a desperate climber.

Ethan was horrified. "In this cold? We'll be dead in an hour! We've got to keep descending!"

Dominic didn't have the strength to argue. But it was becoming increasingly clear to him that descent would not be an option much longer. They had been on the go for a solid day. They were both limping, exhausted, half delirious. In the absolute blackness, how long would it be before one of them took a fatal fall?

The gully seemed to widen as they slogged along, or at least Dominic wasn't bumping into its sides anymore. Eventually, he felt his crampons crunching hard ice instead of snow-covered rock. His heart sank. This only proved that they were hopelessly lost. He could not recall reading about a glacier this high up on the north side.

He was never really sure if he saw the crevasse, because that would have been impossible in the dark. More likely, he noticed his companion starting to stumble. He grabbed Ethan around the midsection, but it was too late. Ethan fell forward into the chasm with Dominic clamped on behind him. At the last second, the older boy flailed desperately at the lip of ice. His ax struck something solid and he held on for dear life. There they hung — Dominic onto Ethan, Ethan to the edge.

Dominic wanted to reach for his own ax, but he didn't dare release his grip on the older boy. Ethan clung to the mountain's rind. They were stuck — stuck until he lost his purchase, and they plummeted to depths unknown.

And then Ethan felt a front point scraping against hard ice below. "I'm letting go."

THE SUMMIT

"Are you crazy?" rasped Dominic. "No!"

"Hang on!"

Dominic closed his eyes and steeled himself for the end. The drop was about six inches. The pounding of his heart reverberated in his ears. The pit was only seven feet deep.

He looked daggers at Ethan. "Why didn't you tell me?"

Ethan managed a thin smile. "You didn't ask."

By the meager light of Dominic's watch, the two investigated their surroundings. The shallow crevasse widened on the left side of the opening. There they found a small cavelike area, enclosed by a roof of ice. The refuge was still desperately cold, but it was protected from the punishing wind.

"Bivouac?" asked Dominic.

"Right."

They sat down on the rime, huddled together for warmth. Both knew they were lucky to find shelter from the elements. They could not have lasted much longer against the storm. But a night outside in the notorious Death Zone was by no means a sure thing. They were bone weary, and had no oxygen to warm and sustain them.

"No sleeping," Ethan shivered. "Sleep here and you'll wake up dead."

"Gotcha." Teeth chattering, Dominic didn't say what both of them felt: *I'm not going to miss out on a second of what little time I have left.*

Tired.

The word had become Tilt's universe. He was too tired to climb. Too tired to descend. Too tired to talk. Too tired to breathe.

He sat in the fresh snow — where? He had no idea. Seven hours of wandering had brought him no closer to the depression that was the route between Camp Four and the Balcony. He was barely aware of his physical body, a being of pure fatigue.

Sitting — that was where the trouble had started. He had plunked down in a snowdrift abruptly when his oxygen had cut out. It was no big deal — ice buildup in the regulator tube. But as of this moment, he had not yet cleared it. And it was just beginning to come through to his muddled mind that he had been stalled there for a long time.

His walkie-talkie crackled to life — Babu, hailing Cicero. "Cap, I'm on the Balcony. No sign of him. No sign anybody's been here for a while."

"Crowley!" bellowed Cicero, and kept on yelling.

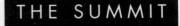

THE SUMMIT

Tilt had been ignoring the team leader's calls all night. But something told him the situation had changed.

Pressing the TALK button on the handset took all his concentration. "Hi, Cap."

"Kid, where the blazes are you?"

"I'm — I'm sitting down," Tilt mumbled.

"Get up!" Cicero almost screamed. "Climb up, down, sideways — just *move!*"

"Funny thing," Tilt replied in an almost amused tone. "I *can't.*"

"You have to!" Cicero begged. "That's hypothermia talking! Climbing's the only way to fight it off!"

"I feel pretty warm," Tilt said in slight surprise. And he did. The bone-cracking chill of a few minutes ago seemed to have let up. His hands and feet felt numb rather than cold. Numbness of the extremities — that was important somehow. A serious problem. But he couldn't for the life of him remember why. Nor did he remember the first rule of the Himalayas — that Everest's deadliest weapon was not a crevasse or an avalanche or a collapsing serac. It was what was happening at this very moment: An exhausted alpinist, every milligram of energy wrung from his soul by a monstrous and indifferent mountain, simply ceases to fight.

Cicero was still yelling, but the voice seemed distant now. Had Tilt looked down, he would have noticed that the walkie-talkie had slipped from his mitt to the snow.

The weather was still unbelievably bad. Tilt wasn't worried for himself. He was a powerful climber with incredible stamina — the youngest ever to summit this pile of rocks. But the shrimp probably wasn't going to make it. On the way to the summit, Tilt had passed bodies, frozen solid, far too high ever to be recovered. The poor little kid would be one of those — the smallest.

But Tilt was strong. He had to be to feel comfortable in conditions like these. Odd — the warmer he felt, the less he seemed able to move his arms and legs.

Maybe all he needed was a short bivouac — a power nap. It might not be too late for the shrimp after all. When Tilt was fresh and rested, he would climb up and find Dominic. Wouldn't that be something — the youngest summiteer in Everest history coming down off the mountain with a lost boy under his arm? An impossible rescue!

As Tilt drifted off into the sleep from which he would never awaken, he was in the bright lights of that press conference. A jumble of microphones sat on the table in front of him. Reporters

THE SUMMIT

hung on every word to come out of the mouth of the great hero of Everest. His mother glowed with pride. The nobody from Cincinnati had traveled far and climbed high and finally reached his dream. Tilt Crowley would not be delivering papers anymore.

Flashbulbs went off until all he could see were spreading blobs of color, disappearing into a background of black.

CHAPTER TWENTY-ONE

The next thing Dominic felt was a sharp pain in the center of his forehead. It was a familiar sensation. Almost like . . .

Brain freeze! From gobbling too much ice cream too fast. Only — the growling of his stomach told him that he hadn't eaten ice cream — or anything else — for a long time. Where was he?

He sprang up with a jolt, banging his head on the ice roof of the crevasse. A cloud of fresh snow flaked off him. No wonder he had brain freeze. He'd been breathing the stuff in all night! A half-inch layer of powder had settled over him from head to toe while he was asleep —

"Asleep?" he cried in horror. "No!" Sunlight streamed in through the chasm's opening. It was morning! He checked his watch: five thirty-three A.M. They had spent an entire night outside at nearly twenty-seven thousand feet!

Ethan came awake, shaking off his own frosty coating. "What?"

Dominic wiggled his fingers and toes. "I can feel everything! You?"

The older boy did an inventory of his extremi-

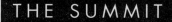

THE SUMMIT

ties. "No frostbite. This crevasse saved our necks!"

Dominic tried to exhale and found himself puffing on the thin air. "We are so lucky!"

"Not yet," Ethan said gravely. He checked his pack, still lashed around the wound on his thigh. "I feel pretty good, but that's only compared with how I felt last night. I'll bet we're too weak to realize how weak we are."

Just *how* weak became clear when they tried to get out of the crevasse. Two alpinists who had reached the top of the world yesterday were unable to extricate themselves from a seven-foot hole. Finally, Dominic worked his way to the surface by means of his front points and two ice axes. He helped Ethan up after him. Elapsed time: thirty minutes. It should have been thirty seconds.

As for where they were, that was another mystery. While the upper mountain was in bright sunlight, a layer of mist hung below them at about twenty-five thousand feet. The summit of Cho Oyu, poking up through the fog, confirmed that they were on the Tibetan side of Everest. But more than that they could not tell. Their crevasse was in a hollow in the mountain's flank, so their view of the great North Face was blocked.

"But if this is the north, what happened to the second cliff?" Dominic asked.

Ethan shrugged. "We must have worked around it somehow. Who knows where we were going in that crazy storm? Just be happy we can see again."

As it turned out, sight was of little value to two climbers who barely had the strength to walk. They had only descended a hundred feet when they found themselves in a steep rock depression, plowing through thigh-deep powder. Each step was a wrestling match — a war against snow, against fatigue, against breathlessness, against pain. *Pain — there's plenty of that.* Dominic's sprained ankle stiffened with every movement.

The ditch seemed endless, cutting diagonally to their left before disappearing into the mist a thousand feet below. The morning disappeared with it, hour by hour, swallowed up by this interminable descent from light into fog.

Struggling a few yards ahead, the figure of Ethan suddenly blurred as Dominic began to sob. The feeling of hopelessness that came over him was so all-consuming that he was left completely hollow. He was less than an empty shell; he was *nothing* — the faintest wisp of life force propelling two robotic legs through deep snow.

"Hey, Dominic!" Ethan was pointing.

But Dominic had retreated inside himself. At

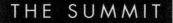

THE SUMMIT

that moment, he was only the sound of his footsteps. Crunch . . . crunch . . .

"Dominic, look!"

And there it was, appearing out of the haze like a ghostly, jagged highway — a great rocky ridge.

"It must be the north ridge!" cried Ethan.

But to Dominic it was much, much more.

It was hope.

Perry awoke to two kinds of ache. Broken ribs and . . .

Tilt.

This time he didn't cry. There had been plenty of tears last night — from climbers and guides alike. They had all heard the whole terrifying process over the radio: the comfortable warmth, the lethargy, the sense of well-being — right up to the moment when Tilt had spoken no more. According to Dr. Oberman, death would have come within hours in the unimaginable cold.

Perry's sorrow was made anxious, edgy as his thoughts turned to Dominic, somewhere on the north side with Ethan Zaph. Two teenagers, lost on unfamiliar ground, far beyond the rescue range of anyone on the Col.

But Tilt! If anybody was bulletproof, I would have guessed him.

In the months Perry had known the boy, he had experienced many emotions toward him — rage, hurt, envy, even admiration. Mourning — that had caught him off guard. Tilt was the best of them. The biggest, the strongest, the most determined. And yet, Perry was going home, while Tilt would remain on the mountain.

Cicero and Babu had searched until four o'clock in the morning. The team leader would have been out there still if Babu hadn't physically dragged him back to Camp Four. Perry was still haunted by their heated conversation, inadvertently broadcast to the Col by a walkie-talkie frozen in speak mode:

"Killing yourself won't bring Tilt back!" Babu had shouted. "People die here, Cap! You know that better than anybody!"

"Fourteen-year-old kids don't!" came the exhausted reply.

"Only because nobody ever brought them before!"

It had seemed heartless last night. Now Perry understood that Babu had been merely stating a fact. If kids were going to attempt Everest, it stood to reason that sooner or later one of them would perish on the mountain.

It turned out to be sooner rather than later. It turned out to be Tilt Crowley.

I never even said good-bye.

But of course, no alpinist ever knew in advance when he or she would be saying a final farewell to a teammate.

Perry thought of his school chess club back home. He had always enjoyed the game for its mental challenge. Now he appreciated its *predictability* more than anything else. Chess was governed by a set of rules that applied to all players. But to tackle Everest was to take on an opponent with a pocket full of extra queens that could appear anywhere on the board at a moment's notice. Poor Tilt had suddenly found himself surrounded by an overwhelming show of Everest's hidden firepower. He was checkmated before he knew what hit him.

Cicero and Babu slept for just ninety minutes. Babu set out to organize a team to look for Tilt's body. Every Sherpa on the Col volunteered to help, even Pasang, who had just recovered from snow blindness.

Cicero would be unavailable for the search party. In yet another cruel twist of fate, the forecasting services had officially called the start of the summer monsoon. Last night's storm was just the beginning, they said. It was time to get off the mountain. So the expedition leader's first responsibility became guiding Sammi and Perry down to Base Camp.

"Which happens right now," Cicero said firmly. "The weather only gets worse from here on in."

"But we can't — " Perry left the rest of his protest unsaid. No one had particularly liked Tilt Crowley. But leaving the Col felt like abandoning their teammate.

Cicero blew his stack. "Since when is this expedition a democracy? *I* decide when you climb! *I* decide when you don't! *I* decide when you eat, sleep, and go to the bathroom! And right now I decide that you *shut up!*"

The SummitQuest climbers and guides regarded him uneasily. Ever since Tilt's death, their leader had been as volatile as nitro. He had just gotten off the radio with the British North Face expedition. Four Sherpas were now on their way to the high camp to bring down Ethan and Dominic — *if* the lost summit party had even made it.

The strain seemed to be getting to Cap Cicero. Would the legendary alpinist be brought down by the very mountain that had made him famous?

Descent. The SummitQuest team's climb was far from over. The wind had died down, but it was foggy and bitter cold. Slogging through this freezer of misery, they would be tackling several

THE SUMMIT

of Everest's most celebrated nightmares — the Geneva Spur, the Yellow Band, and below that, the mile-high sloped ice of the Lhotse Face.

They were approaching Camp Three, hanging off the rope like a frost-nipped procession of clothespins, when the grim word came over Cicero's walkie-talkie. Babu, Pasang, and two other Sherpas had located Tilt's body. Their teammate had died only a few hundred yards from the rock gully that led back down to the Col. But in the zero visibility of last night's howling blizzard, he might as well have been on the moon.

He'd be better off on the moon, Perry thought bitterly. *At least then NASA could send a rocket to bring his body back to his family.*

At twenty-seven thousand feet, Tilt's remains could never be safely removed from the mountain. Even the most skilled Sherpas could not maneuver so much weight on a six-foot frame down two vertical miles of the toughest descent in the Himalayas. It was too much of a risk for the living to recover the dead. Babu and Pasang wrapped the frozen body in the fabric of a small tent they had salvaged from Camp Four. It was all the burial that Tilt Crowley would ever receive.

SummitQuest reached the upper Cwm around three o'clock, and the temperature jumped seventy degrees. Shedding clothing and stuffing snow under their hats, they staggered into ABC late in the afternoon. The British North Face expedition was already trying to radio them.

A team of four Sherpas had ascended to twenty-seven thousand feet to look for Ethan and Dominic. They found the high camp deserted. There was no sign that anyone had been there for at least a week.

CHAPTER TWENTY-TWO

The ridge was notched and craggy — an exhausting series of rock climbs. Cruel and unusual punishment for two teenagers already pushed beyond the limit of human endurance. Was some malevolent god reshaping Everest just to destroy them?

No conversation had passed between Ethan and Dominic since they had reached the ridge. It wasn't that they had nothing to say to each other. Dominic had been formulating the sentences for the past three hours: *I'm done. I have to stop. Tell Chris I got his sand to the top.* The image of his grieving family brought a sharp stabbing pain to a body that fatigue had dipped in Novocain. Picturing them — Mom, Dad, and Chris — drove his stumbling progress. *I can't quit. Not yet.* His gas tank was bone-dry. He had nothing more to give to this mountain.

Below them, a massive snow-covered shoulder was appearing out of the thinning mist. It had been a shock at first, but now he recognized it for what it really was — a death sentence. There *was* no North Shoulder of Everest. Which meant

this was not the north ridge. They were still lost — they had always been so. And lost they would remain. Forever.

Ethan was also bewildered by the titanic bulge in the mountain's bulk, but he lacked the strength to wrestle his confusion into the form of a question. Where were they? What was going on? What was this colossal buttress — itself the equal of all but the world's highest peaks?

The two boys continued to climb down. It made no sense; this was clearly the wrong path. But there was no thinking anymore, no logic. Only will — the will to keep moving.

Finally, they dropped to the shoulder, staggering together in an awkward embrace. It was not a celebration — they fell into each other for support, and found that neither had the power to offer any. After twelve hours of descent, this relatively flat ground seemed strange and disorienting.

Twenty-four thousand feet. They had left the summit a vertical mile above them. Yet Base Camp lay farther still in the opposite direction. They were nowhere — a place that was likely to be their tomb.

Reeling, Ethan and Dominic wobbled arm in arm across the shoulder and gazed through the mist over the valley below.

THE SUMMIT

It was . . . Dominic blinked —

It was . . . *no, impossible! It's a mirage — the final hallucination of a dying climber!*

The Western Cwm!

Ethan saw it, too. The expression on his famous face spoke volumes, but all he could manage aloud was a croaked "How?"

And Dominic had the answer. Oxygen-starved and close to shutdown, his fevered brain made the leap almost immediately. They had *never* been on the north ridge! Somehow in the storm, they had gotten themselves turned around and traversed to the *west* ridge — the most difficult, least traveled route up Everest! And now they were on the West Shoulder, a vertical half mile above the Cwm!

No wonder we never hit the second cliff. We were off the North Face!

He wanted to explain it to Ethan, to scream it all over the mountain. But there was so much to say, so much to do — and so little energy left. They were right above Camp Two, but the tents looked like Monopoly houses twenty-seven hundred feet below. It would be a challenging descent for a well-equipped climber on two days' rest. They were out of rope and out of strength.

At last, Dominic found the only words worth

wasting precious breath on. "We can do it," he barely whispered.

"We can do it." Ethan nodded.

They started down the rounded crest of the West Shoulder.

In all his years of climbing, Cap Cicero had never known such bottomless despair. Sure, he had lost teammates before — friends, even a couple of clients.

No kids. Never kids.

And now the mountain had devoured three teenagers, two of them under his care.

He didn't blame himself. Years of experience had taught him that. Everest chose when and where it would exact its toll, and from whom. The youth of these three victims had nothing to do with their fate. Ethan and Tilt had the size and strength of adults. And Dominic? He was small, but his smarts and stamina made him the toughest alpinist Cicero had ever seen.

I wish I could blame myself. Three kids are dead. Somebody should have to pay for it. Savagely, he drove his ax into the hard ice where he sat, feeling the temperature plunge minute by minute as the sun set on the Western Cwm.

His emotion went far beyond finger-pointing

THE SUMMIT

and recrimination. He was staring at this mountain he knew so well as if he had never laid eyes on it before. *What are we doing here? What's the point of it all? What kind of people are we if we think it's worth this sacrifice to stand on the summit and take pictures with frozen fingers?*

"It doesn't make sense," he muttered aloud.

"Probably not," came a soft voice.

For the first time Cicero realized that Sammi was sitting beside him. She added, "But if it made sense to anybody, it would have been those three." She gave him a watery smile. "At least that's what I tell myself every time I think I'm going to lose it."

It's not enough, he said to himself. *At a certain point the price is just too high.* "Get some rest," he told her. "We've got the Icefall tomorrow."

"Okay." She stood up. "Cap? This Way Up, the Germans, and us — that's all there is on this side of the mountain, right?"

He looked at her. "So?"

"So who are those two guys up there?"

His eyes followed her pointing finger. There, halfway down the hulking West Shoulder, two tiny figures were descending. They looked like ants against a vast expanse of white.

Cicero wrenched the binoculars from his pack. The magnification brought the alpinists closer, but he could not make out faces. Yet he knew. A big guy and a little guy, their movements labored, their exhaustion plain. An extra-small red wind suit.

Unbelievable — no, that wasn't strong enough. *Miracle!* It was the *kid*, back from the dead! Dominic, and Zaph with him!

"*Andrea!*" he bellowed. "*Lenny!*"

And they were climbing, a blur of pure purpose. Cicero could not remember strapping on crampons, but there they were on his boots, biting into the ice and snow of the West Shoulder. Nor could he recall picking up rope. But an entire coil was slung over his shoulder. As he sprinted ahead of his guides, tears streamed down his cheeks. Cap Cicero had never wept at any tragedy on any mountain in a legendary thirty-one-year career. But the emotion of this moment welled up inside of him until a single body could not contain it anymore. Mighty Everest had given one back.

He could see their faces now — two young people, aged decades in forty-eight tumultuous hours. He shouted; they didn't. They *couldn't.* They were close to collapse.

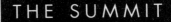

THE SUMMIT

Cicero reached for Dominic's harness, and brought the boy to his embrace. Dr. Oberman and Sneezy flanked Ethan, each supporting an arm. The ordeal was over.

Camp Two waited below. Hot food, warm sleeping bags — life.

EPILOGUE

The memorial service was crowded. Tilt had come friendless to SummitQuest. He left the expedition much mourned by his teammates, the climbing world, and a nation that had read on the front pages of newspapers about his achievements and tragic death. The fourteen-year-old had reached his goal. Tilt Crowley was a household word.

There were more than a hundred people jammed into the small chapel, and that didn't include the horde of media camped in the parking lot outside. The SummitQuest team had been mobbed by reporters upon their arrival. Dominic, in particular, found himself besieged by cameras and microphones.

"Dominic, how does it feel to be the youngest human to stand on top of the world?"

"Do you think your new record has been overshadowed by Tilt's death?"

"Are you haunted by the fact that Tilt died trying to rescue you?"

Cap Cicero handled all questions for the team, and his message was short, if not sweet.

"Bug off!" And he slammed the door in the reporters' faces, shattering the long telephoto lens belonging to the photographer from the *National Daily*.

"Nice shot," whispered Sammi. "Hey, Cap, did you ever find out who was spying on us for those jerks?"

Cicero regarded his three surviving climbers. "No," he said evenly. "I guess we'll never know." Tilt Crowley had been no angel. But what was to be gained by speaking ill of the dead? The boy had paid for his crimes. And then some.

Dominic barely heard a word of the brief service. His mind still reeled from his introduction to Tilt's grief-stricken mother an hour before. The bereaved woman had looked at him with horrified loathing. He could tell that she held him responsible for her son's fate. Even now, seated in the second row of uncomfortable wooden chairs, he could feel her accusations filtering through the black lace kerchief that covered her hair.

A sympathetic hand patted Dominic's shoulder. Chris sat behind his younger brother, his shirt and tie concealing his vial of sand from the Dead Sea, now a few grains lighter. To his left were Ethan Zaph and Nestor Ali of This Way Up, and Bryn Fiedler, a former SummitQuest teammate. On the other side, Mr. Alexis, Sammi's parents, and Joe Sullivan himself paid their respects. As the sponsor of the ill-fated expedition, the billionaire CEO was also under fire from the media. But he had hardly left his nephew's side since Perry's return from Kathmandu.

The last of the speakers was Cap Cicero. He pointed to the life-size photograph of an exultant Tilt on the summit of Everest. "Look at that face and tell me Tilt Crowley was a victim. Not in a million years. He beat the mountain, not the other way around." He turned to the poster and flashed Tilt a thumbs-up, the alpinist's signal for success. "Congratulations, kid. You always told us you could do it."

An uncomfortable, almost hostile murmur rippled through the chapel. That was it? That was all this man had to say about the terrible death of a child entrusted to his care? What kind of callous monster was this so-called legend?

But the climbers in the room understood perfectly. Their backs straightened and their jaws set. Dominic could feel his right hand curling to the grip of an imaginary ice ax. Inside his stiff dress shoes, his feet formed to the contours of heavy mountaineering boots.

He was aware of a flicker deep inside that was half forgotten, yet instantly familiar. It had been extinguished during his descent of the West

Shoulder — at the awful moment when Cicero had told him the news about Tilt.

It was the urge to turn the axis of motion vertical. To defy gravity and leave the ground in search of some impossibly distant summit.

To *climb*.

ABOUT THE AUTHOR

GORDON KORMAN is the author of more than forty books for children and young adults, including the Island series, *Book One: Shipwreck*, *Book Two: Survival*, and *Book Three: Escape*, as well as *The Chicken Doesn't Skate*, the Slapshots series, and *Liar, Liar, Pants on Fire*. He lives in Long Island with his wife and children, and usually stays close to sea level.